**Here's what people are saying about
Traci Andrighetti's books:**

"Traci's writing is sharp and funny; the world she paints leaps off the page and makes the reader laugh out loud…A thoroughly enjoyable new voice in fiction!"

—Kristin Harmel, Internationally bestselling novelist (*The Sweetness of Forgetting*)

"Traci Andrighetti's *Limoncello Yellow* had me tickled pink! Her smart, sassy heroine, wacky cast of characters, and vividly original settings had me glued to the page. I can't wait to read more from this author!"

—Gemma Halliday, *New York Times* bestselling author

BOOKS BY TRACI ANDRIGHETTI

Franki Amato Mysteries:

Limoncello Yellow

Prosecco Pink

Rosolio Red
(holiday short story)

PROSECCO PINK

a Franki Amato mystery

Traci Andrighetti

To my beloved grandmother, Annie Lee Andrick, for saving those old Nancy Drew books just for me

Acknowledgements

Prosecco Pink would not have come into being if it weren't for Gemma Halliday. When I sent her a sample of *Limoncello Yellow*, the first book in the Franki Amato Mysteries, I never dreamed that it would be published. Not only did Gemma publish it, she convinced me to make it a series. And I am forever grateful.

I am also thankful to my family for their role in the writing of this book. A very special thank you goes to my son Dmitriy for being as patient as he could while I wrote; to my mother, Carolyn Andrighetti, for being my biggest fan and for catching my mistakes (She has *always* had a special talent for that, btw.); and to my husband, Graham Kunze, for reading various passages and listening to me drone on and on about plot issues.

Speaking of the plot, I owe a huge debt of gratitude to Detective Ruben Vasquez and Wally Lind, both of whom graciously spend their free time answering the questions of writers like me, and to my friend Gregg Charalambous for inspiring the character of Troy. (He knows why.)

I would be remiss if I didn't extend a sincere *grazie* to my longtime friends Elio Guida and Corinna Semorile and their freaking *adorable* children, Alberto and Vittoria. Not only did they allow me to spend part of our vacation in New Orleans writing *Limoncello Yellow*, they're responsible for my return to Oak Alley plantation, which served as the inspiration for *Prosecco Pink*.

Last but not least, I'd like to thank all my friends who lent me their names for *Prosecco Pink*. You know who you are, and if you don't, you'll have to read the book to find out!

CHAPTER ONE

"Who takes their secretary to a working dinner at a freaking bed and breakfast?" I asked aloud as I sped down Great Mississippi River Road in Louisiana plantation country. I didn't usually talk to myself, but the stress of the situation more than justified it.

"I mean, what's wrong with a restaurant in the French Quarter? People travel from all over the world to eat there."

I steered my 1965 cherry-red Mustang convertible out from behind the 18-wheeler to make sure the black BMW was still up ahead. As soon as I'd spotted it, I dropped back behind the hulking truck. I couldn't let Bradley know I was following him.

Bradley Hartmann was the president of Ponchartrain Bank on Canal Street in New Orleans. With his shocking blue eyes, full lips, and chiseled jaw, he was without a doubt the sexiest bank executive this side of the Mason-Dixon line. And he was mine. We'd been seeing each other for the past three months, ever since his divorce was finalized. Okay, maybe we started seeing each other a bit before then, but that was an accident. I promise.

The problem was, now that his ex-wife was out of the way, his sexy new Chinese-French secretary was in the way. All six feet of her. And at five feet ten inches myself, I wasn't used to looking up to a woman, especially not one as lowdown as Pauline Violette. She did everything she could to keep me away from Bradley—including scheduling these weekend working dinners at bed and breakfasts outside of town. And judging from the way she batted her violet, almond-shaped eyes at him, it was clear why.

"How is it even possible that her eye color matches her last name?" I asked as I hit the gas. "Her boobs are clearly manmade, so those eyes have to be too."

I glanced out the passenger window to try to catch another glimpse of Bradley's BMW, and a flash of pink caught my eye. But it wasn't the coral-pink hue of the thousands of oleanders that framed a stunning, three-story, columned plantation home. It was the pink crinoline skirt of the woman standing on the balcony. It was a hauntingly beautiful image, like something you'd see in an old oil painting.

Unfortunately, the road started to curve sharply, but I was too busy staring at the Southern belle to notice. My tires hit the soft shoulder, and I jerked the steering wheel hard to the left. But it was too late. My car slid sideways right into a swamp.

"*Mamma mia!*" I exclaimed as I realized what had happened. And I did want my mother. Because when I restarted the engine and tried to drive to land, I discovered that I was stuck in the filthy swamp mud.

I threw open my car door, mentally whispered a farewell to my new boots, and stepped into the black swamp water. I trudged around to the back of the car and saw that the rear passenger tire was the problem. I needed to find some wood or stones to put beneath it to try to gain traction. Just as I was about to turn around and head for shore, I made a horrifying discovery. The water was moving.

That's when a bumpy black reptile lifted its moss-covered head above the surface of the murky swamp water, and I came face-to-face with an alligator.

The unsightly beast opened its toothy, cavernous mouth and made a loud hissing sound.

Make that an angry alligator.

"G-good gator," I stammered, frozen with fear.

The alligator lowered its head back into the water and began swimming in a circle, its large cat-like eyes trained on me like the sight of a gun.

"Nice b-boy, Al," I said as I began inching backward through the watery, foul-smelling mud. In case the alligator decided to charge at me, I needed to make it to the driver's side taillight to have a clear shot at the open car door. "Or, maybe you're an Alli?"

As though confirming my suspicion, she slapped her tail hard against the surface of the water.

I estimated her to be around six feet in length—precisely Pauline's height. Then I promptly reminded myself that during my rookie cop days in Austin, Texas, I'd once tackled a male ostrich that was getting frisky with some mothers at a petting zoo. Plus, I'd seen the Gator Boys *and* the Swamp Men wrestle alligators on TV, so I figured that I could take her if push came to shove, er, thrust came to lunge.

Alli stopped near the stump of a bald cypress tree and opened her mouth, revealing eighty or so two-inch-long yellow teeth.

Okay, maybe not.

I took another step backward, and she resumed circling.

"That's right, girl. Just keep swimming," I whispered, advancing another inch or two. "It's good for your waistline." I took another step, and my right foot sunk into what felt like a muddy mass of tree roots. I tried to pull it out, but it was stuck solid. Just like the rear tire of my Mustang.

I felt a fresh wave of fear wash over me, but I knew I had to keep calm. I took a deep breath of the putrid swamp air and tried again to free my foot.

"Franki?" a male voice called.

"Bradley," I breathed. "Oh thank God." My relief quickly gave way to dismay, however, when I realized that he must have seen me following him and Pauline before I ran my car off the road. But surely he would overlook that minor detail now that I was standing in filthy, mosquito-infested swamp water *and* being stalked by an alligator.

"Don't move," he said in a calm, even tone. "You don't want to startle him."

No, I most certainly don't, I thought.

"As soon as he turns to swim away, make a dash for the other side of the car."

"Don't you think I would've done that by now if I could?" I asked, trying to control my increasing hysteria.

"Why can't you? What's wrong?"

"Let me see… Where should I start?"

"Franki," he began, a note of tension creeping into his voice, "why can't you get to the car door?"

"My shoe is caught on something." Should I add that my new boots were the knee-high lace-up kind—with triple buckles?

"Okay, then slip your foot out of your shoe," he said through clenched teeth.

No, now was clearly not the time to tell him. "Um, it's not exactly the slip-your-foot-out-of-your-shoe kind of shoe."

There was a heavy silence.

"Then we're going to have to wait him out," he said.

I gasped. Was he seriously not going to come into the water and pull me out? I mean, saving me from an alligator was the least he could do after planning to take his secretary to a B&B, right?

"If I move, he could attack," Bradley explained. "And you're his closest target."

Before I could protest, I heard an ear-splitting bellow behind me. I jerked my head to the left and saw the largest alligator I'd ever seen. At roughly fifteen feet in length, he was practically a dinosaur.

Terror shot through my body like a white-hot flash of lightening. But I fought to keep my wits about me because the gargantuan gator was standing near Bradley. And as mad as I was about Pauline and the whole leaving-me-to-the-gator thing, I could hardly let Bradley be eaten by a Tyrannosaurus alligator on my account. I had to do something. And fast.

I started jerking my trapped foot as hard as I could. But each time I did, I sunk deeper and deeper into the gooey swamp bottom. The water level was now above my knees, and my panic level was considerably higher.

"You've got to stay still," Bradley warned. "He's extremely dangerous."

"No kidding."

"April is mating season. I think he's looking for a mate."

"Well, tell him Alli isn't interested. And neither am I," I added, just in case.

The big gator bellowed again, causing the hair to stand up on my arms.

Had my refusal offended him or something?

"He's headed toward the water now," Bradley said. "Stay calm."

"Easy for you to say," I muttered under my breath.

I heard a splash as the alligator entered the swamp. At that same moment, Alli dipped beneath the surface of the water. Now there were two of them. Lurking.

Oh God, oh God, oh God. I promise I'll never lust after an alligator handbag or shoes again for as long as I live if you let me survive this, I thought. Then I held my breath and waited.

The swamp was deadly silent, except for the croaking of some green tree frogs.

I started when I heard the sound of a car door opening.

"Bradley, get back in the car!" Pauline called. "It's not safe."

No need to worry about me, *Pauline*, I thought. Not only was the sultry secretary trying to steal my boyfriend, now she was also trying to convince him to leave me for gator food.

"I need you to stay in the car, Pauline," he replied. "I can't have anything happen to you."

Wait a minute. He can't have anything happen to her? *What about* me? I felt a sudden surge of anger-induced adrenaline course through my body. With a steely calm, I crouched down, unbuckled and unlaced my boot and pulled my foot free. Then I yanked the boot out of the tangled roots and rushed around to the driver's seat. I'd paid three hundred bucks for those boots, so there was no way I was leaving one of them in the swamp—gators or no gators.

The second I got into the car, I pulled my 9mm purple Ruger from the glove compartment box. I looked out my driver's side window and saw Bradley kneel down to examine my rear tire.

"Start the engine and press the accelerator," he called.

I did as I was told and watched through the rearview mirror as mud flew from the spinning tire.

He motioned for me to stop. "Let me find something to put under the tire, and then I'll have you try again."

"Be careful," I said.

With my gun in hand, I surveyed the area for hungry—or horny—alligators while Bradley gathered a few small cypress branches.

He arranged the branches beneath my tire and stood up, wiping his hands. "Okay, now."

I hit the gas full throttle and felt my tire gain traction. The car started forward and then spun out to the right, just as something struck the side of my car. I had a terrifying thought. *One of the alligators had lunged for Bradley and hit my car instead!* I threw the car into park and leapt out with my gun drawn.

"Are you crazy?" Pauline screamed. "You could kill him!"

Oh, so now she was worried about the alligator too? Ignoring her protests, I scoured the scene for the offending creature, and that's when I saw him. Bradley, that is. Covered in mud and propped up on his elbows in three-inch-deep swamp water. That was no gator I'd hit, it was my boyfriend. At least, I really, really hoped he was still my boyfriend.

I rushed into the water and knelt at his side. "Are you okay?"

He spit something brown and slimy into the water. "Fine," he replied, a tad tersely.

"Let me help you."

"Now there's an offer you can refuse," Pauline said. I shot her a look. Was that a Mafia jab?

Bradley stood up in silence and did a quick body check before walking to the shore.

"Let me see if I have a towel or something in the car," I said. I ran to the Mustang, but all I could find was a travel-sized package of Kleenex.

I hurried back to Bradley and began dabbing at the mud on his shirt with a tissue. "I'm so sorry about your suit."

He pulled away.

I blinked, surprised. "I said I was sorry."

"It's not about my damned suit, Franki."

"Oh?" I asked, doing my darnedest to feign innocence. But I knew exactly what this was about.

"What were you doing out here on River Road, miles from New Orleans?" he demanded.

Pauline sauntered over and folded her arms across her chest. "Yes, what *were* you doing? Shopping for a plantation home?"

I met her arrogant gaze straight on but avoided her question. "Nice of you to finally get out of the car."

Bradley looked from Pauline to me and sighed. "Never mind, Franki. We'll talk about this later."

Pauline glanced at her smartphone and turned to Bradley, instantly dismissing me. "We still have twenty minutes before your meeting with Mr. Stafford, and according to Google we're only about twenty-five miles from the bed and breakfast. We can still make it if we hurry."

Bradley looked down at his wet, mud-stained clothes. "I can't go looking like this."

"Well, you have that extra shirt and your suit coat in the car, and I have a bottle of Perrier in my purse. If you slip off your pants, I can have some of the more visible stains out before we get there."

Bradley nodded and started for his car.

I gasped. "You're not actually going to take your pants off for her, are you?"

He turned to look at me. "Franki, it's business. This meeting is critical to the future of the bank, and it's my job to do whatever I can to make sure it's a success. I've got to go."

As Bradley climbed into his car, Pauline spun around to face me. She was standing so close that her long, black hair lashed across my face like a silken whip, and her heavy perfume stung my nostrils. "Well, I hope you're satisfied," she said. "Thanks to your little spy game, you've not only ruined Bradley's thousand-dollar suit, you've also potentially cost him a multimillion dollar business deal."

I stared at her open-mouthed. When Bradley told me that he couldn't come over because he and Pauline were having a working dinner at a B&B outside of town, I'd assumed it was just the two of them. I had no idea that they were meeting a client there, not to mention such an important one.

"Now close your mouth and go get cleaned up," Pauline continued. She narrowed her undoubtedly fake violet eyes and looked me up and down. "You're a hot mess."

She did a runway-model turn and strutted to the car.

Oh, I was hot all right. With shame and blinding rage.

* * *

Still smarting from Pauline's smackdown an hour later, I kicked open my front door and threw my mud-caked boots onto the floor.

"Well, look what the cat dragged in," my landlady, Glenda O'Brien, said from a backbend position on the bearskin rug on my living room floor. For a sixty-something-year-old woman, she was startlingly flexible, no doubt due to her forty-something-year career as a stripper.

My best friend and employer, Veronica Maggio, was on the floor beside Glenda, looking exactly as she had when I first met her in our freshman dorm at The University of Texas at Austin. She had her tongue sticking out one side of her mouth as she put the final strokes of Raspberry Fields Forever nail polish on her pinky toe. When she finished, she gave me the once-over. "What happened to *you*?"

I sighed and tossed my purse onto the velvet zebra print rococo chaise lounge. I'd forgotten that Sunday was movie night, or "ladies' night" as Glenda had christened it, and that it was my turn to host. "Oh, not much. I spied on Bradley and Pauline, I nearly got us all killed by a couple of alligators in heat, and then I hit Bradley with my car and pulled a gun on him."

"Oh, sugar," Glenda said, kicking her skinny, veined legs forward out of her backbend and coming to a standing position. "That sounds sexy."

I rolled my eyes. "I'm dead serious."

A coy smile formed at the corners of her mouth, and then she took a long, sensuous drag off her signature Mae West-style cigarette holder. "So am I, child. So. Am. I."

I didn't bother asking her not to smoke since she owned the fourplex that all of us lived in as well as the rather unique bordello-style furnishings in my not-so-humble abode. But I did make a mental note to ask her to stop letting herself in to my apartment.

"Why would you spy on Bradley?" Veronica asked, her brow furrowed. "You said you trusted him."

She never ceased to amaze me. "So, the trust thing is what you're worried about? Not the part about the gator or the gun?"

Veronica screwed the cap on the bottle of nail polish. "Well, you're in one piece, and you're not in jail, so I assumed that those other things got worked out somehow."

"Well, you could at least *act* concerned, you know."

"I'm sorry," she said, fidgeting with the ribbon on her pink baby doll pajamas. "It's just that I thought you were finally over your trust issue with men. That's all."

"I was. I mean, I am," I hurried to add. "I trust Bradley, but I don't trust Pauline around Bradley."

Veronica cocked her head to one side. "Well, isn't that the same thing?"

"No, it isn't. You have no idea how manipulative she is. Plus, she's always so perfect and prepared. I mean, the woman carries a bottle of Perrier water around with her just in case she needs to remove a stain."

"Perrier?" Glenda asked, wrinkling her mouth. "I don't get women who drink bubbly water when they could be drinking champagne. This Pauline sounds suspect, if you ask me."

I cast Veronica a triumphant look. "See? Glenda doesn't trust her either."

Veronica shook her head. "Trusting Pauline isn't the issue. The problem is that you're underestimating Bradley, and it's not like he's stupid."

"No, but he's a man, and she's drop-dead gorgeous. She's built like a model, and she looks like Lucy Liu. To top it all off, she has violet eyes, just like Elizabeth Taylor. And you know how good Liz was at stealing other women's men."

Glenda batted her inch-long, blue false eyelashes. "You know, Ronnie, I think Miss Franki's right. If there's one thing I learned while I was stripping, it's that even the smartest man is no match for a cunning woman."

I nodded, vindicated, although I wasn't entirely sure that you could compare my Harvard-educated, bank president boyfriend to the average strip club patron. But then again, maybe you could.

"You know what I think, sugar?" Glenda continued after taking a long, thoughtful drag off her cigarette.

"What?" I asked, eager to hear her opinion. Glenda was a little rough around the edges, but she often had sage advice.

"You need to make sure that she doesn't put nothin' over on you," she replied, exhaling a cloud of smoke. "So you're gonna have to stick to this Pauline like a pastie on a titty."

Veronica cleared her throat. "Franki, will you let the dogs in? My toes are still wet."

"I'll do it," Glenda said, hopping to her five-inch-high-heeled, slipper-clad feet. "I need to freshen up my glass of champagne, anyway."

As Glenda paraded past me to the kitchen, I noticed that she too was wearing baby doll pajamas—in tight black fishnet with large holes cut from beneath her armpits all the way down to below the hip. It was quite possibly the most clothing I'd ever seen her wear.

Glenda opened the back door, and my brindle Cairn Terrier, Napoleon, bounded over to me, his tail wagging.

"There's my good boy," I said, bending over to greet him.

Napoleon skidded to an abrupt stop, gave a quick sniff of my feet, and took a giant leap backward.

"So much for the unconditional love of pets," I said. "I guess I'll take that as my cue to go shower the swamp off me."

Veronica adjusted the bowtie on her cream Pomeranian, Hercules. "Hurry up so we can start the movie."

"What did you get?" I asked, even though it really didn't matter what the movie was. The only thing I'd be watching were the images of Bradley's hurt face and Pauline's haughty one that kept replaying in my head.

"*Zombie Strippers*," Glenda called from the kitchen.

Obviously her turn to pick the movie, I thought.

"By the way," Veronica began, "I made sugar cookies, and Glenda brought an extra bottle of champagne. Isn't this going to be fun?"

I gave her a blank stare. "Yeah. Tons."

Veronica placed a reassuring hand on my arm. "I know you're worried about Bradley, but try to relax and enjoy the evening."

"I can't. On top of everything else, I might have cost him an important business deal. Do you think I should call and ask how it went?"

"No," she replied. "Let him have tonight to cool off. Then tomorrow you can apologize and explain how you feel about Pauline. I'm sure he'll understand."

I nodded, but I wasn't so sure about the understanding part, especially after my jealousy had almost gotten him killed— first by the alligators and then by me. I set off for the shower thinking that it was going to take a lot more than champagne, sugar cookies, and strippers to get me through the night.

CHAPTER TWO

———

I parked in front of the old brown brick building at 1200 Decatur Street in the French Quarter and glanced up at the bright green, shuttered windows of Private Chicks, Inc. It was the fifth time in two weeks that I'd been late to work, so I was hoping that Veronica hadn't made it to the office yet. There was no sign of her White Audi, but just in case she'd parked on one of the side streets, I tiptoed up the three flights of stairs. As I pushed open the main door, the lobby bell blared like a foghorn.

"You're late!" Veronica shouted from another room.

I walked into her office, my head hung low. "I know. I'm sorry."

"Sorry?" she hissed, sounding remarkably like a Parselmouth from a Harry Potter movie.

I raised my eyes and was surprised to see that in place of her usual designer business attire, Veronica was wearing a dress that looked like something straight out of Glenda's stripper costume closet. She was also really pale—gray, actually. "Are you feeling okay?"

In reply, she stood up from her fuchsia leather chair, threw back her head, and let out a blood-curdling howl.

Wait. A howl? I opened my eyes and realized that a) I was still and bed, and b) Napoleon was the one doing the howling.

I lifted my head to scold him, and it felt like a hatchet had just been buried deep into my skull. "Bad boy, Napoleon," I whispered.

He cocked his head to the side, probably confused by my unusually soft tone.

I settled back into the pillow and wondered whether my dream was some sort of sign that I shouldn't be working for my best friend. But then I quickly decided it was more likely an indication that I needed to lay off the Limoncello. And the zombie strippers.

Rather than lift my head again, I felt around on the nightstand until I found my phone. I glanced at the display—seven a.m., no missed calls, and no texts. The realization that Bradley hadn't tried to contact me hit me like a sledgehammer.

I tossed the phone back onto the nightstand, and, as if on cue, it began to ring.

Certain it was Bradley, I sat up—through the pain—and grabbed the phone. It was my parents. If they were calling on a Monday before they went to work at our family deli, it spelled bad news. I laid down in preparation for the undoubtedly deflating conversation to come.

"Hello?" I replied, trying to hide my concern.

"Francesca? It's your mother, dear." Her shrill voice bore into my head like a drill, as did her habit of stating the obvious.

"Yeah, I know that, Mom."

"You didn't call us last night. Is everything okay?"

I thought about the alligator almost eating me and me almost killing Bradley. "Everything's fine, Mom."

I heard the sound of the receiver slamming down on what I knew to be the kitchen counter.

"Joe!" she shouted. "Francesca's fine!"

I waited for the inevitable grumbled response of my father.

"Tell her that just because she's in New Orleans now doesn't mean she can forget about her family here in Houston," he said.

And there it was.

"Did you hear your father, dear?"

"Yes, but why do you guys get so worried when I miss one phone call?" I asked, even though I already knew the answer. Worrying was my parents' favorite pastime, after Yahtzee.

"Because you usually call us on Sunday, dear."

"I know that, but I was watching a movie with Veronica and Glenda, and it ran late."

"How nice. What did you see?"

This was one of those times when honesty was not the best policy, so I threw out the first innocuous movie that came to mind. "*Gone with the Wind.*"

My mother let out a dreamy sigh. "I've always loved that movie! My favorite part is when Rhett looks at Scarlett and says, 'Frankly, my dear, I don't give a damn.'"

"I'm pretty sure that's everyone's favorite part, Mom."

"Did you know that Clark Gable was bisexual, Francesca?"

This conversation was taking an alarming turn. "Listen, Mom, I need to start getting ready for work. Were you calling to tell me something?"

"Oh yes, dear. Do you remember your cousin Giovanna? The one who's only twenty-four and is already an attorney?"

I put the back of my arm over my eyes. The fact that my mother was bringing up my cousin's age and profession meant one of two things. Either she was calling to tell me that Giovanna was engaged or that she'd been promoted. I was betting on the former. "Of course I remember her. She's my cousin."

"Well, you're not going to believe this, but she's engaged to a judge!"

"*Tombola,*" I said aloud.

"Are you playing Italian bingo, dear?"

I sighed. "It's seven o'clock in the morning, Mom."

"Well, I distinctly heard you say '*tombola.*'"

"I know, I just... Never mind. When's the wedding?"

There was a long pause, and then I heard muffled voices and the sound of a scuffle. I knew from years of experience that my eighty-three-year-old Sicilian grandmother, Carmela, was trying to wrest the receiver from my mother's hands.

"First she's gonna have-a the *festa del fidanzamento,*" my nonna announced, breathless from the struggle.

I should've predicted that my nonna would be listening in to a conversation about a wedding. She'd been trying to get me married for the last thirteen years, since I was sixteen.

"She found a nice-a Sicilian boy," Nonna continued, "so they gonna get married in a church in-a *Sicilia.*"

I couldn't help but feel a tinge of resentment toward Giovanna. By announcing her plans to get married in a Sicilian church, of all damned places, she'd opened up a world of grandma hurt for me. My nonna had already accepted the fact that Bradley wasn't Sicilian, reasoning that a twenty-nine-year-old *zitella* like me couldn't "have-a it all-a." But I wasn't sure how she was going to react to the news that a church wedding to Bradley—provided that he ever proposed to me, that is—was out of the question in light of his divorce. Of course, I avoided the issue and muttered a polite, "That's nice."

Nonna gave a bitter laugh. "'That's-a nice,' she says. Well, if-a you think it's-a so nice, then why you no wanna date those-a Sicilian boys I find-a for you?"

I thought of the string of Sicilian-American chauvinists and mammas' boys she'd given my phone number to a few months before. "Uh, they weren't exactly my type."

"No? And-a what's-a your type, Franki? This I want-a to hear."

I was treading on dangerous ground. If I wavered in my response, she would sick her army of Sicilian suitor-soldiers on me again. "My boyfriend, Bradley Hartmann," I replied in no uncertain terms.

"Okay, and-a when is-a this-a Bradley gonna come-a to meet-a your mamma?"

"Nonna, we've only been dating for a few months."

"That's-a plenty of time. I got-a engaged to your *nonnu*, God rest-a his soul, after two-a weeks.

"But that was in Sicily during Fascism. This is the United States, a democracy, sixty years later."

"And-a you see where all-a this-a freedom has-a gotten you, eh? Twenty-nine years old without-a no husband. *Una tragedia.*"

These calls from home were always so uplifting. "Nonna, I've really got to go. I have a list of things to do before I go to work this morning."

"Well, you add-a this to your list. Tell-a Bradley to meet-a your mamma. Because I'm-a hearing the tick-a tock-a tick-a tock-a of-a your clock all-a the way here in-a Houston."

If I stayed on this call a minute longer, my brain—and my biological clock—were going to explode. "I'll do that," I gushed. "*Ciao Ciao!*"

Happy Monday, I thought as I threw the phone onto the nightstand. I kicked off my hot pink velvet duvet and climbed out of the French bordello-style bed. Thanks to my family, I was now painfully aware that I was old, husbandless, and quickly closing in on barren. So I figured that there was no time like the present to drop by Ponchartrain Bank to find out whether I was boyfriendless too.

* * *

An hour and a half later, I was strolling down Canal Street toward Ponchartrain Bank, taking in the sights and smells of the busy thoroughfare. Unlike the narrow, shop-and-bar-lined streets of the adjacent French Quarter, Canal was one of the main arteries of the city. In the colonial era, it was the dividing line between the French and Spanish portion of the city and the newer American Sector, which is now the Central Business District. Four lanes across with a two-way trolley line in the center, Canal looked more like something you would see in an urban metropolis such as Los Angeles than in a small Southern city like New Orleans. And the same could be said about its hordes of tourists and bums.

As I approached the foreboding black slate walls of the bank, I felt a growing sense of anxiety. I wondered whether Bradley was still mad about the alligator-accident-gun thing. But then I reasoned that the fact that he hadn't called me didn't necessarily mean anything. After all, it was entirely possible that he hadn't been able to call because his meeting ran late. And, looking back on the whole swamp incident now, the only real harm done was a little muddy water on his suit and possibly a lost business deal. But life was about so much more than work. Surely he could see that.

Feeling a surge of newfound confidence, I pushed open the heavy glass door and glanced toward the teller area on the right. Despite her petite 4' 10" frame, I immediately spotted Corinne Mercier, a teller who had helped Veronica and me solve a homicide case at the nearby LaMarca luxury goods store a few months before. She was just finishing up with a client, so I started in her direction to say hello.

"Why, Franki," Pauline's pompous voice boomed from behind me as I was enveloped by a cloud of her perfume. "I'm surprised to see you here."

I turned around and saw Pauline sitting at her desk in front of the row of offices on the left side of the room. "I hardly think it's surprising that I would drop by my bank," I said. Then I added, with emphasis, "And my boyfriend's place of work."

She blinked. "I couldn't agree more. It's just that I thought you'd be hard at work wrestling alligators or gunning down innocent people."

I sighed and slung my hobo bag over my left shoulder to free up my right arm. You know, for gesturing. "Listen, Pauline. I don't have time for this."

She rested her chin on her folded hands and looked me straight in the eye. "Neither do I."

I shifted in my slingbacks. This woman had a lot of nerve. "Could you buzz Bradley and let him know I'm here?"

"He's in a meeting," she replied. And, as though dismissing me, she picked up a jar of opaque white glitter and began sprinkling it into a stuffed envelope.

I gave an impatient toss of my hair. "Okay, what time will it end?"

"No clue." She picked up another envelope and added the white flakes.

"Can you at least tell me how the meeting went with Mr. Stafford last night?" I asked through quasi-clenched teeth.

She ceased sprinkling and glared up at me. "I'm not at liberty to discuss confidential bank business."

I'd set myself up for that one. "All right, then. Just tell Bradley I stopped by."

"That'll be number one on my to-do list." She flashed a false smile.

Somehow, I doubted that. I started to walk away, but my curiosity got the better of me. "What are you doing, anyway?"

Pauline turned up her nose with a self-important air. "Not that it's any of your business, but I'm putting together the invitations for the 'Shoot for the Moon' charity event I'm organizing for the bank. It's to raise scholarship funds for kids who were victims of Hurricane Katrina."

"So, what's the white stuff?"

"It's supposed to be moon dust," she replied, rolling her eyes.

"You sure it's not anthrax?"

She smirked and shook her head in disgust. "Everything's a crime to you, isn't it? And we saw where that got you last night."

I felt a wave of anger rise in my chest, but I fought to maintain my composure. I couldn't cause a scene at Bradley's bank, especially not after the events of last night. "Think what you want, but a lot of people are going to open those envelopes and panic when they see white powder."

"Oh, and I see you're also a cynic," she said, raising her eyebrows in mock surprise. "How charming."

I narrowed my eyes. "Coming from someone like you, I'll take that as a compliment."

She fluttered her eyelashes and faked a mournful frown.

My hands balled into fists. I needed to leave before my free right arm did something I would regret. I spun on my heels and stomped toward the teller area.

"See ya later, *alligator*," Pauline intoned.

I froze in my tracks but didn't turn around. I had no intention of giving her the satisfaction. Instead, I headed straight for Corinne's friendly face.

"*Bonjour*, Franki," Corinne said in her thick French accent. "I see you meet Pauline."

I took a deep, calming breath. "Yeah," I said, casting a hostile glance in her direction, "I had the great pleasure of meeting her a few weeks ago when you were on vacation."

"Ah." Corinne looked down. With her pixie haircut and big blue eyes, she looked like a sad Tinker Bell.

I rested my arms on the counter. "What's the matter?"

She looked up. "I sink she does not like me very much."

Even though I was convinced that Pauline was evil incarnate, I was surprised that she'd take issue with a sweet person like Corinne. "Honestly, I don't think she likes anyone very much, so I wouldn't take it too hard if I were you."

"*Peut-être*," she said, her chin quivering.

"Did something happen between the two of you?"

She wiped away a tear. "I suppose I can tell you. But please, do not tell Bradley."

"Of course not," I said, leaning forward.

She took a deep breath. "On Friday, zere was money missing from my teller drawer. Pauline say I took ze money. But I did not."

Now I was shocked. I didn't know Corinne very well, but I knew she wasn't the type to steal money from her place of work. "How much was missing?"

"Five hundred dollars."

I gasped. "What happened? Do you think you made some kind of mistake?"

"I don't know, but I repay ze money."

"Out of your own pocket?" That was a sizeable chunk of change on a bank teller's salary. And on mine, for that matter.

She nodded. "But now Mr. Hartmann sinks I steal."

"I doubt very seriously he sinks—I mean, *thinks*—that. He knows what an honest, loyal employee you are."

She shook her head. "No, he does not. Pauline say she *saw* me take ze money."

"Oh, Corinne. I'm so sorry." I couldn't imagine why Pauline would go so far as to accuse Corinne of theft. I didn't think it likely that she was after Corinne's job since she struck me as the type who would set her career sights much higher. But what other reason would she have had for saying Corinne took the money? And what had happened to that five hundred dollars, anyway?

"Franki," Corinne said, shaking me from my thoughts. "Yes?"

"Be careful. Zis Pauline, she is not a nice person."

I thought of her potential influence on Bradley, and my jaw tightened. "I will. And you do the same. Keep your eyes on your teller drawer at all times, and let me know if anything else happens."

* * *

As I headed down Canal Street toward the Mississippi River, I couldn't stop thinking about that missing money. I really hoped that Bradley was looking into the situation. Because even though I had no idea what was going on at Ponchartrain Bank, my gut was telling me that something wasn't right.

My gut was also telling me, loud and clear, that it was time for breakfast. And for me, breakfast in the French Quarter, and often lunch and dinner, meant only one thing, beignets. But it was already nine, so the world-famous Café du Monde was out of the question. By this time, the line to get in usually stretched all the way down to the Civil War era, model cannon in neighboring Washington Artillery Park. I took a left on Decatur Street and stopped instead at the less renowned but optimistically named New Orleans Famous Beignets and Coffee Café and ordered a dozen of the powdered-sugar pastries. To share with everyone at the office, naturally.

Ten minutes later, I exited the restaurant cradling a bag of piping hot beignets. When I looked down to grab my sunglasses from my purse, I ran straight into a little woman with the body type of the Pillsbury Doughboy and a Chanel handbag the size of a sixth grader. The impact was so strong that we bounced off one another.

"Oooh!" the woman exclaimed. She straightened her purple knit poncho and then smoothed her platinum-highlighted, bouffant brown bob. Her stubby fingers were tipped with white, paddle-shaped acrylic fingernails decorated with tiny replicas of the same silver and gold moons and stars that adorned her charm bracelet, necklace, and earrings.

"I'm so sorry," I gushed. "Are you okay?"

She stared at me with green eyes as big as saucers and raised her pudgy hand to her small mouth. "I'm fine," she said in a honeyed voice. "But you're obviously not."

I felt my face and did a quick check of my limbs. Everything seemed in order, that is, except for that twenty extra pounds in my mid-section and backside. "Um, I'm not sure I understand."

Her round face grew serious. "I wasn't referring to your earthly body. I meant your *aura*. It's black."

That explains the moons and stars, I thought. "Yeah, I've had kind of a rough morning."

She shook her head, causing her jewelry to jingle like Santa's sleigh bells. "It's not about your morning. And I know, because I talk to spirits."

My first inclination was to tell her that the only spirits I wanted to know about were those of the alcohol variety. But in the short time I'd been in New Orleans, I'd learned to treat the drunks and the crazies in the Quarter courteously—and then flee. "How interesting," I said with a polite nod. "But, I'm late for work, so I'd better be on my way."

"Wait!" she shouted. "This could be a matter of life and death."

At that precise moment thunder rumbled overhead.

I glanced up and saw that dark clouds were quickly obscuring the sunny sky of moments before. I looked back at the woman, and an uneasy feeling came over me. I didn't like the turn the weather was taking, not to mention the turn of this conversation.

"Stay still." She grabbed my left arm, and then her eyes rolled back into her head.

My jaw dropped. I couldn't tell whether she was about to commune with spirits or have a seizure.

As I was pondering what to do, the woman's left arm shot into the air, and her charm bracelet began to vibrate.

Definitely a seizure. I pulled out my phone to call 9-1-1.

"It's worse than I thought," the woman wailed. "Much worse."

"What is?" I asked, alarmed. "Are you going to faint?"

She opened her eyes and dropped my arm. "No," she said in a surprisingly wail-less tone. "I told you, I'm fine. But the spirit I'm talking to isn't. She's in complete hysterics."

The spirit's not the only one, I thought as I slipped my phone back into my purse.

The woman began wringing her hands and pacing back and forth in her denim mini miniskirt and four-inch-heeled, leopard-print boots. "The spirit wants you to know that she did something bad for a family member, and it got her *killed*." She stopped and grabbed hold of my arms. "She was *murdered*."

"O-kaaay." I contemplated shaking free of her grip and making a break for it, but then I opted for a more rational approach. "Well, tell her that I just happen to investigate murders for a living, but only for clients who are alive."

She let go of me. "The spirit knows *thaaat*. Why do you think she's trying to warn you?"

"Warn me? Why on earth—I mean, why in heaven—would she need to do that?"

"What she did has put you and possibly even your friend Valerie or Vicki—no, Veronica—in grave danger."

Veronica? I got goose bumps on my arms. This wasn't crazy anymore; it was downright creepy.

"And the worst part of it is," she continued, "that there's nothing she can do to help you now. You're on your own."

I stared at the ground, trying to process what I'd just heard. I didn't believe in psychics, but where the supernatural was concerned, I made it my policy to be safe rather than sorry. And since I didn't know how this woman knew about Veronica, I decided to err on the side of caution and consider her warning. Now, even though the "you're on your own" part of her message was troubling, it hardly came as a surprise. My solitary state had been the theme of the day, starting with the reminder of my *zitella*-hood from my nonna and ending with Pauline's refusal to let me anywhere near Bradley. But was I really in some kind of danger?

As though in reply from the spirit herself, a bolt of lightening flashed as thunder cracked in the blackened sky. Then a hard rain began to fall.

CHAPTER THREE

———

Seizing upon the downpour as my opportunity to escape the whole psycho situation with the psychic, I shrugged and said, "Gotta run!"

As I dashed beneath the green-and-white striped awning of the café's covered patio, the strap of my hobo bag caught on the back of a wrought iron chair. I lurched forward, narrowly missing a table of Japanese tourists who started screaming as though they were witnessing a real-life version of *The Return of Godzilla*. When I regained my balance, I turned to free my purse strap. And then *I* let out a scream. The odd little woman was standing right in front of me, rooting around in her colossal Chanel bag.

"I wish I would have known it was going to rain," she whined, pulling out an entire box of tissues.

"Yeah," I muttered. Apparently, her metaphysical abilities didn't extend to meteorological phenomena.

"I *just* had my hair done this morning," she added as she began dabbing at her Texas-sized tease.

"That's a bummer," I said, staring fascinated at her huge hairstyle. It had a peculiar sheen to it, like it was gleaming. Not in a rain-spattered or even an otherworldly way, but in a freshly applied varnish one.

She sighed and reached into her bra. "Anyway, take this," she said, pulling out a business card. "You're going to need it."

I took the moon-embossed card—using only my fingernails—and read aloud, "Chandra Toccato, Crescent City Medium."

"'Chandra' is Hindi for 'shining moon.'"

And your last name is Italian for "touched," I thought.

"Well," she prodded. "Do you get it?"

I glanced up at her. "What?"

"Chandra? Crescent City Medium? They both refer to the moon!" she said, beaming. "So, becoming a psychic was literally in the stars for me. Or in the cards—as in, tarot cards?" She put her chubby fingers to her lips and giggled, exactly like the Pillsbury Doughboy does. "And you're not going to believe this, but I'm also a Cancer. You know, a moon child?"

I nodded and then scrutinized her moon-pie face, yet another aspect of her lunar life theme, looking for signs of insanity.

"I need to be honest with you, though," she continued, touching my arm. "I'm originally from Boston. But after Katrina, I felt called to the Crescent City, which is only natural given my celestial essence and all. So I convinced my husband Lou—we were high school sweethearts—that we had to move to New Orleans because the people here were in desperate need of our services."

"He's a psychic too?" I wasn't really interested—just coerced into conversational compliance by her incessant chatter.

"No," she said, furrowing her brow. "A plumber."

"Oh."

Chandra reached into her purse and pulled out a compact. "I was talking about the living *and* the dead," she explained as she examined her hair in the mirror. "Hurricanes are murder on plumbing, and they're terribly stressful for spirits, what with the atmospheric changes and high winds."

The high winds? I had a mental image of a gaggle of Caspar the Friendly Ghosts clutching their heads and screaming in fear of their non-lives while getting tossed around by a hurricane. Clearly, it was time to shake myself out of my Chandra-induced stupor. "So…about that warning. Can you give me some specifics?"

She snapped the compact shut. "Not right now."

"Why not?"

"The spirit's just too upset to speak," she said, depositing the compact into her bag.

"Oh, she is, is she?" I asked, annoyed. This spirit, provided she was real, of course, was something else.

"Try to understand her point of view," Chandra said, putting her hand on her hip and gesturing with her free hand. "She just had to fess up to some pretty rough stuff, so naturally she's embarrassed."

I frowned. I should have been biting into a beignet by now, but instead I was bickering with a selfish spirit via her mad medium. "Tell her that I'm kind of upset *myself* now that I know she's put me in danger."

She pursed her lips. "That wouldn't help. Spirits are really temperamental beings, so I don't want to push her. And, between you and me," she whispered, shielding her mouth with the back of her hand, "spirits kind of freak me out."

Now I was really taken aback. "You're a psychic, and spirits make you uncomfortable?"

Chandra glared at me. "It's not like I chose this profession. It was preordained. Besides, how would you react if a spirit was yelling at you?"

I wanted to tell her that I'd probably see a psychologist, but to be polite I went with, "I'd run like hell."

"You see?" she said, raising her brow. "So, we'll just have to wait until she feels like talking again."

"Whenever that is, please let me know." I handed her my card.

"I most certainly will." She took the card and looked at the front and back. "Franki Amato, Private Investigator. Private Chicks, Inc.," she read. "I don't get it."

Now it was my turn to get defensive. "You know, there's the two references to 'private,' and 'chicks' rhymes with 'dicks'—as in, 'detectives?'"

"Hm." She sniffed and dropped the card into her purse. "Well, it's stopped raining, so I really should be going."

As I watched Chandra walk serenely down Decatur Street, I pulled the bag of now lukewarm beignets closer to my chest. Even though I had my doubts about her psychic abilities, I couldn't help but feel concerned about my personal safety—and my conspicuous lack of business card symmetry.

* * *

I slunk into Veronica's office a good hour late and silently deposited the bag of beignets on her desk. I saw it as a kind of peace offering, albeit a cold and soggy one.

Veronica eyed the bag and then looked up at me. "What's the matter with you?"

"Huh?" I asked, startled by her unusually harsh tone. I felt like I was dreaming about zombie-stripper Veronica again. But one look at her healthy glow and crisp pink Donna Karan suit confirmed that she wasn't undead.

"You look like you've seen a ghost," she replied, leaning back in her chair.

"Oh, it's probably powdered sugar," I explained, wiping my mouth. "I ate a couple of beignets on my way in to the office." Okay, so I really had five or six. But who could blame me after my anxiety-inducing encounter with that psychic?

"No, you're pasty," Veronica said. "Are you feeling okay?"

"I think so," I whispered as I felt the lymph glands in my neck.

"Now don't go all hypochondriac on me," she warned. "It was just an observation."

"I'm not," I fibbed, casually moving my hand to my earring. It was a well-established fact that where contracting illnesses was concerned, I was open to suggestions. And now that she'd mentioned it, I *was* feeling kind of sick to my stomach. Not that it had anything to do with those half-dozen beignets.

"Wait. This is about Bradley, isn't it? Have you talked to him yet?"

I flopped down into a chair in front of her desk and let out a deep sigh. "No, I went by the bank, but he was in a meeting. Or, at least, that's what his protector, Pauline, claimed."

"Ah," Veronica said, crossing her arms. "That explains it."

"What?" I asked.

She smirked. "You're still feeling threatened by her."

"I am not," I snapped. "Pauline is hardly threatening. Controlling and deceitful, yes, but nothing I can't handle."

"Well, I've known you long enough to be able to tell when something's wrong. So, what is it?"

I debated whether to tell her about Chandra and the spirit. In keeping with her incredibly disciplined, workaholic nature, Veronica had a strictly practical, non-mystical approach to life. But on the positive side, you could always count on her for down-to-earth advice. Plus, I was terrible at keeping secrets. So I blurted out, "Something really freaky happened at New Orleans Famous Beignets and Coffee this morning."

"What? The cashier predicted you'd order a dozen beignets without you even telling her?" She snickered.

I shifted uncomfortably in my seat. How did Veronica know I'd ordered twelve beignets? "No," I replied, refusing to confirm or deny the specifics of my order. "I met a psychic who said a spirit told her I was in danger."

She rolled her eyes. "Well I hope you did the *scongiuri* because if a psychic said it, you know it's true."

Scongiuri was an Italian hand gesture used to ward off the evil eye. It looks like The University of Texas' hook 'em horns sign, but with the index and pinky fingers pointed toward the ground. My nonna taught it to me when I was little, and Veronica never missed an opportunity to make fun of me for doing it. The thing was, I didn't think I'd made the gesture after Chandra told me I was in danger, so I immediately dropped my hands to my side, out of view of Veronica's judgmental eyes, and did so. Then I gave her a pointed look and said, "I wouldn't be so blasé about this if I were you, because that spirit knew your name."

"Come on, Franki. Psychics make it their business to know people's personal information. That's how they reel them in."

I resented the implication that I was a sucker, so I retaliated with a sure-fire comeback. "Okay then, explain to me how she would've known that I had a friend named Veronica."

"Hm, let me see." She pressed her index finger to her temple in mock concentration. "Our Private Chicks television commercial?"

"Oh. Right." I'd completely forgotten that our first-ever commercial was airing this week. In all likelihood, Chandra had seen us on TV, which meant that the Crescent City Medium was nothing but a Crescent City Con Artist.

No sooner had I reached that conclusion than thunder boomed in the sky so violently it shook our building. I jumped in my seat and told myself that those eerily timed thunderbolts couldn't possibly be messages from the spirit. Could they?

Veronica stood up and looked out the window just as the lobby door slammed hard.

I instantly recognized the exuberant slam as that of David Savoie, our nineteen-year-old, part-time employee.

"Will David ever learn to close the door like a normal person?" Veronica asked.

"Not until he gives up those Red Bulls and his testosterone stops surging," I replied.

A drenched David burst into the room holding a dripping wet Tulane backpack. "*Dude*, what's up with the *rain*?"

Veronica frowned at the water pooling around him on the hardwood floor. "Let me get you something to dry off with."

David moved aside to let her pass and turned to face me. "Like, the rain totally came out of nowhere. When I was parking my car, it was sunny and clear. But then when I got out, it was instant downpour."

"It happened to me too," I said. "It's kind of weird, isn't it?"

"I'll say," he said with a brisk nod.

Veronica returned with two towels and handed one to David. "Well, it *is* the rainy season. You know the old adage about April showers."

"I dunno," David said, as he began to towel dry his hair. "I've lived here all my life, and I've never seen anything like it."

I shifted in my chair. So, I wasn't wrong in assuming that the weather was bizarre, even for New Orleans. There was something unusual in the air today. But was it even remotely possible that it was a spirit?

"Hey, speaking of weird," he continued, "are you guys expecting a client?"

I looked at Veronica, who was crouching in the doorway and sopping up the water.

"There's nothing on the books," she replied. "Why?"

"Because there's this really creepy lady out front in a black Cadillac DeVille," he replied.

I felt my stomach lurch as I thought of Chandra. "She's not, by any chance, a doughy little woman with a Dallas-style do, is she?"

"Nah," David replied. "From what I could tell, she's way skinny, and her hair is black and white and spiky. Oh, and she's got a crapload of dogs."

Veronica stood up and walked to the window overlooking Decatur Street. "I see the car, but I don't see her."

"That's because I'm right here," a deep feminine voice drawled from the doorway. "I've been waiting in the lobby for the past five minutes."

We all turned, and I stared open-mouthed at the woman. Not because she'd startled me with her brash manner of speaking but because of her imposing appearance. She was sixty-ish and rail thin with skin as pale as the pearls around her neck. But her high cheekbones and prominent chin, not to mention her blood-red lips and fingernails, made it clear that she was anything but delicate.

"I'm sorry about the wait," Veronica said as she walked over to greet the woman. "We didn't hear you come in. I'm Veronica Maggio and—"

"Delta Dupré," she interrupted, extending her hand like she was expecting it to be kissed rather than shook.

Veronica took her hand and awkwardly shook-raised it up and down. "What can we do for you, Ms. Dupré?"

Delta cocked an eyebrow à la Cruella De Vil. "That's 'Mrs.' And the first thing you can do is have your boy take my coat."

"Uh, yes, Mrs.—I mean, uh, ma'am," a red-faced David stammered as he took her white floor-length fur and scurried away.

Delta frowned. "I hate to be cliché, but it's just so hard to find good help these days."

I was fuming at her rudeness. "Actually, David isn't our servant."

She turned and looked me up and down. "And you are?"

"Franki Amato."

"Interesting name," she said in a decidedly disinterested tone. Rather than extending her hand, as she had for Veronica, she began toying with a Gothic black cameo brooch that was pinned to the bodice of her red silk dress. It was framed in diamonds and depicted a skull in a top hat against a backdrop of guns and roses.

I glanced at Veronica and realized that she was oblivious to Delta's arrogance. Whenever jewelry was in the vicinity, she zoned out on her surroundings and zoomed in on the sparkly object.

"What an unusual brooch!" Veronica exclaimed. "Who is that supposed to be on the cameo?"

"It's Baron Samedi, a degenerate voodoo god who leads depraved souls to the underworld. I wear it because it reminds me of my late husband, Jackson Dupré."

Must have been some guy, I thought. *Much like his wife.*

Veronica cocked her head to one side. "That name sounds familiar. Was your husband in local politics?"

"He was the chief of police for twenty-five years. And now that I need him, the SOB isn't around. That's why I'm here."

"Please, have a seat," Veronica said, ignoring Delta's jab at her not-so-dearly departed. "I'm sure we can help you."

"I think you can too," Delta said, taking a seat in one of the two chairs facing Veronica's desk. "I saw that skinny old prostitute on the evening news a few months ago—the one who did all the interviews after you girls solved the murder of that shop girl?"

"Her name is Glenda, and she's an ex-stripper," I said as I reluctantly sat down beside her.

Delta waved her hand. "Prostitute...stripper... Same damn difference. Anyhow, I have an unusual case on my hands, so I need investigators who can think outside the box, unlike the ones currently employed by our police department. And since you two outsmarted the cops on the shop girl strangling, you're perfect for my predicament."

"Can you tell us more about your, uh, predicament?" I asked.

"I'm the executive director of Oleander Place, the antebellum plantation on River Road?" She looked at Veronica and me for signs of recognition.

I recognized it all right. It was the very plantation home that had distracted me and caused me to swerve into the swamp. "I just drove past it yesterday. You've got a really eye-catching place there."

"Yes, well, I'm afraid its beauty has been marred by a rather unfortunate incident," she said, fiddling with her brooch. "You see, three days ago, a twenty-eight-year-old woman named Ivanna Jones was murdered there. I found the body when I opened the plantation at eight o'clock the next morning."

"I heard something about that on the radio last night," Veronica said.

"Unfortunately, it's all over the news," Delta replied. "As you can imagine, the cancelations have already begun— weddings, craft fairs, even a TV show. And the problem is that Oleander Place isn't just my livelihood—it's my heritage. I'm a descendent of the original owner, General Knox Patterson. So, I'll do whatever it takes to protect my income and my family name."

I had no doubt she was telling the truth. She was no sweet Southern belle. She was a surly Southern beast. "Do you know how the victim got to the plantation?"

"She drove. Her car was in the parking lot, unlocked, with her purse on the front seat." Delta reached into her black Louis Vuitton and pulled out a manila envelope. "This is a copy of the police report and photos from the scene."

I looked at her in surprise. "How did you get those?"

"Thanks to my Jackson, I still have important connections on the police force."

Veronica took the envelope and began to examine its contents. "This will be a tremendous help to us."

I turned to Delta. "Did you know the victim?"

"No, but she took one of our plantation tours a few weeks ago. I'm sure it was her, but I can't prove it because she didn't pay with a credit card or sign the guest registry."

"Was anyone with her?" I asked.

"I don't know. Our tour groups are often fairly large, and I wasn't really paying attention."

I looked at Veronica. "Anything interesting in the report?"

She scanned the information on the first page and then looked at Delta. "The cause of death is listed as 'undetermined.'"

"Which is why I need your help," Delta said. "The police are dilly-dallying around with this investigation because they think the woman committed suicide. And as a business owner, I don't have time to waste. Every day this crime goes unsolved is a day I lose money."

By now it was clear where Delta's priorities lay. This woman was a real steel magnolia. "What makes you think it wasn't suicide?"

"It has to do with the placement of the body and the plantation's history," she replied.

"Take a look," Veronica said, handing me a photo.

It was a shot of a beautiful young woman with long, golden-blonde hair and rose-red lips. If I didn't know better, I would have said she was asleep. "Wow," I breathed, "she looks just like Sleeping Beauty."

Delta shook her head. "No, she's the spitting image of Evangeline Lacour."

"Who's that?" I asked.

"She was Knox's second wife. He spent a fortune building Oleander Place for her, and then the tramp went and cheated on him. You know how those French women are," she said with a knowing look.

I couldn't resist asking, "Are you related to her, as well?"

"Certainly not!" Delta replied, her eyes wide with alarm. "I'm descended from Knox and his first wife, Caroline Landry. He and Evangeline had no children, thank heaven."

Veronica cleared her throat. "Why do you say the victim looks like Evangeline?"

"Well, for one thing, she's the spitting image of the oil painting Knox commissioned of Evangeline when they were married. And for another, she was found lying in Evangeline's bed in the exact same position Evangeline was in when she died in 1837, and she was wearing her pink crinoline dress."

I immediately thought of the woman I'd seen on the balcony of Oleander Place. But I knew that it couldn't have been Ivanna Jones, because she was killed the day before.

"You mean, the dress Evangeline was wearing when she died?" Veronica asked.

Delta nodded. "We have it in storage at Oleander Place. It's the one we always see Evangeline wearing when she appears."

Now *my* eyes opened wide in alarm. "Come again?"

"Evangeline's spirit still resides in the house," she replied.

I swallowed hard. "The plantation is haunted?"

Delta raised her chin and gave a smug smile. "As haunted as they come. Oleander Place ranks among America's top ten most haunted buildings."

To say that my mind was reeling would be putting it mildly. I simply couldn't process the possibility that I'd seen the ghost of Evangeline Lacour on the balcony of Oleander Place yesterday. Surely it was one of the plantation tour guides, right? And then I thought of Chandra. Despite my better judgment, I wondered whether there was any connection between the spirit she'd claimed she was talking to and Evangeline. Or was it just one big transcendental coincidence that two people had approached me about incidents involving spirits on the same day? Either way, I was starting to get the distinctly ominous feeling that the inhabitants of the netherworld—or their earthly representatives—were trying to tell me something. And I didn't like it. Not one bit.

CHAPTER FOUR

———

I cocked my head to the side. "When you say 'as haunted as they come,' what do you mean, exactly?"

"What do you think I mean?" Delta snapped. "I mean we have a lot of ghosts floating around Oleander Place."

"Whoa!" David exclaimed—from a safe distance in the hallway.

"You can say that again," I muttered. I was starting to feel like I was in a speeding "doom buggy" on Disneyland's Haunted Mansion ride, and I wanted it to slow the hell down.

"Besides Evangeline," Delta continued, "Knox and Beauregard are the main spirits on the plantation."

"Who's Beauregard?" Veronica asked as she began typing notes.

"He's Knox's brother, and he was a decorated army colonel," Delta said with pride. "But then when Knox made general before him, he turned pirate."

"Pirate?" I squirmed in my seat. Of course, I'd never met a pirate, alive or dead. But if I were a betting girl, I'd wager that a pirate ghost was not the friendliest of souls.

"They called him 'Beau the Black,' and he was notorious for his ruthlessness." Delta touched her pearls, and the corners of her mouth turned upward into a Joker-like smile. "I'm assuming you girls have heard of him?"

I looked questioningly at Veronica.

"I'm sure he's very infamous," she began politely, "but I'm afraid we're not well versed in pirate lore."

Delta frowned. "He was one of the pirate Jean Lafitte's right-hand men. In fact, Beau and Lafitte helped General Andrew Jackson defeat the British at the Battle of New Orleans. You *have* heard of Lafitte, I presume?"

"Oh, sure," I replied as I grabbed the stack of photos from Veronica's desk. "When I went to that bar 'Jean Lafitte's Blacksmith Shop' in the French Quarter a month or so ago. And if he was anything like that purple voodoo drink they serve there, then he must have been a real swashbuckler."

The room fell silent. I looked up from the pictures and saw both Delta and Veronica staring at me. I felt my face flush, probably similar in color to that drink. "So...how was Evangeline killed?"

Delta raised her brow. "She was poisoned."

Veronica's fingers began flying over her keyboard. "How do you know? Are there any records?"

"Yes, the *Times-Picayune* reported on her death. And we also have Knox's journal in our plantation archives. Both sources indicate that Evangeline was found with an oleander flower in her hands. At first, everyone thought it was because she loved oleanders. It was well known at the time that she was the one who had them planted on the grounds." She looked hard at Veronica. "And for the record, she just insisted on that coral pink. Had it been me, I would have selected a less vulgar shade."

Veronica nodded. She'd always turned up her nose at coral jewelry because she didn't approve of orange in her pink.

"But then they discovered oleander in a half-empty cup of tea on the table beside Evangeline's bed." Delta paused and curled her lips. "As far as I'm concerned, that flower was a message that Evangeline was as toxic as the oleander plant."

Talk about the pot calling the kettle black, I thought as I flipped through the pictures.

"Who did they think poisoned her?" Veronica asked.

Delta exhaled deeply. "Knox blamed Antoinette, the house slave who'd served her the tea, and the police agreed. Of course, she fled the plantation, and the case was closed. Nevertheless, a rumor persisted that Knox had done it."

I looked up at Delta. "Why would anyone suspect Knox?"

"Because the day before the French tart was killed, he found out that she was planning to run off with his brother," she explained with a pointed look. "Apparently, he came across a letter she was writing to Beau that detailed their sordid affair.

And everyone knew about it, too, because Knox woke the whole plantation that night."

"What for?" I asked.

Delta snorted. "He was tearing the place apart looking for a pink diamond Beau had given Evangeline."

Veronica leaned forward, her eyes sparkling like a precious gem. "There was a pink diamond?"

"Yes. In the letter Evangeline mentions an emerald-cut diamond that Beau had secretly given her as a promise of his intent to marry her. Like her beloved oleanders, it was that tacky coral pink," she said with a dramatic eye roll. "He told her he would come for her as soon as he'd made enough money from smuggling to buy some land and build her a house."

Veronica sighed. "That's so romantic!"

Delta threw her head back and gave a raucous laugh, revealing a row of yellow teeth that clashed with her alabaster skin. "Foolish, if anything. But men are blind when it comes to a beautiful woman."

I instantly thought of Bradley and Pauline and grudgingly found myself agreeing with her. "What ever happened to the diamond?"

"No one knows," Delta replied. "The only record we have of it is what Evangeline wrote in the letter. She said that she would sit on the balcony holding the stone in her hand while she waited for Beau's ship to come down river. And that's where we usually see her, on the balcony."

I shuddered. *Was that what I had seen? The spirit of Evangeline waiting for her buccaneer beau, Beau?*

"What happened to Knox and Beau after Evangeline's death?" Veronica asked as she resumed typing.

Delta picked a white hair off her blouse. "Knox died in 1838, presumably of a broken heart." She straightened in her chair and raised her chin. "But Beau died valiantly in 1862 in the capture of New Orleans, trying to defend our beloved city from those dreadful Union forces during the Civil War."

I got the distinct feeling that Delta was prouder of the pirate than the general.

"Today, Beau's spirit roams the grounds of Oleander Place looking for Evangeline—Knox had the trollop buried in an unmarked grave, naturally. And Knox storms the halls looking for Beau."

Great. A ruthless pirate and *an angry general*, I thought as I studied a photograph of Ivanna's body. *Can't wait.*

"Do you know where Evangeline was buried?" Veronica asked.

"I don't, nor do I care to," she replied, crossing her arms.

The more I looked at Ivanna's body, the more something seemed off about the picture. And then it hit me. "You said that Ivanna was found in the exact same position as Evangeline, but I don't see an oleander flower."

Delta clutched her creepy cameo. "Oh yes. That's because she was holding a bottle of lip gloss."

Veronica began turning the pages of the police report. "That's mentioned here, but it says the bottle was unmarked. Do you know who made it?"

She shrugged. "Who knows?"

"Wait a second," Veronica said, returning to the first page. "The report has a business listed as Ivanna's personal address. Lickalicious Lips. I wonder if it was one of their brands."

I sat up straight in my chair. "Hey! They make that flavored lip gloss I used to wear in college, remember? The one I had to stop buying because I couldn't stop licking my lips?"

"Yeah." Veronica grinned. "That was the semester you sprained your tongue on Bailey's Irish Crème Brown."

Delta curled her lips in disgust. "The victim made liquor-flavored lip gloss? No wonder someone up and killed her."

Veronica and I exchanged a look.

"Anyway," Delta continued, "that lip gloss is one of the things that makes me think this wasn't a suicide. If this Ivanna woman was just some nutcase who wanted to recreate Evangeline's deathbed look, then why in the world would she be holding a bottle of lip gloss instead of an oleander flower?""

I held up the picture of Ivanna. "Did the bottle match the shade of red she was wearing?"

"No, it was coral pink. Just like her dress."

I bit my lip. "That's odd."

"Indeed," Delta conceded.

"What about the cup of tea?" Veronica asked.

"There was no tea. But since there was no obvious cause of death, the coroner's office is testing for poison among other things."

Veronica flipped through the police report. "I don't see any interrogation records. Have the police questioned your employees?"

"They haven't bothered because they think it was suicide and because the plantation was closed at the time of death. But that's another thing that makes me think this was a murder. We have an alarm system at the plantation, and it was on the night this happened. Yet this woman got inside without setting it off."

I had to agree with Delta. Unless Ivanna had somehow managed to get a key to the plantation and the code to the alarm, then someone had let her in.

"Has anyone from Ivanna's family contacted you?" Veronica asked.

"Not so far. I don't even think the police have talked to them yet. From what I understand, her father is overseas."

"We'll need to talk to your employees," Veronica said. "When would be a good time for us to come to Oleander Place?"

"It'll have to be tomorrow." She glanced at a diamond-encrusted silver watch. "In about an hour we have to start setting up for a dinner. Fortunately, the charity hosting the event didn't cancel on us, but they did demand a discount, the cheap bastards. Anyhow, it's getting late, so I'd best be on my way."

As if on cue, David popped around the doorjamb with her fur coat.

She scowled at him as she rose to her feet and snatched the coat from his hand.

Seeing Delta's fur reminded me of something we'd forgotten to ask. "Wait. I have one more question."

"Make it quick," she snapped as she slipped on her coat.

"Did you find Ivanna's clothes at the scene?"

She blinked. "No, just her purse. Like I told you before."

"Thanks," I said, puzzled. That implied that Ivanna had arrived at Oleander Place already wearing the dress, which raised a lot more questions than it answered.

"Now, you girls can come to the plantation at one o'clock tomorrow," she said. Then she narrowed her eyes and pointed a bony finger at Veronica and me. "But come alone. And don't even *think* about talking to the press."

I watched in a mixture of awe and fear as she spun on her heels and exited the room, her fur flying behind her. The second I heard the lobby door slam shut I turned to David. "So, those dogs you saw in Delta's car...they weren't Dalmatians, were they?"

* * *

I tugged at the handle of my front door to make sure it was locked and then headed across the street to Thibodeaux's Tavern. As I walked, I averted my gaze to avoid seeing the spooky cemetery that was next to the bar. It might sound childish, but living by tombs, sarcophagi, obelisks, and gothic statues didn't exactly raise your spirits. In fact, some days it damn near drove me to drink. But for reasons I simply couldn't fathom, Veronica had no problem with it, which is why she arranged for me to live next door to her in Glenda's fourplex. If I'd known about the burial ground before I'd signed the lease, I would have told her to go straight to hell.

The sounds of Amy Winehouse's "Rehab" greeted me as I arrived at the bar and pulled open the heavy wooden door. Once inside, I scanned the dimly lit room for Veronica, but there was no sign of her. It was ten after six, and we'd agreed to meet at six o'clock for dinner. Unlike me, Veronica made it a habit to show up at least fifteen minutes early to an appointment. But for the past week or so, she'd been showing up late, and I was starting to wonder why.

"What can I get you, Franki?" the bartender, Phillip, asked in a monotone voice as he ran a wet dishrag over the stainless steel bar.

I slid onto a bar stool and placed my Gucci knockoff bag on the counter. "How about an Italian margarita?"

He nodded and reached across several rows of bottles for the Amaretto.

I studied his face as he poured the amber liqueur into a shaker. Veronica said he resembled a young Kurt Cobain, probably because he was in a grunge rock band, albeit an environmentally conscious one. But I thought he looked and sounded exactly like the stoner Jeff Spicoli in *Fast Times at Ridgemont High.*

"How's your music coming along?" I asked, tapping my knuckles on the bar to the beat.

Phillip shook his stringy dishwater blond bangs out of his eyes. "Aw, I quit Saving Pumpkins. Making it in the industry these days is such a long shot, man. I decided it was time to focus on something more secure."

"Smart move," I said, impressed. "What are you working on now?"

"My skateboarding career," he replied, wiping his nose on his sleeve. "I think it's finally gonna be an Olympic sport."

I stopped tapping. "Yeah, the Olympics are always a good fallback plan," I replied. But the irony was lost on him.

Philip handed me the margarita just as Veronica rushed into the bar.

"Sorry I'm late," she said, slipping her powder blue Prada bag off her shoulder. "How'd the research go today?"

"Well, I spent some time online going over the media accounts and some articles on the history of the plantation. I didn't find anything we don't already know, but I'm starting to think this case has something to do with obsession."

Veronica took a seat and grabbed the drink menu. "Why do you say that?"

"When I was at the police academy, we studied something called Obsessive Love Disorder. People who have it usually start out by idealizing someone. But then they feel jealousy and resentment when the object of their affection can't live up to their unrealistic expectations. That's when their so-called love can turn violent."

"Okay, but I don't see the connection between this disorder and Ivanna's death."

"Think about the way her body was neatly laid out on that bed. If she swallowed a bunch of sleeping pills, I think her arm or her head or something would have shifted. But instead it's like someone carefully arranged her hair, her dress, even her hands to make her look as beautiful as possible. Someone who put her on a pedestal."

"Or someone who wanted to make her look like Evangeline."

"Could be," I said, stirring my drink. "But why?"

"I don't know. That's what you're going to have to find out."

I froze in mid-stir. "Wait. *Me?*"

She smiled. "Yeah, I've decided to make you the lead on the case."

I stared at her, stunned. Veronica was so type A that even her blood type was A, so it was shocking to say the least that she was assigning me the case when I was still new to the company.

"I'm going to help you, of course," she continued. "But, I think you're ready. Plus, we've gotten busier, so I'm going to have to handle some of our smaller cases."

Phillip slid a bar napkin in front of Veronica. "What'll it be, Ronnie?"

She looked at the drink list. "Hm. One of the Italian sparkling wines…"

While Veronica pondered the Proseccos, I pondered my promotion. It just didn't make sense that she was turning down the lead on a case that involved a legendary diamond, and a pink one at that. If there was such a thing as Obsessive Love Disorder for diamonds, then Veronica had it. Her favorite song was "Diamonds are a Girl's Best Friend," and one of the last vacations she took was to Crater of Diamonds State Park in Arkansas to dig for the dazzling gems.

"I'll have a glass of the Riondo, please."

Phillip nodded and turned to get her drink.

I took a long sip of my margarita. "Hey, so, is there anything you want to tell me?"

She twisted a lock of hair around her finger. "Why would you ask?"

"Because you've been really distracted lately. And because you've decided to let me handle a case that potentially involves a pink diamond."

"What's this about a pink diamond?" Glenda asked from behind me.

I turned to reply but stopped short. I wasn't prepared to find her wearing an ensemble that vaguely resembled exercise attire. Nor was I ready to discover that her red shorts were so short they were practically panties. Ignoring her question, I asked, "Have you started exercising?"

"Hell no, child," she said with a red cigarette holder between her teeth as she unzipped a sporty red hoodie—cropped directly beneath the breasts—to reveal a matching jog bra that was more like a sweatband. "I'm teaching a boot camp for strippers."

"How fun!" Veronica said, clapping her hands together. "I want to Strippercise."

Glenda placed the cigarette holder on the bar beside Veronica. "This is no strip aerobics class, Miss Ronnie. My old manager down at Madame Moiselle's on Bourbon Street asked me to whip some of his girls into shape. And it's a good thing he did, because I never saw a sadder bunch of strippers. Today one of the sorry fools went and slathered herself with lotion right before pole practice. So, when she cartwheeled into an upside down leg hold, she slid right down the pole and popped a damn breast implant on the stage."

I crossed my arms over my chest even though my boobs were real and, I sincerely hoped, unpoppable.

Phillip placed the Prosecco in front of Veronica and turned to Glenda, keeping his eyes downcast. "What would you like, Miss Glenda?"

"A tall drink of water," she replied with a sultry wink.

A shade of red that matched Glenda's jog bra spread from his cheeks down to his neck.

Glenda leaned over the counter and looked at me. "Now tell me about this diamond."

"We've been contracted to investigate a suspicious death at Oleander Place," I replied.

"So you girls are talking about the Lacour diamond," Glenda said.

"How'd you know that?" I asked, surprised. Although I shouldn't have been. Where local legends were concerned,

Glenda was a walking encyclopedia, probably because she was one herself. In the sixties and seventies, under the stage name Lorraine Lamour, she'd stripped for the biggest names in politics, show business, and organized crime.

"I make it my business to know about jewelry, sugar. And I'm sure the same was true for that woman they found at that plantation."

Veronica took a sip of her Prosecco. "What do you mean?"

"I mean I'll guaran-damn-tee you that pink diamond is why she was there. Diamonds are to women what hookers are to men."

I took a swig of my margarita. Glenda's analogies, while impressive, always left me speechless.

"What woman can resist a pink diamond?" she continued. Then she licked her lips with gusto. "And especially one from a lusty pirate."

I wrinkled my nose. Whenever I thought of pirates, *lusty* was not a word that came to mind. *Crusty,* yes.

"Like that pirate on TV," Glenda said.

"You mean, Captain Feathersword from The Wiggles?" I asked.

Glenda batted her red eyelashes. "What in heaven would I do with a pirate whose sword is made of a feather, sugar?"

"I think she means Captain Jack Sparrow," Veronica explained.

Glenda looked at Veronica. "Is he the one who wears the sexy black guyliner?"

She nodded.

"Well, he can shiver me timbers any day of the week," she said with a flip of her long platinum Cher hair. "Ooh, now I have a hankering for a pirate something awful." Balancing the six-inch heels of her stripper-style tennis shoes on the rungs of her bar stool, she rose up and waved her arm at Phillip. "Bring me a Salty Dog, sugar."

Phillip went from red around the collar to green in the gills.

"Speaking of manly marauders," Glenda said, "isn't that your banker beau, Miss Franki?"

I followed her gaze out the window and saw Bradley walking toward Thibodeaux's. My stomach did a little flip, not because I was happy to see him, but because I could see the frown on his face from inside the bar. "I'd better go talk to him."

"Need any help, Miss Franki?" Glenda asked with a tinge of hopefulness in her voice.

I shot her a look. Then I downed the rest of my drink and pulled my wallet from my purse.

Veronica put her hand on mine. "I've got this. You go."

"Thanks," I said as I rushed outside.

"Hi," Bradley said coolly as the tavern door closed behind me.

I flashed him a smile. "I wasn't expecting you."

He put his hands into his pockets. "I thought I'd swing by on my way to the airport."

I blinked. "You're going out of town?"

"Yes."

I gathered from his curt one-word reply that it was time to apologize. "Listen, I can understand why you're mad and—"

"Can you?" he interrupted. "First you follow me, then you almost get yourself and me killed. And all because I was going to a meeting with my assistant."

"Well, in my defense, the location of that meeting was a little suspect."

"The place isn't the point, Franki."

"Actually, I think it is," I huffed. "What was I supposed to think when you took Pauline to a bed and breakfast?"

"You were supposed to think exactly what I told you— that it was a business meeting," he said, throwing his hands into the air. "Franki, Pauline is my assistant, and she's a damn good one. She worked on Wall Street. Now, there's a lot riding on these meetings, including my job. So I can't have the two of you at each other's throats. I need you to find some way to tolerate her."

I looked at the ground and desperately tried to think of something nice to say about Pauline—for Bradley's sake, not hers. I managed to choke out, "Well, she did do me one favor."

His face softened. "What's that?"

"She told you I dropped by the bank this morning."

Bradley stared at me blankly.

I felt tension rising in my chest. "Pauline did tell you I came by, right?"

He looked away. "She must have forgotten."

My hands balled into fists, one finger at a time. "Oh, I'm sure that's what happened," I said in a convincing tone. But I thought it in a sarcastic one.

"Anyway," Bradley said, glancing at his watch. "I'd better get going. I'll be out of reach off and on. But if you need me, call Pauline. You know her number."

He bent down and gave me a quick and completely unsatisfying peck on the cheek before crossing the street and climbing into his car.

Oh, I've got her number all right, I thought as I watched him drive away. *And before long, she'll have mine.* I was going to prove to Bradley that Pauline was a snake if it was the last thing I did.

CHAPTER FIVE

———

At ten a.m. the next morning, I strode through the French Quarter filled with a new resolve to get a handle on the out-of-control events of the past few days, starting with the out-of-this-world experiences. My first order of business was to question Chandra about the suspicious spiritual goings-on before Veronica and I went to Oleander Place to begin our investigation of Ivanna Jones' death. My second and most immediate objective was to navigate Bourbon Street, where Chandra's office was located, without incident.

As I turned onto the famous party street, I buried my nose in my scarf to escape the unpleasant odors produced by the bacchanalia of the previous night. I also made it a point to walk down the middle of Bourbon despite the crunch of Mardi Gras beads and broken plastic drink cups beneath my feet. That way I was able to dodge the restaurant, bar, strip club, and souvenir shop employees who were spraying the sidewalks and surrounding street with much-needed disinfectant as well as the lingerie- and bikini-clad strippers and waitresses who were already stationed outside their respective establishments selling sex and neon-colored test-tube drinks.

After I'd walked a couple of blocks, I began scanning the addresses of the balcony-lined, two-story structures until I spotted the one listed on Chandra's business card—626 Bourbon Street. It was a cute little building painted terra cotta with a large, white-trimmed twelve-pane window. There were bright red steps with black wrought-iron railings leading to a small covered porch, and fronds of potted ferns hung charmingly from the balcony above.

I bounded up the steps and pushed open the glass door to my left. As I entered, I was greeted by a wall of T-shirts, boas, shot glasses, voodoo dolls, and countless other New Orleans souvenirs. I thought I had the wrong address.

"Can I help you?" a male voice asked.

I turned and saw a forty-something-year-old with a tremendous Afro and a goatee hanging a hand-painted Mardi Gras mask on the wall behind the cash register. Based on the sheer height of his hair, I had a feeling he was Chandra's colleague. "I'm looking for the Crescent City Medium."

"In the back," he said, gesturing with his head.

I nodded and set off for the rear of the shotgun-style shop, wondering whether the "Just Deux It" T-shirt he was wearing was available in the store.

I arrived at two doors, one of which said *Restroom* and the other *Cartomancy and Crystallomancy*. Although I had no idea what the latter terms meant, I didn't have to be a private investigator to know they had something to do with the paranormal.

"Come in, Franki," Chandra's sugary voice called from inside—before I knocked.

She probably heard me talking to the cashier, I rationalized as I entered the closet-sized room.

Apart from a crystal ball, nothing in Chandra's office was what I'd expected. The walls were bare and painted a dull ivory color, and the furniture consisted of an ordinary gray card table and three folding chairs. Instead of patchouli, the aura of Chanel weighed heavily in the air, thanks to Chandra's Chanel No. 5 perfume and her suitcase-sized handbag.

"I haven't had time to decorate," Chandra announced from her seat behind the table. She was wearing the occult version of the ugly Christmas sweater. It had all the planets of the solar system in brightly colored sequins. In place of the stereotypical psychic turban, she had her huge hairdo.

"That's cool," I said, really wishing she'd stop reading my mind and anticipating my presence.

"How can I be of service?"

Wish granted, I thought with relief. "It's about that spirit you were talking to yesterday. Can you tell me her name?"

"I have no earthly idea."

I cast her a blank stare. "Do you have a heavenly idea?"

She shook her head, causing her moon and star earrings to swing like pendulums. "People who've crossed over don't always identify themselves. Besides, I'm not good with names, and it's hard work keeping up with all these spirits."

"Right." The more I talked to Chandra, the more surprised I was that she actually managed to earn money as a medium. "Is there any chance the woman was an older spirit, like from the early 1800s?"

She cocked an eyebrow. "Do you really think that a female spirit who doesn't want to tell me her name would reveal her *age*?"

I sighed. These spirits were driving me crazy with their vanity. "How about this," I said, folding my arms on the table. "Could you look in your crystal ball there and tell me if you see a female spirit at the Oleander Place plantation on River Road?"

"That's going to cost you twenty dollars." She placed her hands in her lap and looked at me expectantly.

"Fine," I muttered, as I pulled a twenty from my wallet.

In a move reminiscent of Glenda, Chandra took the money and shoved it down the neck of her sweater into her ample bra. Then she began waving her plump hands over the ball. As she moved, her charm bracelet jingled so loudly that it sounded like a wind chime.

"Well?" I asked, after several minutes had passed.

"I see a woman."

"Interesting," I said, thinking that I could *so* do her job for a living. "What's she doing?"

"She's pulling at the handle of a French door."

"I guess she wants out," I theorized. "What does she look like?"

Chandra squinted and leaned closer to the crystal ball. "She's blonde."

I rolled my eyes. I'd heard that psychics conned their customers by speaking in vague generalities, but this was ridiculous.

"Oh, and she's wearing a pink crinoline dress," Chandra continued.

I sat up straight in my chair. That was no generic detail. "What else can you tell me?"

"Nothing. Everything went black."

"Would it help if I took you to the plantation?" I offered. "I'm going out there in a couple of hours."

She frowned and leaned back in her chair. "I don't do onsite readings. I told you before, ghosts scare me."

I put my head down for a moment, and then I looked her straight in the eyes. "No offense or anything, but you need to get over your fear of ghosts if you're going to work in this profession."

She jerked her head backward an inch. "I've done very well for myself, thank you."

"Okay, but will you please think about it? This is really important. I've been assigned a case at Oleander Place, and it's looking like it involves a murder."

Chandra gasped as she drew her paddle-shaped fingernails to her mouth. "Murder? Oh, no. I couldn't!"

The spiritual angle was looking like a dead end. But since she'd hit on the color of Evangeline's dress, I did have one more pressing question for her. "Just for curiosity's sake, could you look into your crystal ball and tell me what my boyfriend Bradley's new secretary is up to?"

"You need a tarot card reading for that," she explained, folding her hands back into her lap. "That's an extra twenty bucks."

"Of course," I grumbled, reaching back into my nearly empty wallet. I handed her the cash.

She stuffed the money into her bra and then handed me the cards. "Shuffle and cut the deck."

I followed her instructions and then watched as she laid out three cards. I felt instant anxiety when I noticed that one of them was upside down. "What does that card mean?"

Chandra's lips tightened into a thin line. "It's the Three of Cups. As the middle card, it represents your present. When it's upright it means that friendships and relationships with loved ones are in harmony. But when it's reversed, it usually indicates that you've had a falling out with your friends or that there's a third person in your relationship."

Everything was fine with Veronica, so that could only mean one thing. Pauline was trying to turn my circle of love with

Bradley into a love triangle. *I knew it!* I jumped up and threw my hobo bag over my right shoulder.

Chandra looked up at me with wide eyes. "Don't you want me to read the other two cards? They're your past and future."

"Uh-uh. I definitely don't want to revisit my past, and I already know that I'm woefully unprepared for the future." I turned and opened the door. "I'll be in touch."

I left Chandra's office feeling a weight in the pit of my stomach. It was one thing to suspect Pauline of trying to steal my boyfriend, but it was quite another to have my worst fear confirmed, even if it was by a pseudo psychic.

As I rushed past the merchandise, I bumped into the cashier, who was on his knees putting black and gold "Geaux Saints!" scarves onto a low-hanging rack.

"Hey, now," he said. "Watch where you're goin'."

I turned and read his nametag. "Sorry, Xavier. I just got some surprising news during my reading, and I was trying to figure out what to do about it."

He rose to his feet and began to break down the empty scarf box. "Well, whatever you decide, remember one thang. This ain't Disneyland, this is Noo Awlins. And it's a war zone out there."

"I'll keep that in mind." I pushed open the door and headed out onto Bourbon Street, steeling myself for the battle to come.

* * *

"You still haven't told me what you found out from the Psychic Friends Network," Veronica said as she steered her Audi onto River Road.

I snorted. "You know, Chandra's not part of any clairvoyant company. She's just an ordinary woman working from an office."

"Precisely. You remember that before you get all worked up about something she says."

"It's not like I'm buying in to this whole psychic thing,'" I said, scratching my nose and visualizing Pinocchio. "But I *am* paying attention to the fact that she knows things about me and this case."

"Okay, but this is the information age," Veronica said with a pointed look. "She can go online and find out pretty much anything she wants to know, starting by looking at your meticulously maintained Facebook page."

My text message tone chimed.

Saved by the bell, I thought as I reached into my bag for my phone. When I read the display, I got a fluttery feeling in my chest.

Back in town tomorrow. Dinner at 7? Missing you, Bradley.

I smiled. Maybe I'd overreacted to my tarot card reading just a smidge. After all, Bradley *did* tell me in no uncertain terms that Pauline was just his secretary. And one person didn't make a love triangle, right? I texted him an enthusiastic "It's a date!" and tossed the phone into my bag. "Speaking of information, do we have background checks on the Oleander Place employees?"

"David finished them late yesterday. Everyone was clean except for one of the tour guides, Scarlett Heinz. Last year she was charged with assaulting a woman."

"I wonder if it was because the woman teased her about her name," I said. "I mean, it's essentially 'Red Ketchup.'"

Veronica shot me a look. "I seriously doubt it."

I looked out the passenger window and mused, "So Miss Scarlett has a colored past…"

"If you're thinking about moving on to Clue jokes, don't," Veronica said, leaning menacingly toward me.

I moved closer to the passenger door, just to be safe. "Did you have David run a check on Delta too?"

"Yeah. Nothing."

"So, assuming Ivanna was murdered, do you think there's any chance that Delta's involved? She seems kind of proud of the fact that her plantation has a murderous history."

Veronica shook her head. "When your business is weddings, charity dinners, and craft fairs, you don't want this kind of publicity. You heard Delta say that the media coverage is costing her clients, and she practically threatened us if we went to the press."

"True," I said, again glancing out the window. We were approaching Oleander Place, and the view was spectacular. Oleander bushes dotted the grounds like pink flamingos, and there were two rows of centuries-old Southern live oak trees that dutifully lined the walkway leading to the plantation like soldiers standing at attention. Now that I was focusing on the house instead of the back of Bradley's BMW, I realized that it was painted the palest shade of pink, as was the colonnade that wrapped around the three-story home. I shifted my gaze uneasily to the balcony, and to my relief there was no sign of Evangeline.

Veronica pulled into a long driveway and parked in a lot in the back of the house that was conveniently located next to a ticket booth. Directly in front of the parking lot were the slaves' quarters and a gift shop with a restaurant. Beyond the gift shop were two old sugar mills and the sugar cane fields.

"Any special instructions, *capo?*" Veronica asked.

I got a little thrill from being called "boss," but I acted casual. "Yeah, look for any evidence that Ivanna's death was actually a murder."

"On it."

As I stepped out of the car, I saw Delta and an older Southern gentleman in a seersucker suit standing on the back porch beside a magnolia tree. I felt like I was on the set of the *Murder, She Wrote* episode where Seth Hazlitt's plantation-owner cousin is battling a perfume company over the scent of the flowers from his secret magnolia tree. But I was quickly reminded that Delta was no Jessica Fletcher when I saw her shake her fist at the man, who cowered and held up his straw hat like a shield.

"You leave this property at once, Floyd Buford!" she shouted. "I don't want to see your face around here again."

"I'm sorry you feel that way, Delta," he said with a slight warble in his voice. He placed his hat on his head. "But if that's what you want, then good-day."

Veronica and I ambled toward the porch as Delta watched the man hurry away.

"Is everything okay?" I asked.

"That was the president of the Antebellum Plantation Historical and Preservation Society," Delta replied. "He just canceled a luncheon they'd scheduled here for next week."

"I'm sorry," Veronica said.

"I'm not," she snapped. "Believe you me, it's no picnic catering to a bunch of snobbish geriatrics with digestive issues."

Veronica and I exchanged a look.

Delta turned and opened the door. "You girls come on in. I'll show you around."

"I'd love to," Veronica said as we entered a wide hallway with gleaming hardwood floors.

I was less enthusiastic about seeing the house. It was beautiful, but the tarnished history of plantation homes— specifically the fact that they were operated on slave labor— made me uncomfortable.

"This place is gorgeous!" Veronica exclaimed.

Delta stopped and turned to face her. "It is *now*. Knox designed the home in the Greek Revival style to make that nitwit Evangeline happy. But thankfully one of his descendants had the good sense to strip the house of the garish cornices, crown moldings, and ceiling medallions to bring it in line with the Federal style."

"What happened to those things?" I asked.

"They're stored in the little mill," she said with a dismissive wave of her hand. "Now, my office is here on the left. And on the right is the kitchen, which used to be the house-slaves' quarters. The original kitchen was located in a separate building to keep the odors and the heat to a minimum."

I nodded and followed Delta to the front of the house.

"This is the parlor," she said, gesturing to the left. "And across the hall is the dining room."

Veronica and I peered into the parlor, which was protected by a cordon. A gold-plated crystal chandelier, a large gilt mirror, and several bronze candelabra gave the room a sumptuous look. In front of the fireplace was a courting area with Empire-period seating covered in blue velvet. Above the black marble mantel was an enormous oil painting of a beautiful blonde woman with delicate features. She was dressed in coral pink and painted against a dark background of bluish black.

"Is that Evangeline?" Veronica asked, as though reading my mind.

"Yes," Delta said drily, clutching her pearls.

"She was lovely," I enthused. "Like a real-life Disney princess."

Delta scowled. "I'll take you up to her room."

We climbed a tall wooden staircase to the second floor.

"On either side of the hallway are the guest bedrooms," Delta said, "and the children's bedroom is in the middle. In keeping with the custom of the era, Evangeline and Knox had separate bedrooms in the front of the house." She turned to Veronica and me. "I don't know why we ever did away with that tradition."

I flashed a wry smile at Veronica as we followed Delta the length of the hallway to the master bedrooms.

"Those French doors lead to the front balcony," she explained, pulling a set of keys from her pocket. She unlocked the door to the left. "And this is Evangeline's bedroom, otherwise known as 'the pink room.'"

Veronica, a connoisseur of pink décor, gasped and covered her mouth with her hand. "It's pink perfection."

I had to agree that it was a beautiful room, but I'd always been partial to purple. "Can we go past the cordon?"

Delta raised an eyebrow. "Just don't touch anything."

I smirked and entered the spacious bedroom with Veronica in tow. On the right was a seating area with a pink armchair and matching chaise lounge. Between the windows was an imposing armoire with decorative wood inlay and a white marble bust on the top. But the most impressive piece of furniture in the room was a canopied bed covered with pink pillows and draped in sheer pink netting.

"Is this the original furniture?" Veronica asked.

Delta nodded. "Evangeline died in that bed."

"It's awfully small," I remarked. It reminded me of the dainty Princess furniture Veronica used to have before she redecorated her apartment like Elvis Presley's Jungle Room at Graceland.

"People were smaller back then," Delta said, eyeing my 5' 10" frame with evident disapproval.

I made a point of turning my back to her and began inspecting the area to the right of the bed, next to the windows, while Veronica searched the area to the left. On a white marble–covered night table beside the bed sat a stunning bronze snuff box adorned with a picture of Marie Antoinette.

"Is this box an original too?" I asked.

"Yes, it's from France. So is the trio of perfume bottles."

I looked at the delicate pink glass bottles with gold filigree. "I only see two."

Delta frowned and rushed to my side. "I don't understand," she muttered. "Where's the other bottle?"

"Could someone have moved it?" Veronica asked.

"That's impossible. I have the only key to this room, and no one has been allowed in here since the body was found." She knelt and looked under the bed.

I stared at the night table, deep in thought. "Are you sure the bottle was here that night?"

Delta stood up and brushed some dust off her navy blue dress. "I think so."

"Hold on," Veronica said, reaching into her beige and leopard-print Furla tote. "I have the police photos with me. There's one of the nightstand, remember?"

"That's right!" I said.

Veronica began flipping through the pictures with Delta looking on.

Meanwhile, I glanced beneath the table but didn't see anything. Then I pulled back one of the heavy, pink silk damask drapes and noticed a two-inch tear in the white sheer curtain underneath.

"It's not in the picture," Veronica said. "There are only two bottles on the nightstand."

"Wait a second!" Delta said, snapping her fingers. "That bottle was here on the day of the murder. I know it for a fact."

"How?" I asked.

"Because a French antique dealer on the same tour as Miss Jones made a comment about the trio. He said he'd never seen the full set intact."

I chewed my lip. I was starting to think there was a connection between Ivanna's death and the missing perfume bottle. "What about this?" I asked, pulling aside the drape to reveal the tear in the sheer curtain. "Did you know it was torn?"

"No, I didn't," Delta replied, her eyes smoldering with anger.

I stepped aside as she stomped up to the drapes and jerked them away from the window, causing a small object to propel across the floor.

Veronica bent down and retrieved the item. "It's a piece of pink glass!"

"That's part of the perfume bottle," Delta said, her pale skin blanching as white as the curtain.

"Was the room cleaned after the tour?" Veronica asked.

"No, the cleaning crew came the morning after I found the body, but the police had me send them away." Delta lowered her head. "I suppose it's possible that a member of my staff could have broken it, but I don't know what reason they would have had to go into the room after a tour, and especially to go behind the cordon."

I thought about the torn curtain and the broken bottle, and in my mind they added up to one thing. "I don't think that's what happened," I said. "There was a struggle in this room the night Ivanna Jones died, which means that your hunch about this being a murder is probably right."

CHAPTER SIX

———

Delta crossed her arms and curled her lips. "Of course I'm right. Like I told you, that girl was murdered in this house. The only thing you two need to worry about is finding out who did it."

"We're just covering our bases," Veronica explained.

"This isn't a damn baseball game," she snapped. "This is my business, and I'm paying you to find the killer. No more no less."

I narrowed my eyes and opened my mouth to reply, but Veronica silenced me with a shut-it look.

"And you'll do it soon," Delta added. "I'm losing money by the minute thanks to this disaster."

I'd had enough of Delta and her demanding demeanor. Mentally repeating *the customer is always right* with the intensity of Dorothy when she was trying to will herself and Toto back to Kansas, I exited the room and opened one of the French doors to take in some desperately needed fresh air. As I stepped onto the balcony, I saw an old rocking chair to my right. I took a seat and let my gaze follow the striking tree-lined walkway straight to the waters of the mighty Mississippi River. I wondered how many times Evangeline had done the same as she held her pink diamond and waited for Beau.

The door flung open giving me a start, and Delta popped her head around the side. "Sorry to intrude on your quiet time, but we have a tour starting in half an hour. So, if you're going to question my tour guide, you'd better get started."

I bit my lip to keep from saying something I would only partially regret and rose from my chair. Once inside, I glanced at the narrow flight of stairs leading to the third floor. "What's upstairs?"

"Storage. It was a walk-in attic even when the plantation was functional. Now it houses our document archives as well as some antique furniture and vintage clothes."

I was about to ask whether I had time to take a quick peek when we heard a dull thud followed by a woman's scream. It sounded like it had come from the end of the hall.

"What in the *hell*?" Delta exclaimed as she rushed toward one of the guest bedrooms.

I followed her with Veronica hot on my heels. When I entered the room, I saw a petite young woman in a waist-pinching corset and an old-fashioned white petticoat. She was kneeling and examining a large bronze pineapple.

"I'm sorry, Miss Delta," she said with a distinct Southern twang. "I dropped it on accident."

"Scarlett, you fool! That's a priceless antique!"

"I know, but I didn't realize how heavy it was." She pushed a lock of frizzy, dishwater-blonde hair behind her ear and started to lift the bulky bronze fruit.

"Leave it be!" Delta shouted as she scooped up the pineapple with a single hand. "Aren't you supposed to be getting dressed for a tour?"

"Yes ma'am," Scarlett said, rising to her feet and taking a step backward. "But I remembered that I hadn't dusted the stuff on the bed."

"Never mind that now," Delta said as she deposited the pineapple at the end of the bed next to a gray feather duster. "Where's your hoop skirt?"

"On the back of the door."

Delta stormed over to the door and pulled it back. She stiffened suddenly and turned to Scarlett with a look of pure rage. "What did I tell you about hanging up vintage clothing?"

"That I shouldn't use no wire hangers?" Scarlett ventured.

I felt my body tense in preparation for a Mommie Dearest moment.

"That's right," she said through clenched teeth. "No. Wire. Hangers!"

I halfway expected Delta to pull a Joan Crawford and start beating Scarlett with the hanger. Or with the pineapple.

Instead, she inhaled deeply and looked at Veronica and me. "Scarlett earns extra money doing some light cleaning here at the plantation," she explained. Then she turned to her and gave her an icy stare. "But if she continues to drop two-hundred-year-old artifacts, I'll have to relieve her of her duties, both as a maid and as a tour guide."

Scarlett lowered her head and began biting the fingernail on her middle finger.

I wondered whether she was discreetly flipping Delta off and smiled inwardly at the notion.

"At least nothing was broken," Veronica said.

"Not yet, anyway," Delta remarked, putting her hands on her hips. "Now, I've got to get downstairs to see that everything is ready for the tour. Scarlett, Ms. Maggio and Ms. Amato need to ask you some questions about the murder. You make sure you cooperate, you hear?"

"Yes, Miss Delta."

Delta frowned at her and left the room.

I looked at Scarlett and noted that her hands were trembling. I couldn't tell whether it was because of what had just transpired or because she was afraid to talk to us. Either way, I knew I had to try to calm her down to have a chance at getting any information she may have. "Scarlett is the perfect name for a plantation tour guide." I smiled. "I'll bet you hear a lot of Tara jokes."

She stared at me, expressionless.

Time to try another tactic. "What's up with the pineapple?"

"It's a symbol of Southern hospitality, isn't it?" Veronica chimed in.

Scarlett nodded. "Yes ma'am. But in the old South, if you were a guest in someone's home and you woke up and found one at the foot of your bed, it meant you'd overstayed your welcome."

"Awk-ward." I laughed.

She pressed her lips into a thin line. "Miss Delta said you had some questions about that woman that was killed?"

Clearly, Scarlett was in no mood for jokes. "Uh, yeah," I said. "Were you here between five p.m. last Friday and eight a.m. the next morning?"

"I came in at eight thirty on Saturday for the nine a.m. tour," she said, her eyes narrowing. "Why?"

"We're not accusing you of anything," Veronica began, "we're just trying to find out if you know anything that could help us."

"I don't," she said hotly.

It appeared that Scarlett had a scrappy side, like her *Gone-with-the-Wind* namesake. "Did you see the body after it was found?" I asked.

She nodded. "Miss Delta told me what happened when I came to work. I went into the room to see for myself."

"Did you recognize the victim, Ivanna Jones?" Veronica asked.

Scarlett glanced at the floor. "I seen her here before."

I felt my heart skip a beat. "When?"

"A week or so ago."

I remembered that Delta said she'd seen Ivanna two weeks before. I wondered whether Ivanna had returned to the plantation a week later. "Can you give us a more precise date?"

She tugged at the top of her corset. "Uh, actually, I think it was two weeks ago."

Veronica furrowed her brow. "You're sure?"

"You think I'm lying?" she asked, raising her chin.

"I want to make sure we have the correct information, that's all," Veronica replied.

Scarlett stared at Veronica and said nothing.

Changing the subject, I asked, "Was Ivanna on one of your tours?"

"Yeah." She paused and played with the fabric of her petticoat. "And..." Her voice trailed off as she looked out the window. Then her face clouded over. "I'd better go." She grabbed the feather duster from the bed and pulled her hoop skirt and a red dress from the back of the door. "It's almost time for my tour."

"Okay, but let us know if you think of anything else," I said.

Scarlett left the room without a word.

"Did you see that?" I asked as I hurried over to the window. "She was about to tell us something, but she changed her mind."

"Yeah," Veronica replied with a toss of her hair. "And from the way she kept messing with her clothes, I'd say she was lying about when she saw Ivanna."

I stared out onto the grounds below and immediately locked eyes with a stocky, thirty-something male standing near the back porch. He turned away and headed in the direction of the sugar mills. "I just saw a man looking up at this window. Let's go find out who he is."

I rushed downstairs with Veronica close behind. When I opened the back door, seven miniature pinschers rushed in and circled me with their teeth bared like tiny land sharks preparing for a foot-feeding frenzy. I immediately froze in my tracks and feared for my Dolce Vita wedges and my toes.

Veronica sprung into action. "Bad dogs!" she shouted, clapping her hands. "Shoo! Shoo!"

But the mini mongrels stood their battleground.

Using my best Southern canine speak, I yelled, "Go on, now! *Git!*"

Delta emerged from her office wearing her standard scowl. "What's all the damn fuss about?" she asked, waving an antique candlestick like a club. "We have a tour going on, you know."

"This pack of wild Dobermans!" I said, desperately wanting to gesticulate but holding my body mummy-style still.

Delta looked down as though she hadn't realized the dogs were there. Then she dropped to her knees and drew the dogs into a collective embrace. "Mamma's sweet babies!" she cooed in a manly maternal tone as she kissed each dog on the mouth.

I felt my jaw drop from the shock of Delta's unexpected display of affection.

She looked up, beaming with pride. "These are the seven dwarfs."

More like the seven deadly sins, I thought.

Veronica walked around me. "Delta, we need to identify

a man who was staring up at the window when we were questioning Scarlett a few minutes ago."

She used her right knee to hoist herself back to her feet. "It was probably that good-for-nothing Miles McCarthy, our groundskeeper. He's always poking around in the bushes and whatnot, sticking his blasted nose where it doesn't belong."

I noted that Delta had made a quick recovery from her bout with maternal warmth. "Does anyone else help with property maintenance?"

"No, but our historian, Troy Wilson, gives tours of the grounds. He's not here today, though."

Veronica pressed a finger to her cheek. "Hm. We'd planned on questioning everyone while we were here."

"I told him that," Delta said as she began twisting the candle in its spiral-shaped metal holder. "But he said he had some business to attend to at Tulane, something to do with his PhD dissertation. You should ask him about his research, by the way. It's fascinating."

"When can we talk to him?" I asked, glancing down at the Disney-named demon dogs.

"The day after tomorrow," she replied. Then she unceremoniously deposited the candlestick in my hands. "Here. Hold the base while I pull this candle out."

"That's a funky-looking candlestick," I said.

"It's a courter's candle." Flexing the muscle she'd exhibited earlier with the bronze pineapple, Delta gave a hearty tug and the candle slipped free from the metal spiral.

"What's that?" Veronica asked as I handed the candlestick to Delta.

"A courting timer. When a gentleman came calling for one of the eligible young ladies of the plantation, her father would light the candle. When the wax burned down to the top of the metal spiral, it was time for the young man to leave. If the plantation lord felt he was a good prospect he would turn the handle to raise the candle before he lit it to give the couple more time together. But if he didn't, he would lower it."

"Talk about getting the short end of the stick," I joked.

Delta raised an eyebrow and stared at me. She might have a secret human side, but she had no sense of humor.

Veronica peered around Delta's shoulder. "Why are you replacing the candle?"

"One of my staff lit the damn thing, and the wax dripped all over the holder. Probably Scarlett," she added, shaking her head.

"Speaking of Scarlett," I said, "what time does her tour end?"

"In about thirty minutes. There are only six people— foreigners who are blissfully ignorant of the murder, I'm sure."

"Okay, thanks," Veronica said, walking to the door.

I held back until Delta and all seven of the devil dwarfs had retreated into her office. Then I rushed out after Veronica.

"Let's go to the larger mill first," I said.

"Yeah, the smaller one is probably the storage shed."

Veronica and I walked past the slave quarters and the gift shop and veered left in the direction of the big sugar mill. As we approached the rickety old wooden structure, we saw four huge cast iron kettles arranged in order from largest to smallest in front of the building. The tallest kettle was at least five feet high and seven feet across, and the smallest was only about two feet high.

I walked up to the weather-beaten door and knocked. After a minute or so passed, I pressed my ear to the thin wood. "It sounds like a fan or something is running. Maybe he didn't hear me."

"Is the door locked?"

I pushed the door, and its rusty hinges creaked as it opened about a foot. "I'm going in."

Veronica nodded.

"Hello, Miles?" I called as I slipped inside. I followed the loud whirring, which seemed to be coming from somewhere in the back. I passed through a room equipped with several antiquated-looking machines with grooved rollers and arrived in an adjoining room with wooden worktables and shelving.

Miles was standing at a table with his back to me and using an industrial-sized Shop-Vac to remove some pink powder from a clear plastic Tupperware container. When the last of the powder was gone, he turned to switch off the machine.

I couldn't see his mouth because he was wearing a white

surgical mask, but I thought his brown eyes widened when he noticed me. "Sorry, I didn't mean to startle you. My name is Franki, and I'm a PI investigating the suspicious death here at Oleander Place."

He removed his mask and began stripping off his elbow-length rubber gloves. "Where y'at?" he asked in a Brooklynesque accent.

I started to say, "Right here." But then I remembered that *Y'at* is a white, working-class dialect peculiar to the area around New Orleans' Irish Channel neighborhood, meaning *How are you?*, and I cleared my throat. "Fine. And you?"

"Awrite," he replied. "I was jus' cleanin' up some rat poison. Maybe we should step outside?"

I was all too happy to leave the mill. I could almost feel airborne rat poison entering my lungs, and I was a little leery of Miles. With his bushy reddish-brown brow, flattened boxer nose, and hulking frame, he looked like he could have been an Irish Mafia extra for the cast of *The Departed*.

When we got outside, Veronica was leaning over the next to largest of the kettles.

"Careful, now," Miles said. "You don' wanna fall into de *flambeau*."

Veronica blinked. "The what?"

"All dese kettles have a name. Dis big one here is de *grande*, den come de *flambeau*, de *sirop* an' de *batterie*."

"So they were used in sugar production?" I asked, running my hand over the smooth black surface of the *grande*.

"Yeah, to boil de sugar cane juice down 'til it crystalized. But dey also used 'em to make de meals for de plantation hands. And during de harvesting season, dey took de boiled cane juice from de *flambeau* and mixed it wit' French brandy to make hot punch." He rubbed his belly. "It's dee-licious."

I felt my mouth watering. Naturally, I'd been craving a mint julep since I stepped onto the plantation. But some condensed sugar juice and European brandy would do just fine. "Listen, my partner Veronica and I would like to ask you a few questions about the murder. Is now a good time?"

"F'sure," he said, crossing his arms against his solid chest.

"Great," I said, pulling a note pad and pen from my purse. "What time did you leave work last Friday?"

"I went home early dat day, at tree p.m."

Veronica crinkled her nose. "At three?"

He nodded. "Tha's right."

I jotted down the time. "Can anyone vouch for you?"

"How ya mean?"

"I mean, do you have an alibi?"

He looked down. "I stay by myself, and I was dere all night. Pahdon my French, but I had de *fois*."

I had a hard enough time deciphering proper French, so there was no way I could do Cajun. "The *fwas*?"

"I was in de battroom," he said, raising his eyebrows.

I looked at him blankly.

He gave a sheepish grin. "I ate a bad batch o' gumbo?"

"Got it," I said, holding up my hand in a stopping motion. I didn't need any of the gory gastric details. "What about Saturday? Did you come to work?"

"I got heuh at eight."

Veronica pulled a crime scene photo from her Furla tote. "Did you view the victim's body?"

"No ma'am. No one was allowed in de house dat day."

"Do you recognize this woman?" she asked, showing him a photo of Ivanna's body.

Miles stroked his unshaven chin and looked to one side. "Nevah seen her before."

I noted that he didn't flinch at the sight of her corpse. "Her name is Ivanna Jones. Does that ring a bell?"

He looked down at his worn brown work boots. "Cain't say it does."

"Thanks, Miles," I said slipping the pad and pen back into my bag. "That's it for me. Veronica?"

She shook her head.

"Looks like we're done for now," I said, extending my hand. "If we need anything else, we'll be in touch."

He grasped my hand in a powerful grip. "Y'all have a blessed day."

As Veronica and I headed back toward the plantation, I whispered, "Miles never once looked us in the eye when we asked him about Ivanna."

"I noticed that. Suspicious, huh?"

I was about to reply when I saw something move by the magnolia tree next to the back porch. I squinted and saw Scarlett peeking out from behind the massive trunk. "True to her Clue counterpart, Miss Scarlett is a spy."

"Interesting," Veronica said. "Let's go to talk to her and find out what's going on."

I cupped my hands around my mouth. "Scarlett!"

She glanced in our direction, and then she put her head down and hurried toward the parking lot.

Veronica looked at me. "What's she doing?"

Scarlett climbed into a beat up, red Ford pickup and started the engine.

"Leaving," I replied as I watched her back up and speed away.

"That's the second time today she's run away from us," Veronica said.

"And both times it was right after she'd seen Miles." Now I was positive that Miles was hiding something, but what? And what about Scarlett? It seemed like she was afraid of Miles. If she was, I had no idea whether it was because of something he knew about her or because of something she knew he'd done. Either way, I needed to talk to Scarlett. And soon.

CHAPTER SEVEN

"Okay, message delivered." I pressed end on my phone and dropped it in the cup holder beside the passenger seat of Veronica's Audi. "Now we just have to hope Scarlett calls us back."

"She will," Veronica said, frowning at the old tan Lincoln Town Car puttering along in front of us on the single-lane highway. "Otherwise, she'll have Delta breathing down her neck."

"Surely she'd want to avoid that," I replied. Although I wasn't convinced she'd call. Scarlett had seemed scared, and fear was a powerful motivator to keep your mouth shut, even when you were mouthy by nature.

Veronica fidgeted in her seat and tightened her grip on the steering wheel. "How could anyone stand to drive so slowly? They're doing 40 miles per hour."

"I think it's an older couple," I said in an attempt to stave off any impending reckless driving on Veronica's part. Ever since she'd driven the Ferrari racetrack in Italy, she thought she was a Formula One driver. And trust me when I say she wasn't. For starters, she could barely see over the steering wheel, and she had to drive in high heels so she could reach the pedals.

"Sunday drivers," she muttered as she craned her neck looking for oncoming traffic. "Don't they know it's Tuesday?"

"You can't pass here," I said. "There's a double yellow line."

Flagrantly ignoring both my comment and the law, she flipped on her turn signal and floored the gas pedal as she steered into the next lane.

I braced myself against the seat and pressed my feet on the floorboard as though that would protect me in the event of a fiery crash. When we'd safely made it around the startled-looking elderly driver and his equally startled-looking passenger, I relaxed a little and glanced at the odometer—85 mph. "Okay, we've passed them. Do you think maybe you could slow down now?"

She gave me a sideways look. "You're such a backseat driver."

"Actually, I'm in the front seat, so I can see that you're speeding. And it's not like we have to be back at the office. It's almost six o'clock."

"I have something I need to do," she said as she eased off the gas.

I wondered whether this "something" was why she'd been acting so weird lately. "What? A date?"

"Just...an errand," she said, tilting her head to the side and running her fingers through her hair.

I recognized that head-hair gesture. Veronica only did it when she was lying.

"Hey," she began in a suspiciously perky tone, "what time did you want to make our surprise appearance at Lickalicious Lips tomorrow?"

A clear diversion tactic. I narrowed my eyes and replied, "First thing in the morning, I guess."

She nodded and looked out the driver side window.

Before I could start systematically prying into her personal life, I was interrupted by the sound of my phone. I looked at the display and saw the main number of Ponchartrain Bank. My heart skipped a beat as I pressed answer. "Hey, babe."

"Do you always answer the phone that way?" the voice of Pauline asked with an audible sneer.

I felt a slow burn ignite in my gut. But I reminded myself that Bradley had asked me to try to get along with her, so I kept my cool. "Only when I think it's my boyfriend calling."

"Classy," she hissed.

Okay, to hell with Bradley's request. "How'd you get this number, Pauline?" I asked with attitude. "My office phone is the only one I have on file at the bank."

"Ancient Chinese secret," she intoned.

"I think you mean 'ancient Chinese snooping through Bradley's personal contact information,'" I snapped.

She gave a haughty laugh. "I don't need to resort to your little tricks. He doesn't keep anything from me."

The slow burn burst into a full-blown flame.

"But while we're on the subject of secrets," Pauline continued, "I thought you'd be interested to know that I just got a call from a fascinating woman named Carmela Montalbano?"

Nonna. The angry fire in my stomach was abruptly extinguished by anxious fear. I started mentally running through all the possible ammunition she could have provided to Pauline.

"She said she was your nonna, and she was calling to talk to Bradley about the *pranzo ufficiale*."

I cringed at her perfect Italian pronunciation and whispered a silent prayer that she'd only dabbled in the language, say, in high school or in preparation for a trip. "Yeah, that's an Italian family thing where the parents meet the boyfriend."

"A fine attempt at understatement," she said in a snide tone. "But my maternal grandmother is from Italy, so I know the score."

Wait. Chinese-French Pauline had a nonna? How multi-ethnic could her freakin' family be? I swallowed hard and squeaked, "Sicilian?"

"No, *calabrese*."

O. mio. Dio. Calabria is the region right next to Sicily at the toe of the Italian boot, which meant that Pauline, for all intents and purposes, had a Sicilian grandmother too.

"So, just out of curiosity," she said, "does Bradley have any idea that you and your nonna are planning his engagement to you?"

Beads of sweat began sprouting on my upper lip like mustache hairs on an old Italian woman. If Bradley found out what my nonna was doing, he might think I was in on her scheme. And even if he didn't suspect my involvement, it was way too early for him to find out how crazy-invasive my nonna was. I mean, he'd barely had enough time to get used to my teensy little idiosyncrasies, much less the masterful meddling methods of my nonna. As distasteful as it was, I was going to have to try to reason with Pauline.

"Um, *hello*?" she pressed.

I took a deep breath and said, "Look, you have an Italian grandma, so you know how incredibly intrusive they can be. I assure you that I had nothing whatsoever to do with this."

"Riiiight. Just like you didn't have anything to do with spying on Bradley and me last Sunday."

Okay, screw reasoning—it was time to beg. "Pauline, I'm asking you woman-to-woman not to give that message to Bradley."

I could practically hear her lips curling into a satisfied smile.

"Why, Franki," she exclaimed in mock outrage, "I'm his executive assistant. It wouldn't be right not to give my boss his messages."

"Oh, really?" I huffed. "Because you didn't give him *my* message the other day."

"Did you call?" she asked innocently.

"No. I came—"

"Precisely," she said, and she slammed down the receiver.

I stared at the phone in shock. And then in a fit of rage clearly influenced by my recent plantation visit, I raised my phone in my fist and vowed, "As God is my witness, as God is my witness, she's not going to lick me."

"Wow," Veronica said. "Did you just lose everything but Tara in the Civil War?"

I looked at her, expressionless. "Pauline's going to tell Bradley that nonna is already planning our engagement party."

"She's *what*?" she shouted as the Audi swerved to the right. "Franki, you're going to have to find a way to rein your nonna in."

After checking to make sure my seat belt was still fastened, I shot her an annoyed look. "Can you really put a harness on a tornado, a hurricane, or a tsunami? Because that's the kind of force I'm dealing with here."

She sighed. "I know, but what about your dad? She's his mother. Can't he help you get her under control?"

"Are you kidding? You know my family's like a bad 1950s sitcom. Only, instead of *Father Knows Best* it's more like

Nonna Knows Best. Whenever I complain about her to my dad, he says she's looking out for my best interests, which would be true if I had dreams of being a stay-at-home mom of ten in Fascist Italy."

"Well, you're going to have to do something. Otherwise, you'll end up a *zitella*, which is exactly what your nonna doesn't want.

I put my head in my hands and tried to think. Veronica was right. If I wanted to save my relationship with Bradley, I was going to have to take on my nonna. But she was a formidable foe, so I needed backup. I grabbed my phone from the floor where it had landed during the near accident and pressed my parents' number.

"Hello?" my mother responded shrilly on the first ring.

"Hi, Mom."

"Is that you, Francesca?"

I sighed. "Mom, you have two sons and one daughter. What other woman would be calling you 'Mom?'"

"Well, I see *you're* in a mood," she replied.

"Yes, I am. Nonna is up to her usual antics, and she's gone too far this time. She actually called Bradley at the bank to talk about having a *pranzo ufficiale*."

"I know she comes on a little strong, dear, but she just wants to see you settled down."

"A *little* strong, Mom? *Seriously?* To quote an Italian expression, she's like an elephant in a glass shop—after it's had a few gallons of espresso. It's bad enough that she's always trying to run my life, but now she's orchestrating Bradley's too. We have to—"

"Rosemary and I were just talking about the two of you at the deli today," she interrupted in a cheerful tone.

I instantly felt my hackles rise. I'd asked my parents not to talk about my personal life with the deli customers at least a thousand times, but they recognized that request about as often as my Mom recognized me when I called.

"And she wanted me to be sure to tell you the main benefit of marrying early," she continued.

"Oh?" I asked, making sure to sound as disinterested as possible.

"Yes, dear. You have your kids while you're young so that they're out of the house before you go through 'The Change.' That way, you and your hubby have time to recharge your sex life before the hot flashes hit."

"Mm," I said noncommittally. Where my Mom was concerned, I made it a point never to encourage womanly conversations that centered on changing or recharging.

"Take your father and me."

Dear God, no, I thought.

"When you left for college, we made love on the kitchen table for the first time in twenty-five years."

My stomach crawled into my throat, no doubt remembering with horror all the times it had eaten at that table. "Mom, can you please put Dad on the phone?" I asked, before she could drop any other sex bombs. "This is important."

"Well, all right, dear," she said, her voice dripping with disappointment from the sex-talk shut down. "Let me see if I can find him."

I heard the receiver crash onto the kitchen counter.

"Joe!" she shouted. "It's Francesca calling from New Orleans! Get on the phone!"

I looked at Veronica and shook my head in frustration.

She smirk-smiled at me and then shifted her gaze back to the road.

"How's the job going, Franki?" my father's voice boomed. "Are you chasing any cheating spouses?"

"Not right now," I replied, holding the phone away from my ear. "We're working on a murder case."

"Again? This PI business is starting to sound just as dangerous as your work on the police force," he said with a note of irritated worry. "I thought you wanted to get away from all that."

My dad and I had been around and around about my suitability, both as a woman and as an individual, for fighting crime. And even though we'd made some progress on that front, the battle was far from won. "Dad, being a PI is a lot less dangerous than being a cop. Besides, I've told you before that it wasn't the job I wanted to get away from as much as the partner requirement. I mean, my ex-partner, Stan, was about as nurturing as an absentee father."

Veronica glanced at me, her brow furrowed.

"Well, if you're sure about that..." he said.

"I am, Dad," I asserted firmly. "Anyway, that's not why I'm calling. I need to talk to you about nonna."

"Nonna? What's she got to do with your job?"

"Not my job. My life."

He gave an exasperated sigh. "How many times are we going to have to go over this? Your nonna loves you, and she wants to see you happy. That's all."

"Well, if *that's* what she wants, then all she has to do it stop meddling in my relationships, and I'll be ecstatic."

"Franki," he began in a gruff tone, "your nonna is a lonely old woman who just wants to be involved in your life."

I felt my guilt level shoot straight from five—the amount Catholic girls, good or bad, were taught to carry at all times—to ten.

"Maybe if you shared things with her from time to time," he said, "she wouldn't feel like she had to meddle."

Now my guilt was at eleven. He had a point. I hadn't confided in my nonna in years, but it wasn't entirely my fault. I mean, the minute I reached the dating age she went from a gracious grandmother to a Machiavellian matchmaker.

"Are we clear on that?" he asked in a tone that indicated this call was over.

"Yeah, Dad," I said, resigned. "Talk to you soon."

"Well?" Veronica asked.

I pressed end and shoved the phone into my bag. "A complete waste of time."

"He's not going to help?"

"Nope. He just gave me the usual speech about how she's doing this because she loves me, which is beside the point. It really bothers me that neither one of my parents gets how serious this is. But you know what really gets me?"

"No, what?"

"My nonna never once got on the phone."

She shrugged. "So?"

"So?" I repeated, surprised by her lack of insight. "Her whole M.O. is to get on the phone every time I call and try to pressure me into whatever the scheme *du jour* is. The fact that she didn't can only mean one thing. She's up to something, Veronica. Something bigger than the *pranzo ufficiale*."

"What could be bigger than that?"

"I don't know," I said, looking out the passenger window. "But the prospects are terrifying."

* * *

When I opened the door of my apartment at six thirty, I half expected to find Napoleon lying on the floor with a burst bladder. Instead, he was in his now customary position, flat on his back on the zebra chaise lounge with his legs splayed wide open. Ever since we'd moved into the bordello-themed apartment, he'd been exhibiting a newfound animal virility. Lately, he'd taken to humping the leg of the lilac velour armchair. It had long gold fringe—to match the drapery—that clearly brought out his inner lion.

"You look like you need to lay off that chair leg, buddy," I said.

He gazed at me through half-lidded eyes.

I smiled and entered the kitchen, tossing my bag onto one of the Bordeaux-and-gold Dauphine chairs arranged around the rococo dining table. I hadn't eaten since lunch and, to cite Duran Duran, I was "Hungry Like the Wolf." I pulled open the refrigerator door and peered inside. Celery and a pan of re-hardened Zip Wax. I slammed the door and rummaged around in the pantry where I found some rock-hard raisins and a jar of Nutella. Of course, I made the healthy choice—the milk-chocolate hazelnut spread. There was calcium in the milk, cancer-fighting antioxidants in the chocolate, and protein in the hazelnuts. Sure there was no fruit or vegetable, but let's not forget that nuts contain nutritious oils not unlike those of the olive and the avocado.

After grabbing a spoon from the drawer, I flopped onto the chaise lounge next to Napoleon. From his upside down position, he kept one now fully-opened eye trained on the spoon as I raised and lowered it from the jar to my mouth a couple or twenty times.

"I've told you before, Napoleon, chocolate is good for people but poisonous for dogs."

His ear flopped closed as though refusing to listen to any more of my excuses.

I spooned another gob of the silky-smooth ambrosia into my mouth and heard the phone ring from inside my purse.

"*Sonamabiccia,*" I cursed in Italianized English as I jumped up and ran to the kitchen. I placed the Nutella on the counter and threw the spoon into the sink. Then I grabbed the phone from my bag and saw "Bradley" on the display. Instead of the usual chest-fluttering happiness I felt when he called, now I felt nothing but gut-wrenching anxiety. By this time, Pauline had probably given him an earful about me, my nonna, and the *pranzo ufficiale.*

"H-hello?" I stammered, bracing myself for the worst as I carried the phone into the living room.

"Hey, babe," Bradley's sexy voice replied without a trace of animosity.

For a split second, his greeting reminded me of my infuriating exchange with Pauline hours earlier, but I was too relieved to think about the venomous vixen now. I curled up on the chaise lounge and purred, "Hey you."

"When you sound like that," he growled, "you make me want to drive straight to your house and break the door down."

My pulse began to quicken, and I said in a husky voice, "Then it's too bad you're out of town."

"Actually, I just got back. One of my meetings got postponed, so I caught a flight out a day early."
"Oh?" Now my pulse was racing. "Where are you now?"

"I'm getting some takeout on my way to the office. I've been craving Chinese."

Chinese? My blood stopped cold. But then I reminded myself that he was talking about food, not scheming secretaries who were after their bosses.

"Sometime I need to bring you to this place," he continued. "It's a dive, but the food is amazing. It's called 'Oriental Triangle Chinese.'"

I sat straight up. Did he say *triangle* and *Chinese?* My mind flashed to my tarot card reading. Was this a sign that Chandra was right about that Three of Cups card?

"They have some French food too," he added.

The minute he said the word *French* I had my answer. "And a bit of Italian, I'm sure," I muttered.

"Sorry, Franki. The cell signal is weak in here. What'd you say?"

I cleared my throat and replied in a frosty tone, "I said, I *prefer* Italian."

He gave a low, sexy laugh that warmed my chilled blood—and some other parts of me too. "I do too."

"Well, in that case," I began, nestling back into the chaise lounge, "you'd better get right over here so I can serve you my specialty." The second the words came out of my mouth I hoped he understood the euphemism. Because if not, the only thing I could offer him to eat was "ants on a log" with hair removal wax in place of peanut butter.

"I wish I could," he said wistfully. "But something came up at the bank today that I have to take care of ASAP."

I swallowed my disappointment, along with a glob of Nutella that had gathered around one of my molars, and resumed my seductive tone. "I guess you'll just have to wait to sample my specialty on our date tomorrow night."

"About that," he began, "Pauline rescheduled the meeting that got postponed as a video conference for tomorrow night. I'm sorry."

I leapt to my feet and bit the inside of my cheek to keep from blurting out something I would regret. I had no doubt that she'd scheduled that meeting to keep Bradley away from me, but I couldn't tell him that. I needed him to think that I was trying to get along with her, even if I had no such intention. So, through clenched teeth, I uttered a normal-sounding "Thursday, then?"

"I'll try, babe, but I can't guarantee anything. Between the merger and some other things going on at the bank, I've been working nonstop. Even Pauline is working overtime to help me put out fires."

Yes, she is, I thought. *Yours and mine.*

I heard my phone beep. I pulled the phone from my ear and looked at the display—Scarlett Heinz. "Bradley, I have to take this call. It's really important."

"Okay—"

I pressed answer before he could finish speaking. It served him right for letting Pauline cancel our dates. "Hello?"

There was silence on the other end.

"Scarlett?"

"Don't call me again," she said in a low, unsteady voice.

"I'm sorry if I'm bothering you. Delta said it would be all right to call—"

"Well, it's not," she interrupted.

"All I want is justice for Ivanna Jones," I said firmly.

"It's too late for her," she gushed. "But it ain't for the rest of us."

"What do you mean?"

"I mean, you don't know what you're messing with," she replied in a frightened tone. "If you're smart, you'll let it lie."

"What's going on, Scarlett? Please tell me what you know." I waited for her to respond, but I heard dead air on the other end of the line. I looked at my phone and realized she'd ended the call.

I lay back on the chaise lounge, stunned. It had been clear from the start that Scarlett had information about the case. But judging from her warning to me just now, something was going on at Oleander Place—something far more sinister than Ivanna's death. And that was a possibility I hadn't foreseen.

As I stroked Napoleon's belly, I wondered what, exactly, was I "messing with" and whether Miles McCarthy was involved in some way. The bigger question, though, was whether other lives were at stake. Like Scarlett's.

Or mine.

CHAPTER EIGHT

"So what do you want to do about Scarlett?" Veronica asked the next morning as I exited Interstate 10 in the direction of the French Quarter.

"I guess I'm going to have to go to Oleander Place to try to talk to her after her shift. Depending on how long it takes us to question everyone at Lickalicious Lips this morning, I might be able to do it today."

"That reminds me." She pulled a tube of pale pink Chanel lip gloss from her hot pink Dolce & Gabbana Miss Sicily bag and applied a fresh layer.

I turned onto Canal Street. "Where'd you say this place was again?"

She smacked her lips. "On St. Peter."

I nodded and glanced in the direction of Ponchartrain Bank—which we were passing purely by chance, of course. I immediately spotted Corinne's fairy-like figure walking toward the main door with her handbag clutched to her chest and her head lowered. She looked despondent, like a Tinker Bell with drooping wings.

"That's Corinne Mercier," I said, pointing in her direction. "It looks like something's wrong."

"Why don't you pull over?"

"I think I will." I steered my Mustang into a thirty-minute customer service zone in front of a tourist shop.

Veronica rolled down her window, and I leaned across her lap and shouted, "Everything okay, Corinne?"

She turned toward my car and glanced uncertainly at Veronica. "*Bonjour.*"

"Bone-jure," Veronica replied with a polite nod. Like me, she spoke an unofficial Texas dialect of French.

I cleared my throat. "This is my partner, Veronica Maggio."

"I am 'appy to meet you," Corinne said, approaching the window. She was so small that she barely had to bend over to see inside the car. "After yesterday, I am in desperate need of Private Chicks' services."

I killed the engine. "Why? What happened?"

"Zere was more money missing from my teller drawer." Her big blue eyes welled with tears. "Anozer five hundred dollars."

"This has happened before?" Veronica asked.

I nodded. "Did you have to pay back the money again?"

"*Non*. Mr. Hartmann and I were here until midnight. We did not find ze money, but zis time he tell me not to pay."

So that's the bank business he had to take care of ASAP. I pressed my fingers to my lips. "Could one of your customers be a short change artist?"

"I don't sink so. Ze bank train us to recognize such tricks."

"Does anyone else have access to your drawer?" I asked.

"I don't see how, but I suppose it is possible."

"Well, if someone did steal money without you noticing," I said, "then the security cameras would have captured it."

"Yeah," Veronica agreed. "Has anyone checked the surveillance tape?"

"*Oui*, we review ze tape last night wis Pauline."

"Pauline?" I repeated, surprised. And incredibly annoyed. "What's she got to do with this?"

"She is in charge of ze computer wis ze security files."

"That's odd," Veronica said. "You'd think that an IT person or at the very least a manager would handle that sort of thing."

"And not an executive secretary," I muttered. For the life of me, I couldn't fathom how an intelligent man like Bradley could trust a conniving piece of work like Pauline so implicitly. Whatever the reason, I sincerely hoped it didn't have anything to do with her violet, almond-shaped eyes.

"You know Pauline," Corinne said. "She has her hand in everysing."

"Yes," I said dryly, thinking of Bradley's pants. Then a thought occurred to me. Did she also have her hand in Corinne's teller drawer? She certainly seemed to be around every time cash came up missing. But it didn't make sense unless she needed money or had some ulterior motive for wanting Corinne fired.

"It is almost nine o'clock," Corinne said. "I must go in. But I am serious about hiring your firm."

"We can discuss the details another time," Veronica said.

"Yeah, don't worry about that now," I added. "I'll come by the bank this afternoon to see what I can find out. We'll have to keep this arrangement strictly confidential—for your sake and mine. If Bradley finds out I'm poking around in bank matters, he'll ban me from the premises." *And possibly from his life.*

"But of course," she said. "*Au revoir.*"

As soon as Corinne had entered the bank, Veronica turned to me. "What do you think is going on?"

"I don't know, but I'd be willing to bet my eye teeth that it has something to do with Pauline."

Veronica frowned. "I know you don't trust her, but that's a pretty serious accusation."

I sighed. "I know what you're thinking, and you're wrong. This is business—it's not personal." Okay, so maybe it was. But just a little.

She arched an eyebrow and crossed her arms. "Oh, really?"

"Yes, really," I said, mentally crossing my fingers. "Everything was fine until Pauline showed up on the scene. But ever since then, bad things have been happening. At first I thought she was just after Bradley, but now I'm starting to think she wants more than that."

She smirked. "Like total bank domination?"

"Go ahead and laugh, Veronica. But when I prove that she had something to do with the missing money, I'll be the one to laugh last," I said with a pointed look. Then I started the V-8 engine and revved it—for dramatic effect.

"Okay, but are you sure you want to take this case? You've got a conflict of interest here. And if you're wrong about her, it could ruin your relationship with Bradley."

"I don't really have a choice, do I?" I asked, shifting in my seat to face her. "Corinne is my friend, and I want to help her. And Pauline is already trying to ruin my relationship with Bradley. Any minute now, she's going to lay the news of the *pranzo ufficiale* on him and blame it squarely on me. So if I have a chance to show him her true colors, which are black and blacker, I have to take it."

"All right," Veronica said. "Just be careful."

"Around the perilous Pauline? Count on it," I said as I sped away from the curb and tried to figure out how in the hell I was going to investigate Pauline without her or Bradley realizing it.

* * *

After an impromptu stop by the office to retrieve Veronica's laptop, we pulled in front of Lickalicious Lips at nine thirty a.m. I made a quick U-turn in the middle of St. Peter to grab an unlikely parking spot in front of the Gumbo Shop two doors down. The minute I stepped out of the car, my nostrils were filled with the tantalizing aroma of *roux*, a thickener made of bacon fat and flour used as a base in Cajun and Creole cooking. I fervently hoped that the questioning of the Lickalicious staff would last until lunchtime so that I could have a hearty bowl of chicken Andouille gumbo—and a heaping helping of warm bread pudding with whiskey sauce.

"Look, Franki!" Veronica slammed the car door. "Lickalicious Lips is next door to Fleurty Girl, that darling boutique I was telling you about."

I snorted. It figured that she would focus on fashion while I fixated on food. "Maybe we can check it out later," I said as I headed for the cosmetics company. "*After* lunch."

Veronica stopped to admire a tutu on a mannequin outside the shop entryway while I tried the handle of the worn white door to Lickalicious Lips.

"It's locked." I glanced at the windows for signs of life. "I hope they haven't shut down."

"Try the doorbell," Veronica said, arriving at my side.

I pressed the buzzer and took a step back. As I waited, I scrutinized the exterior of the building. I had expected to see brightly painted brick with a cute lip-themed sign. Instead, it was an unmarked stuccoed structure with faded beige paint and the white-trimmed windows and green shutters typical of the French Quarter. I was about to ring the bell again, when the door opened to reveal a tall male in his mid-thirties wearing a wrinkled, white lab coat and khaki pants.

He blinked as though unaccustomed to sunlight. "Can I help you?"

"Yes." I handed him my card. "I'm Franki Amato, and this is Veronica Maggio. We're investigating the death of Ivanna Jones."

He blinked again, this time from surprise. After reading my card front to back, he narrowed his small steel-blue eyes. "Who hired you?"

Veronica stepped forward. "We're representing Oleander Place."

"We'd like to come in and ask you a few questions, if you have a moment," I added.

"I don't know." His brow furrowed. "I've already talked to the police."

"I understand," I said in a gentle tone. "But our client is dissatisfied with the progress of the police's investigation, so we're retracing their steps to make sure all evidence has been uncovered. For Ivanna."

He hesitated and then gestured for us to come inside. "I'm Dr. Adam Geyer. Call me Adam."

"What do you do for Lickalicious Lips?" I asked as Veronica and I entered.

"I'm their cosmetic chemist or, at least, I was. I have no idea what's going to happen with the company now." He exhaled and ran a hand through his short blond hair. "Please, have a seat."

Following Veronica's lead, I sat in one of two black leather armchairs facing the wooden table that served as a desk.

The place looked more like an IKEA showroom than a cosmetics firm. "Is this your office?"

"No," he replied, taking a seat behind the desk. "I work in the next room, in the lab. This was where Ruth Walker sat. She was our administrative assistant, but she resigned on Monday."

I wondered whether Ruth had merely jumped from the proverbial sinking ship or whether there was something more to her resignation. "Would it be possible to speak to her?"

Adam paused and then scribbled something on a piece of paper. "Here's her cell, but I can't guarantee she'll talk to you. She wants nothing to do with this company now."

"Thanks." I took the number and shoved it in my bag.

"Had Ruth been working here long?" Veronica asked, opening her laptop on her knees.

"About three years."

Veronica began typing notes. "What about the other employees?"

"There aren't any. I make the prototypes in house, and then we send them to an outside firm for production and distribution."

That explains the lack of testers here in the lobby, I thought—not without a pang of regret. "How long have you been with Lickalicious Lips?"

"Ivanna recruited me to help her open the company ten years ago. She was working on her Masters in Cosmetic Science at Farleigh Dickinson while I was finishing up my PhD there. She was a student in a class I was teaching, and one day she came to my office hours and said she was going to start Lickalicious when she graduated. I didn't think anything of it at the time, but then a year later she called and offered me a salary I couldn't refuse."

Veronica stopped typing. "She must have had some impressive financial backing."

"She did. From her father, Liam Jones. He's a doctor, and she was his only child. So he could afford to back her."

"Rumor has it that he's been hard to locate," I said. "Have you spoken to him since her death?"

Adam leaned back and crossed his leg over his knee. "No, but I've been trying to reach him. He's works for Doctors Without Borders, so he's often out of contact. Last I heard he was in Syria."

"What about her mother?" I asked.

"She died when Ivanna was a teenager."

"I see." I paused for a moment. "I'm sure the police told you the details of Ivanna's death."

He clenched his jaw and nodded.

I looked him straight in the eyes. "Do you know of anyone who might have done this to her?"

"She didn't have any enemies that I know of." He rubbed his days-old beard. "She was a nice person, and she kept to herself."

"Forgive me for prying," I began, "but was everything okay between the two of you?"

His eyes flashed with anger. "Of course it was," he snapped. "We argued about business from time to time, but that's hardly unusual."

Intrigued by his defensive reaction, I pressed on. "Where were you last Friday night?"

Adam gripped the arms of his chair. "Wait a second," he said rising to his feet. "Do you think I killed Ivanna?"

"We don't think anything," Veronica soothed. "We're just being thorough."

His face relaxed. "Sorry about that," he said, sitting down. "As you can imagine, I've been under a lot of stress."

"Of course," I said. But I was now convinced there had been tension between him and Ivanna. The question was, had it been enough to lead to murder?

"I was here at the lab until midnight on Friday," he explained, "working on the formula for a green lip gloss called Midori Melon."

I licked my lips and told myself that this was not the time to ask for a trial run. "Which shade was Ivanna found holding?"

"That was a pink lip gloss we'd been working on." He began bouncing his right leg. "I can't imagine why she had it with her."

I glanced at his bobbing knee and wondered what had brought on the apparent case of nerves. "What was that shade called?"

"No idea. I just know that it was going to be part of our drink line. But we were having trouble producing the right shade."

Veronica scratched her temple. "How could you mix a specific shade without knowing the drink you wanted to model it after?"

He leaned forward in his chair. "Ivanna was an artist. And like most creative types, she didn't always do things in a way that made sense. Sometimes she would come to me with a color in mind, and then she would wait until I had created just the right shade to announce the flavor."

As he spoke, I tried to think of a brand of liquor that was pink. All I could come up with was a cheap wine I'd found (and may or may not have sampled) in my parents' liquor cabinet when I was thirteen called Boone's Farm Tickle Pink, and I seriously hoped that Ivanna hadn't planned on making a lip gloss version of that. "Could we take a quick look around the lab?"

His eyes widened. "Sure. But there's not much of interest in there."

"That's fine," Veronica said. "We just want to see how the business works."

Adam rose to his feet and opened a door to the right of the desk. "After you."

I entered the lab followed by Veronica. Like the lobby, it was something of a letdown. I thought there would be test tubes, beakers, and maybe even a Bunsen Burner, but instead it was just a kitchen, and a very small one at that. On the left side of the room, there was a sink with cabinets and a small counter on one side and a stove on the other. Next to the stove was a small table with two chairs. And there was still no sign of any testers. "Where do you keep your supplies?"

"In here," he said, opening the wooden cabinet above the counter.

I scanned the contents. Although I was certainly no scientist, I recognized the ingredients from my years of experience as a grocery store makeup buyer (for myself, that is):

lanolin, beeswax, hydrogenated soy glycerides, and assorted bottles of coloring and natural flavors. "There's not much here."

"It doesn't take much to make lip gloss," he said, closing the cabinet door. "You can do it with as little as Vaseline and some powdered or cream blush."

"Or eye shadow or lipstick," Veronica added with a nod.

"Neat," I said, feigning interest. I couldn't be bothered to make myself a sandwich, much less a tube of freaking lip gloss. "What do you keep in the cabinet below?"

He opened the door. "Just kitchen utensils."

"What does that door lead to?" Veronica asked, pointing to the back wall.

Adam walked to the door and opened it. "Ivanna's office and the bathroom. You can look around, if you like."

I followed Veronica into the room, which was decorated with an adorable pink couch and a glass desk with a red leather chair. *Now this is more like it*, I thought.

"The police took Ivanna's computer and her filing cabinets," he said. "So the furniture is all that's left."

"That's too bad," I said, although I'd anticipated as much. I began walking around her office, surveying the scene.

"They also cleaned out her place upstairs."

Veronica turned to Adam. "She lived upstairs?"

He nodded. "She owned this whole building."

"That explains why her business address was listed as her personal address on the police report," Veronica said.

I walked over to the shelving behind Ivanna's desk. There was nothing but a few books and some knickknacks. "Did the police have a key, or did they have the fire department 'spread the door?'"

"Pardon?"

"Sorry." I smiled. "That's police jargon for removing a door without damaging the frame."

"Oh," he slipped his hands into the pockets of his lab coat. "They used her key. Apparently, she'd left it in her car."

"You don't have access to a spare, do you?" I asked.

"I don't know of anyone who does."

I looked around Ivanna's office once more. "One last question, did Ivanna ever talk to you about a pink diamond?"

He rubbed the back of his neck. "Never. Why?"

"Just curious," I said. "Would it be all right if we contacted you with any follow-up questions?"

"Sure," he replied.

I wasn't positive, but I thought I'd seen a look of disappointment in his eyes.

Adam pulled his billfold from his back pocket and extracted a business card. "Call my cell. I'm not sure how much longer Lickalicious will be open."

"Thanks." I took the card. "We'll be in touch."

Veronica and I walked outside into the spring sunshine.

"That was disappointing," I said.

"How so?" Veronica asked, making a hard left toward the boutique.

"Well," I began, close at her heels, "Adam didn't tell us much, and it looks like the police beat us to any evidence."

"Maybe. But you are making progress in the case."

"I suppose." I sighed. "The décor left a lot to be desired too."

She laughed. "You're just upset that they didn't have any free samples."

"Maybe," I said. "I *was* kind of looking forward to a reunion with Bailey's Irish Cream Brown. It's been a long time."

Veronica stopped in front of Fleurty Girl. "Mind if I pop in for a sec?"

I looked at my phone. It was only ten o'clock, which meant that I could kiss my gumbo goodbye. "Nah, we're ahead of schedule. I'm going to stay out here and call Ruth."

"K," she said as she dashed through the doors.

I dialed Ruth's number and started pacing up and down the sidewalk. After several rings, I heard someone pick up.

"Hello?" a matronly voice replied.

"Ruth Walker?"

"Yes. Who's this?"

"I'm Franki Amato. I've been hired to investigate the Ivanna Jones murder."

"Well thank goodness you called," she said in an its-about-time tone.

I stopped in my tracks. "I just got your number from Dr. Adam Geyer. Did he already tell you I'd be calling?"

"No, but I've been waiting for someone besides the police to get involved in this case."

"How come?"

"Because there were some suspicious goings on at Lickalicious Lips between Ivanna and Dr. Geyer right before she was found murdered, and the detective I spoke to doesn't seem too concerned about it."

I spotted a group of oncoming tourists and moved to stand beside the mannequin. "Can you tell me about it?"

"Not on the phone. But I will say that it has something to do with that coral-pink lip gloss Ivanna was found with at the plantation house."

My breath caught in my throat. "Did you say *coral* pink?"

"Mm-hm. It's a shade Ivanna wanted Dr. Geyer to make before she died."

"Yes." *And it was Evangeline Lacour's favorite color too*, I thought. "Any chance we could meet today?"

"Do you know Napoleon House on Chartres Street?"

"No, but I'll find it."

"Can you be there in an hour?"

"See you at eleven thirty." I closed the call.

A million questions were running through my mind, but there was one thing I was certain of. If Ruth knew the shade of pink that Ivanna wanted Adam to produce, then he must have known it too. What I didn't know was why he would lie about it. I mean, I was certain that the lip gloss had something to do with the case, but I hadn't really thought too much about the color. Now I had good reason to believe that Ivanna was trying to match the shade of pink near and dear to Evangeline Lacour's heart. But was it the oleander flowers or her dress that Ivanna was trying to match? And why would she want to match the shade of one of these items for her drink line instead of the liquor itself?

I leaned the back of my head against the facade of Fleurty Girl. The deeper I got into this case, the less I understood what was going on.

CHAPTER NINE

When Veronica and I entered Napoleon House an hour later, I was immediately struck by its old-world charm. The music of Beethoven filled the air, and the main room had a high, wood-beamed ceiling with a hanging light that looked like Thomas Edison had designed it for his newly invented light bulb. There were quaint arched doorways set in distressed plastered walls covered with oil paintings and drawings of various historical figures. Overall, the place had a real colonial vibe—apart from the odor of meatballs and marinara sauce coming from the kitchen.

While we waited for the hostess, my eyes were drawn to a white bust of Napoleon sitting unimperially atop the cash register in the center of the hand-carved wooden bar. He seemed to be looking down his nose at the patrons, as though disgusted that his likeness wasn't somewhere more befitting of an emperor. "Why is this place called Napoleon House, anyway?"

"Because this used to be a house, and the original owner invited Napoleon to live here during his exile," Veronica replied, scanning the clientele. "But he wasn't able to escape from the island of Saint Helena."

"Why would he even want to?" I loved New Orleans and all, but if I had to be exiled, I'd root for the beach over the swamp or the banks of the Mississippi any damn day.

Ignoring my question, Veronica nodded toward a fifty-something female sitting alone in the corner. "Do you think that's her?"

"Let's go find out."

As we weaved our way through the rustic tables and chairs, the woman's head snapped up from her menu. Her tight, graying brown bun didn't move a millimeter, but the chains on either side of her black horn-rimmed reading glasses swung back and forth like jump ropes. "I'm glad you two showed up."

"Of course," I said as Veronica and I sat down. Ruth's familiarity was becoming a little off-putting, to put it mildly.

"I got here a little early, so I ordered us some appetizers and waters." She removed her glasses and let them hang from the chain around her long neck. "They make a good gumbo, and if you're in the mood for a cocktail, this place is famous for its Pimm's cup."

I uttered a silent thank you to the gumbo gods but looked with longing at the bottles lining the bar. "We don't drink on the clock."

"Personally, I never touch the stuff," she said as a waiter arrived with our waters and what looked like an iced tea garnished with cucumber for Ruth.

I had to question why a woman who didn't drink would ask Veronica and me to meet her at one of the most famous bars in America, not to mention work in a place that produced liquor-flavored lip gloss.

"But given what I've been through at Lickalicious Lips," Ruth continued, "I thought a nip of Pimm's would do me good." She took the glass from the waiter and lifted it in a salute. "It's made from herbs, you know."

Question answered, I thought.

The waiter pulled out a pad of paper and a pen. "You all ready to order?"

"Oh, we don't have time to eat," Veronica announced to my utter shock and disappointment. She glanced in my direction. "I just remembered that I have to meet a client at a restaurant near the office at twelve fifteen."

I narrowed my eyes. Veronica never forgot an appointment, especially when it came to business. I was starting to get annoyed with her secrecy—and with the fact that it was the second time that day I'd had to give up gumbo. And now meatballs too.

Ruth waved her hand at the waiter. "I'm good with the appetizers." Then she tapped her glass with a neatly trimmed nail. "But I'll be needing another one of these."

He shoved the pad and pen into his apron, took our menus, and stalked away.

Veronica turned to Ruth. "What can you tell us about the relationship between Ivanna and Adam?"

She pressed her thin lips into an even thinner line. "Well, to start with, they were having an affair."

Veronica and I exchanged a look.

I was surprised Adam had neglected to mention that not-so-insignificant detail. "Are you sure about that?"

"I'd say so, after catching them in the act on the table in the lab."

What was up with sex on the table? I thought, my mind flashing regrettably to my parents.

"Plus, some mornings when I got to work early, I'd see him slinking down the stairs from her apartment." She gave us a knowing look. "In the same clothes he'd worn the day before."

I nodded. It sounded like the walk of shame—not that I had any personal experience with that or anything. "Was he in love with her?"

Ruth sat back in her chair and crossed her arms. "I'm not sure the man knows what love is. But he worshipped the ground she walked on. He used to follow her around like a puppy dog, until they started fighting, that is."

Veronica leaned forward. "Did you ever witness any of their arguments?"

She snorted and reached for her drink. "They were hard to miss. In the two weeks before she died they fought every day."

"Did the fights ever become physical?" Veronica pressed.

"Not that I saw. But it wouldn't surprise me if they had."

"What did they fight about?" I asked.

Ruth sucked down half of her Pimm's cup. "Adam had a taste for gin. He'd been coming into work hung over more and more often, and she confronted him every time. The day before she died, she told him to sober up or get out."

I thought about Adam's disheveled appearance. I'd attributed it to grief, but now that Ruth mentioned it, he could have had a hangover.

"Did he stop drinking?" Veronica asked.

"Nope." She tossed back the rest of her drink and raised her glass to the waiter, signaling the second round.

All Ruth's imbibing was making me thirsty, so I took an unsatisfying sip of my water. "Do you think Ivanna would've fired him?"

She laughed. "That and have him blacklisted too. She made it clear that he was replaceable. And Ivanna was tough. You messed with her business, and she let everyone who mattered know about it. She would've ruined him in the cosmetics industry, and he knew that."

"What can you tell us about the coral-pink lip gloss?" I asked, toying with my table knife.

"Well, I don't know what Ivanna was doing with it at the plantation, if that's what you mean. But I wasn't surprised to hear she had it with her."

I looked up. "Why not?"

The age lines around Ruth's mouth deepened. "There was something weird going on with that lip gloss. I know Ivanna was mad that Adam couldn't get the color right, but it was like she was obsessed with it or something." She stared off into the distance and then shook her head. "All I can tell you was that there was a tension between the two of them over that lip gloss, and it was so thick you could have cut it with a knife."

I dropped the offending utensil. "Do you believe he could have killed her?"

Ruth smirked. "I think all humans are capable of murder, don't you?"

"I don't know," I said with a shrug. "There's a big difference between being capable and actually carrying it out."

"Maybe." She stirred her ice cubes with her straw, searching for one last sip. "But given Adam's recent downward spiral, I wouldn't put it past him."

The waiter returned with Ruth's drink.

"It's getting late," Veronica said. "Is there anything else you can tell us?"

"Yes." She grabbed the Pimm's cup from the waiter's hand. "Keep an eye on Adam Geyer. He's involved in this somehow. You mark my words."

"We'll do that." Veronica rose to her feet. "We really appreciate the information, Ruth."

"And the appetizers we didn't get to have," I said as I stood up and cast a hungry, hateful look in Veronica's direction.

"You let me know if you need anything else," Ruth said before she set to work draining her second drink.

"There is one more thing," I said. "Did Ivanna ever mention a pink diamond?"

Ruth stopped in mid sip. "I can't say she ever did."

As I followed Veronica to the exit, I thought about how Ruth had described Ivanna as *obsessed* with the lip gloss. Why was this particular shade so important to her? And what about Adam? Was his so-called *worship* of Ivanna an obsession? If so, then her criticism could have been a catalyst for violence. Of course, this was all supposition. But Adam's lies and omissions were raising lots of red flags where his innocence was concerned.

* * *

I dropped Veronica off in front of our office at five after twelve. I briefly considered following her to the alleged client meeting to see what I would find out. But then I decided to go straight to Oleander Place. I didn't need a repeat of what happened the last time I fancied myself a spy.

The subject of spying reminded me that I hadn't seen Bradley since he'd returned from his trip. I thought about stopping by the bank to see if he was free for a quick bite, and then I got an idea. If he'd already gone to lunch, that meant I had a forty-five-minute window of opportunity to do some investigating at the bank. I took a left turn and headed toward Canal Street. The plantation could wait another hour.

As I drove, I ran through my plan of attack. I needed to find out two things—Pauline's employment history, so I could do a little digging into her past, and the location of the security room. I didn't know how I was going to do it, but I had to get my hands on a copy of the video files for the days the money went missing from Corinne's drawer.

When I pulled up in front of the bank, I backed into a thirty-minute customer service zone and turned on my hazard lights. I rationalized that I was a) a bank customer in need of service, and b) in an extremely hazardous situation—especially if Bradley or Pauline learned what I was up to.

I exited the car and strolled casually into the lobby, where I saw Pauline hard at work on one of her essential bank tasks—writing on a poster board with a glitter pen. I took a deep breath and approached her desk.

"He's at lunch," she proclaimed without even looking up at me.

"Thanks." I needed to get her talking, so I asked, "What are you making?"

Pauline looked up at me, her gold earrings swaying. "A poster for the children's fundraiser. Now if you'll excuse me, I need to get back to work."

My eyes zeroed in on her earlobes. Those dangles were triangles! *Damn you and that Three of Cups card*, I fumed. But I kept it together and said, "I've been meaning to ask you about the perfume you're always wearing. What kind is it?"

"Pure Poison by Dior," she replied, resuming her drawing.

If ever there was a scent that captured Pauline's essence that was the one, I thought. "Well, I just love it."

She put her glitter pen down and leaned back in her chair. "What do you want?"

"Nothing. Just trying to be nice." I had to bite the tip of my tongue to stop myself from adding, *You should try it sometime.*

"Uh-huh. Well, I'm busy right now, okay?"

I noticed that she had several rows of pictures of herself on her desk (not that she was self-absorbed or anything). This was my chance to bring up her work. "Wow! Is that you?" I gushed, picking up a photo. "You look like a model."

She sighed. "That because I *was* a model. In New York."

"Oh, I thought Bradley said you worked at a bank there. What was it called?" I asked, trying to conjure up a fake bank name in hopes that she would correct me. All I could think of was the unfortunately named, "Brokeman Bank."

"Brehman," she grunted as she added more glitter to the poster.

I felt a little rush. It wasn't her complete job history, but it was a start.

Pauline stared up at me with a scowl. "Listen, I don't have time chit chat. I've got to finish this before lunch."

"Yeah, that's an important poster," I said, unable to resist one tiny jab. "I've got to go make a deposit, anyway."

She rolled her eyes. "Thanks for sharing."

I smiled as sweetly as my tense facial muscles would allow and then headed over to Corinne's teller window. As I waited in line behind a customer, I took a deposit slip and pen from a nearby table and wrote, *Pretend like I'm making a deposit in case Pauline is watching.*

"Next," Corinne called.

I walked up to the window and slid the deposit slip toward her to make it look legitimate.

Corinne read the slip and nodded.

Looking down at the counter, I asked in a low voice, "Are employee resumes kept on file here at the bank?"

She typed something on her keyboard. "If zey are, zey would be in ze employee files in ze left-hand drawer of Mr. Hartmann's desk."

"Last question, where is the computer with the security video files?"

Corinne tore off my copy of the deposit slip. As she handed it to me, she pointed over my shoulder.

I turned and followed her finger to an unmarked door next to Bradley's office—just in time to see Pauline pull her keys from her purse and head to the exit. "Thanks," I said brightly. "See you next time."

She flashed a nervous smile. "You're welcome. Have a nice day."

I put the deposit slip in my bag and glanced at a clock in the lobby. It was twelve thirty, which meant that I had at least twenty minutes before Bradley returned. With my heart in my throat, I walked to his office. When I reached the door, I entered as though I belonged there. I *was* his girlfriend, after all.

Once inside I hurried to his desk and pulled open the left-hand drawer. Sure enough, there were files with the names of employees on them. In the back of the drawer was a label that read "Pauline Violette." I pulled the papers from inside the file and began flipping through them. Insurance information, an annual review, confirmation of a raise (that I was sure she didn't deserve). Then I found it. Pauline's resume.

I shoved the other papers back into the file and sat in Bradley's chair. His desk pad calendar caught my eye. Out of curiosity, I checked to see whether he wrote down our dates. I saw red—both literally and figuratively—when I realized that "Date with Franki," which he'd penciled in for yesterday, had been scratched out with red ink and replaced with "Video Conference" in a decidedly feminine handwriting.

"One of these days I'll cross you out, Pauline," I muttered as I began scanning the list of her previous employers with renewed determination. If her résumé was accurate, which was questionable, she'd worked for two banks from 2010 to 2011 and then from 2011 to 2012. For 2013, she had listed her freelance modeling work. *Because that's so pertinent to the world of banking*, I thought.

"I'll be right with you, Rich," Bradley's voice boomed from outside the door.

I froze in my seat—correction, Bradley's seat—as sheer panic coursed through my body.

"I need to grab my laptop," he continued.

Luckily, adrenaline followed the panic. I leapt up from the chair, kicked the file drawer shut, and stuffed the résumé up my shirt. I had just enough time to tuck the bottom of the sheet into the waistband of my jeans and sit on the corner of his desk before the door opened.

Bradley saw me and started. "Franki! What are you doing here?"

"Uh," I began, pushing a lock of hair out of my eyes, "before Pauline went to lunch, she said I could wait in your office."

He cocked his head to the side for a fraction of a second before removing his suit coat and hanging it on a coat rack. It must have sounded strange even to him that Pauline would be so accommodating.

I fervently hoped that he didn't mention this to her. Otherwise, she'd make good on her threat to out me about the *pranzo ufficiale*.

"It's great to see you, babe," he said as he crossed the room. He put his arms around my waist and pulled me in for a kiss.

For a second, I was seduced into an oblivious state by his touch. Then, remembering the resume, I arched my back like a cat so that his stomach wouldn't press against mine. As a result, his lips landed squarely on my nose.

Bradley pulled away and looked into my eyes. "Is everything okay?"

"Fine, fine," I said, thinking how ironic it was that even Pauline's résumé managed to drive a wedge between us.

Before I realized what was happening, he pulled me toward him again. As his body pressed against mine, there was a loud paper-crumpling sound.

He took a step back, his right arm still encircling my waist. "What was *that*?"

"Um," I said, racking my brains to think of a paper product I would have a logical reason for wearing around my mid-section—besides Depends. "It's a…new…maxi-maxi pad."

He stared my stomach and blinked.

"It goes up to the abdomen," I explained, feeling my cheeks flush. "For when you need that extra super protection."

"Oh," he said, as embarrassed as I was.

I glanced at my wrist—where a watch would have been if I'd been wearing one—and said, "Gosh! I need to go." And then using Veronica's lie as I rushed to the door, I added, "I just remembered that I was supposed to meet a client near the office at twelve fifteen."

"Wait a minute, Franki," he said in a stern tone.

I felt my stomach sink. He knew I was up to something. I turned to face him—and the consequences.

"Have dinner with me tomorrow night," he said softly with that familiar gleam in his eyes.

My knees went weak. I wanted to throw myself into his arms, but instead I smiled and nodded. Then I ran from the room, crinkling all the way.

* * *

Three hours and a wasted trip to Oleander Place later, I stomped up the three flights of stairs to Private Chicks and pushed open the door.

"Hey Franki," David said. He was sitting at his desk in the corner. "That package on the coffee table is for you."

"Awesome." I flopped down on the couch and picked up the cardboard box. "Hopefully someone sent me a rope to hang Delta with."

Veronica walked into the lobby from her office. "Why? What happened?"

"I just went to Oleander Place to talk to Scarlett, but when I got there I found a note saying the plantation had closed early. So I just blew three hours of my afternoon for nothing, and now I have to go back out there again tomorrow."

"That's weird." Veronica put her hand on her hip. "Delta called a few minutes ago, but she didn't mention that."

I narrowed my eyes. "She wasn't at the plantation, was she?"

"She didn't say. She was calling to let us know that the medical examiner said Ivanna died from respiratory failure."

"Do we know the cause?" I asked.

"Well, here's where it gets interesting. Ivanna didn't have any health conditions or injuries, which means that we're looking at a possible drug overdose. Or poisoning."

"Wow." I shook my head. "Then there's a possibility that Ivanna was poisoned—like Evangeline."

David spun around in his chair to face me. "Dude, that would be insane."

"That's one way to describe it," I said, staring at the box in my lap. "I hope they're testing for oleander."

"I would imagine they are at this point," Veronica replied, handing me a letter opener from David's desk.

I started slicing through the tape on the box. "This is just a thought, but Adam would know how to extract the poison from oleander."

Veronica took a seat beside me. "Yeah, but you don't have to be a scientist to poison someone with oleander. Evangeline is a perfect example of that. Whoever poisoned her just boiled oleander leaves in her tea."

I opened the box and stared inside. Then I turned to Veronica, my eyes wide with disbelief.

"What is it?" she asked.

"A pineapple."

"What?"

"In the package. It's a whole pineapple."

Veronica leaned over and looked inside. "Who sent it?"

I pointed to the outside of the box. "There's no sender name or address."

"David, who delivered this?" Veronica asked, visibly upset.

He shrugged. "It was by the front door when I got here."

I removed the pineapple and saw a typed note at the bottom of the box. I picked it up and read aloud, *You've worn out your welcome, Miss Franki.*

"Huh?" David said. "I don't get it."

"Actually, it's pretty clear," I replied in a surprisingly calm tone considering that my heart was hammering my rib cage. "It's a Southern-style threat to stay away from the Ivanna Jones case."

CHAPTER TEN

I arrived at Private Chicks at ten the next morning, exhausted and on edge. Following the shock of the package, I barely slept a wink. It seemed like I'd had the same nightmare all night long. I'd been pushed into a vat of fruit cocktail at the Dole pineapple plantation and was about to be canned alive.

Given the uncertainty of the situation, I kept an eye out for suspicious items as I climbed the stairs. Then I scoured every inch of the office. I felt kind of silly about being wigged out over a pineapple, but after yesterday, I was never going to look at the spiny fruit the same way again.

I'd just pressed start on my laptop when, out of nowhere, Veronica popped her head around the doorjamb.

"You okay?" she asked.

After prying myself off the ceiling, I replied, "How would you feel if you'd received the Southern equivalent of a severed horse head in your bed?"

She pursed her lips and took a seat in front of my desk. "I know you're upset. Believe me, I am too. But a pineapple isn't exactly a *Godfather*-caliber threat."

"Then I should feel good about the fact that I was threatened by an old-school Southerner rather than a mobster?"

"I'm just saying that I think it was a scare tactic. You should definitely be careful, but I don't believe you're in any real danger."

I cast her a sideways look. "All I know is that the next time I get a pineapple, it had better be on top of a piña colada."

Veronica gave a half smile. "So, who do you think sent it?"

"Scarlett comes to mind." I hugged my knees to my chest. "She's the one who told me what the pineapple symbolized in the Old South."

"She wouldn't set herself up like that."

"I'm not so sure. She didn't strike me as the brightest bustle dress on the plantation. But I do think Miles is also a possible culprit."

Veronica examined a fingernail. "Have you considered Adam?"

"If it was Adam, then he's connected to someone at Oleander Place. Whoever sent it had to know about the incident between Delta and Scarlett."

"Not necessarily. Remember, I told him that Oleander Place is our client. And Louisiana is plantation country, so the pineapple custom is well known here. In fact, you can buy pineapple merchandise at kitchen and gift shops all over the state."

"I don't know." I rested my chin on my knee. "It would be quite a coincidence for Adam to send a pineapple without knowing what went down."

"Mornin', miladies!" David exclaimed in a British accent as he appeared in the doorway.

I jumped out of my seat and almost out of my skin.

His face wrinkled in confusion. "Did I scare you, Franki?"

"Nah," I scoffed, picking up my overturned chair.

"We didn't hear your signature door slam," Veronica said.

"Oh! I get it now." He laughed, his head bobbing with each "ha." "I didn't close the door. My vassal did."

Veronica smirked. "Whatever your vassal is, I like it."

"It's a he." David puffed out his chest. "He's, like, my servant."

A short young man with hair slicked to one side and round, coke-bottle glasses stepped from behind David's lanky frame. "'Vassal' is a medieval term for a type of servant."

"Silence, vassal!" David commanded. Then he turned to Veronica. "My fraternity gave him to me. He's a freshman pledge, so he has to do my bidding for the day."

"What kind of fraternity is this?" I asked. "A feudal one?"

"Uh, that would be fairly ridiculous," David replied. "It's, like, a comp sci frat."

The vassal leaned forward. "I wanted to major in Radio, Television, and Film, but my parents wouldn't let me."

David stared open-mouthed at the young man. "Vassal, must I flog thee?"

"David!" Veronica rose to her feet and put her hands on her hips. "There will be no flogging in this office, do you understand?"

"Yes, ma'am. I mean, mademoiselle." He bowed his head. "But I wasn't really going to flog him. Honest."

I held up my hand. "Okay, enough about fraternities, feudalism, and flogging. I need you to do a background check for me ASAP on a woman named Pauline Violette."

David's head shot up. "Yo, she sounds *hot*."

The vassal nodded vigorously, careful to keep his lips sealed.

"Well, she's not," I snapped.

"Right," David said, bowing his head again. "I'll get to work on that now."

"You do that," I said.

David scurried from the room, but the vassal stood there looking at me, slack-jawed.

I realized that he was probably waiting for his orders, so I used a language I knew he would understand, Shakespearean English. "Be off with thyself, vassal!"

He turned and fled.

Veronica stared after him, shaking her head. Then she turned to me. "I see you've stepped up your investigation of Pauline."

"I have, starting with the résumé I snagged from Bradley's desk yesterday."

"Nice work," she said with an appreciative nod. "What's the plan?"

"I'm going to contact her previous employers to see what I can find out."

"Most Human Resources offices won't tell you anything without a signed release from Pauline."

"I know, but I'm hoping I'll get lucky and talk to an unprofessional ex-boss. Most bosses are jerks, you know."

Veronica lowered her eyelids.

"Not you, of course," I hurried to add. "Anyway, there are a few things about her résumé that are interesting." I pulled the document from a file in my desk. "For example, she worked at two different banks in New York in a short period of time, and then she did some freelance modeling."

"So?"

"Well," I began, frustrated that she couldn't see the gaping issues, "why'd she leave the two banks so fast?"

"From the sound of it, because she wanted to be a model."

"Sure, but was that really lucrative enough for her to be able to live in New York for a year? Probably not, because she's not doing it anymore."

She shrugged. "Maybe her family helped support her."

"Okay, then why, after she quit modeling, would she take a bank job in New Orleans and not in New York? That's where all her contacts were."

"Because she wanted to get out of the city, more than likely. New York is famous for burning people out."

I frowned. Maybe there were logical explanations for my questions, but my instinct was telling me that there was more to the résumé than met the eye. "Well, I still say it's worth looking into. I'm going to start by calling..." I scanned the page for the bank Pauline had mentioned. "That's weird."

"What?"

"The bank she told me she worked for in New York isn't listed."

Veronica smiled, her eyes sparkling. "Now that *is* interesting."

* * *

I hung up the phone and looked out my office window. Rain clouds had moved in and turned the sky an ominous black. Just like my mood.

I shivered and zipped up my hoodie. Then I went into the kitchen and poured myself some much-needed French roast. I'm pretty sure my Italian cappuccino mug was offended.

"How's the investigation going?" Veronica asked as she entered and pulled a container of chopped vegetables from the refrigerator.

"Well, it took me half an hour to figure out that Brehman Bank is spelled with an *h*. Then I spent another forty-five minutes on hold with HR only to be told that I needed the signed release form."

"That's what I was afraid of." She took a bite out of a radish.

I grimaced. I was convinced that radishes were as poisonous as the oleander flower. Then I began spooning my customary five tablespoons of sugar—unrefined, of course—into my coffee.

She popped the rest of the radish into her mouth. "Did you call the two banks that were on the résumé?"

I nodded. "Same thing. I need Pauline's signature to get any info."

The lobby bell buzzed.

"Is David still here?" I asked, stirring my coffee sugar sludge.

"He made the vassal drive him to class."

"At least the vassal went with him this time." I picked up my mug. "I'll go see who it is."

I walked into the lobby and saw Chandra. She was standing by the door in a white plastic rain poncho that did nothing for her dough-ish figure. "Hey, Chandra. What brings you to Private Chicks?"

Her jewelry jingled as she pulled the poncho over her head and smoothed her over-styled do. "That spirit came to me again."

"She did?" I sat down on the couch, cradling my coffee cup. I hated to admit it, but I was excited.

"Uh-huh, and she was calm this time," Chandra said, flopping down beside me. "Maybe it was because Lou and I were in our yard, enjoying nature. It's planting season, you know, and he just installed a sprinkler system in my flowerbeds." She stared at her chubby flip-flopped feet, which were dangling over the edge of the sofa. "Being married to a plumber certainly has its advantages."

"I'm sure." There was something to be said for a lifetime of good water pressure and unclogged toilets. "But what about the spirit?"

"Well, this year I wanted to plant moonflowers and starflowers, but they're both white. So Lou insisted we add a touch of color. He just loves bright things, that one. He picks out all my outfits," she said, gesturing toward her yellow sunburst-themed T-shirt and bright orange short shorts.

"How romantic," I said, picturing a stocky, balding man with a closet full of Hawaiian shirts. "But what does any of this have to do with the spirit?"

She put a hand on my arm. "I'm getting there. Be patient."

Patient? I thought. *Who has time for that?*

"Anyway, Lou went to the nursery to get the plants. And I had him get some extra mulch and fertilizer too."

I was seriously starting to worry that planting season would be over by the time she finished this story.

"And do you know what he came back with?"

"Um, the stuff you asked for?"

"Impatiens."

Go figure. "I still don't see what this has to do with the spirit."

Chandra sighed. "They were pink, exactly like the flowers at Oleander Place."

I placed my mug on the coffee table. *Now we were getting somewhere.*

"I didn't notice the similarity of the pink, but the spirit sure did. She came to me on the spot and told me to warn you about Oleander Place. She said that it may seem like a welcoming place, but it's downright inhospitable. Dangerous even."

"Yeah, I've gotten that message," I said, thinking of the pineapple package.

Thunder rumbled in the sky, as though underscoring my precarious position.

"She also said not to be fooled by the oleander flowers."
I leaned forward. "What did she mean by that?"

"How should I know?" Chandra pulled a family-sized
bag of Zapp's New Orleans Kettle-Style Voodoo chips from her
Chanel bag.

"Um, because you're the medium who talked to her?" I
suggested, observing the bag with a certain interest—the Zapp's,
not the Chanel.

"It's not my job to interpret messages. I'm only supposed
to relay them. That's what 'medium' means."

She had me there. It was up to me to decipher the
meaning. But was the spirit telling me that oleander had nothing
to do with the case? There was only one way to find out. "Listen,
I wish you would reconsider coming out to the plantation."

Chandra nibbled on a chip. "I have."

"Really?" My stomach rumbled as I watched her chew. I
wanted some chips. With a ham po' boy. And a slice of bourbon
pecan pie. Or just the bourbon.

"After the spirit came to me in the flowerbed I said to
myself, 'Now Chandra, it's just plain silly to be scared of spirits.
You came to The Crescent City to serve them. They're your
cosmic clients.'" She bit into another chip.

I licked my lips. "That's so true."

"Then I said, 'Chandra, the spirits will keep you safe.
The only one in danger here is Franki.' And that made me feel
better about everything."

Gee, me too. "So, can you go to Oleander Place with me
later this afternoon?"

"With the lunar eclipse coming, I've got clients
practically beating down my door."

I imagined a pack of half-men, half-werewolves trying to
claw their way into her tiny office.

"But I suppose I can make some time tomorrow before
noon." She rose to her feet and gathered her bags. "I never do
business during lunchtime."

"That's a good policy," I said, consulting the lobby
clock. I had just enough time to run over to Tracey's bar in the
Irish Channel for that po' boy. And some gravy cheese fries. I

ushered her to the door and said, "I'll pick you up at your office at ten."

"Okay." She stepped into the stairwell. "But make sure you bring a hundred bucks. Cash."

As the door closed behind her, lightening lit up the room like a kind of meteorological exclamation point.

I collapsed onto the couch, certain that the weather—or maybe the spirit—was mocking me. One hundred dollars was a lot to pay for something as unscientific as a psychic reading. But I told myself it was worth the price to see what Chandra would discover at the plantation—provided that she wasn't a fraud, of course. I wanted to find out the identity of the spirit that was contacting her and that of the blonde in the pink crinoline dress she'd seen in her crystal ball. It had to be either Evangeline or Ivanna, and I needed to know which.

First, however, I needed lunch. I hurried to my office to grab my bag, hoping that Veronica would let me bill Delta for Chandra's services. Otherwise, after today, there would be no more po' boys for me.

The lobby bell sounded.

"*Porca miseria,*" I cursed in Italian. And I was in "pig misery" because something or someone out there didn't want me to have my pork po' boy.

When I returned to the lobby, I gave a start. I saw what looked like a werewolf in transition—human flesh and patches of gray fur with two ears and a long tail—holding a cardboard box about the size of the pineapple package. But then I saw the cigarette holder between its teeth and realized that it was just Glenda.

"That wasn't left outside the door, was it?" I asked, eyeing the box with concern.

Glenda placed the container on the coffee table and removed the cigarette holder from her mouth. "Nah, these are a little something I made for you girls."

"How nice," Veronica said as she entered the lobby.

I relaxed and went back to my spot on the couch.

"I just finished teaching my stripper boot camp class, so I thought I'd run them by."

"How's that going?" Veronica asked.

Glenda sighed and sat down beside me, crossing her fur-leg-warmer-clad calves and adjusting her matching loincloth. "I tell you, those girls are gonna drive me to drinkin'. Today they had to present a three-minute routine in costume. I went first to show them how it's done."

"What are you supposed to be?" I asked, scrutinizing her fur wrist warmers.

Glenda batted her inch-long orange eyelashes. "Why, I'm sexy Big Bad Wolf."

"Gah, Franki," Veronica chided, as though sexy Big Bad Wolf costumes were as common as blue jeans.

"Sorry," I muttered. "But why not sexy Little Red Riding Hood?"

Glenda exhaled two lungsful of smoke. "Sugar, do I look like a sexual victim to you? No self-respecting woman would play the part of that red-hooded idiot."

"Definitely not," Veronica huffed.

"Wow," I said, reeling from the red-riding-hood revelation. "I just thought it was a children's story about stranger danger."

Veronica and Glenda stared at me like I was the red-hooded idiot, even though my hoodie was purple.

"Anyway," Glenda said with a flip of her platinum hair, "this one girl put together a sexy maid routine. Not very original, but hey, she's a beginner so I kept an open mind."

"Good for you," Veronica said.

"But then what does the fool go and do? She sashays onto the stage in three-inch heels."

Veronica gasped and put her hand on her heart.

I looked from Veronica to Glenda, unsure of "the fool's" faux pas.

"Once I recovered from the shock," Glenda continued, "I said, 'Sugar, are those tap dancing shoes?' To which she replied, 'They're my strippin' shoes.' So I went, 'Child, anything less than six inches is just plain sad. And that goes for the boudoir too."

Veronica nodded.

"And do you know what she proceeded to inform me?" Glenda asked, waving her cigarette dangerously close to my cheek. "That platform heels hurt her feet, so she needed a *sensible* stripper shoe. Can you imagine such a thing?"

I shook my head. In all honesty, I really couldn't.

"So, I told her, 'Well, if you want to sell sensible, sugar, go get yourself a job at the Naturalizer store, because here we sell sex.'"

Veronica patted Glenda's bare thigh. "Those girls are so lucky to have you as their teacher."

"Thank you, Miss Ronnie." Glenda stood up and took another drag off her cigarette. "But this younger generation just isn't willing to suffer for their art. And if that doesn't change, I'm afraid they're going to cheapen the whole stripping profession."

"We can't have that," I said.

"Speaking of stripper shoes," Glenda began, reaching into the box, "I made this for you, Miss Franki." She handed me a white, ceramic stripper-shoe planter with a prickly pear.

I stared speechless at the item. *Was everyone in New Orleans planting but me?*

"And this is for you, Miss Ronnie." She handed Veronica a cute little pink handbag planter with sweet-smelling white jasmine.

Veronica squealed. "It's adorable!"

I looked at her planter with envy. Why did she get the precious purse while I got the slut shoe? With a cactus, to boot.

"Anyway, girls," Glenda said, picking up the box, "I don't want to keep you from your work, especially since it involves a pink diamond."

As Veronica walked Glenda to the door, I thought about Glenda's comment. Could the diamond be the key to this case and not the oleander? That would certainly fit with the spirit's warning not to be fooled by the flowers—that is, *if* I wasn't being duped by Chandra.

"Bye Miss Franki," Glenda said, snapping me out of my thoughts.

I turned as she opened the door and saw Delta standing on the other side in a dramatic floor-length black mink. If there were ever two personalities destined to clash it was the proper southerner and the promiscuous stripper. I held my breath and watched the standoff with a mixture of fascination and fear.

Glenda made the first move. She narrowed her eyes and took a deep drag off her cigarette.

In reply, Delta grasped her pearls and raised her chin.

Given their attire, I felt like I was watching a Louisiana-style territory-marking ritual on Animal Planet.

Glenda exhaled. "Nice fur."

"Likewise," Delta said, jerking her head backward to avoid the fumes.

Seizing upon Delta's submissive posture, Glenda nodded and—with her cigarette holder in one hand and her tail draped over the other—made a triumphant exit.

Breathing a sigh of relief, I thanked heaven for their mutual fur fetishes.

"Hello, Delta," Veronica said, closing the door behind her.

I rose to my feet. "I didn't realize we had a meeting."

"I didn't realize I had to set up a meeting to talk to you," she said, waltzing into the room and taking a seat on the couch.

"Oh, you don't," Veronica hurried to add.

I really wished Veronica hadn't said that. Something told me that being at Delta's beck and call could be brutal. I sunk down onto the couch beside her. "So what brings you away from the plantation again?"

"Again?" she repeated.

"Yeah, yesterday I went out there to talk to Scarlett, but it was closed."

She touched her Baron Samedi brooch. "Why would you need to talk to her? Is something wrong?"

"That's what we're hoping Scarlett can tell us," Veronica said.

"We think she has information about the case," I explained. "She was acting strange when we were at the plantation."

"Strange?" Delta threw her head back and laughed. "That's because the girl's as dumb as a stump. But if you think it's worth your time to question her again, her last tour ends at three o'clock today."

Sidestepping the stump issue, I asked, "So, the plantation is open?"

"Yes, I closed early yesterday because we didn't have a single tour booked for the afternoon, and I had to meet with my informant about the coroner's report. Naturally, he can't discuss the investigation over the phone."

I nodded.

"Anyway, there's been a development in the case. The test results came back on the lip gloss. It contains a significant amount of oleander."

Veronica gasped. "So, Ivanna might have been poisoned just like Evangeline?"

"It looks that way," Delta replied.

I was almost inclined to agree. But I reflected on the spirit's warning, and a thought occurred to me. Ivanna wasn't wearing the pink lip gloss—she was wearing red. So, unless she ingested the lip gloss as a taste test or something, it couldn't have caused her death. If that was the case, then why was the lip gloss poisoned? And what killed Ivanna?

CHAPTER ELEVEN

———

"Anyhow," Delta said as she rose and made her way to the door, "I've got to get over to Arnaud's for a luncheon." She flashed her yellowed teeth in something that resembled a smile. "I just adore their Filet Mignon Charlemond."

My stomach growled at the mention of meat. "Before you go, has your informant said anything about the results of the mass spectrometry?"

"The mass what?" she asked, drawling the word *what* for a good three syllables.

"It's a type of test done in forensic toxicology for cases of possible drug overdose or poisoning."

"Those must be the results we're still waiting for," she said, pulling her Cadillac keys from her Louis Vuitton. "I assume they'll show that Miss Jones died of oleander poisoning."

"Yeah," I said despite my doubts. "I'd like to see them, just the same."

As Delta reached for the doorknob, the vassal entered with two carryout bags.

My stomach instantly recognized the Johnny's Po-Boys logo on the bags and let out a mighty roar—more from outrage than hunger.

"Well, excuse you, young man," Delta huffed.

The vassal looked at her with his coke-bottle-lens-enlarged eyes and stepped to the side, leaning against the door to hold it open.

"Greetings, good ladies," David bellowed as he strode big-man-on-campus-style into the room. His strut went straight to slump when he caught sight of Delta.

She wrinkled her nose in disgust and looked from David to the vassal. "What *is* that ghastly odor?"

The vassal blinked but maintained his fraternity-imposed silence.

David stood at attention, more like a common footman than a feudal lord. "Uh, it's three french fry po' boys with gravy and two hot dog po' boys with chili, ma'am."

"Well, it smells like road kill," she snarled.

The vassal pushed up his glasses with his index finger and proceeded to stare at Delta in his mouth-breather manner.

She gathered her mink around her neck and scowled at him as though he were a vulgar voyeur. Then she turned to Veronica and me, her lips thinning into a straight line. "I don't know how you two can work in these appalling conditions."

The second she went out the door, Veronica shot me a wry smile.

David relaxed and resumed his fraternal-feudal air. "Vassal, I'm ready to be served."

I watched with envy as the vassal pulled the sandwiches from the bag and laid out a po' boy picnic on David's desk.

"What are you thinking, Franki?" Veronica asked.

"That I would kill to have the metabolism of a college male."

"Well, that goes without saying," she said, glancing at David as he licked brown gravy from his fingers. "I meant about the oleander in the lip gloss."

I sighed. "I don't know what to think. Nothing makes any sense."

"Let's go talk it out in my office." Veronica turned to David. "When you're finished feasting, could you research the effects of oleander poisoning on the body?"

David nodded with french fries protruding from his mouth like cigarettes.

I took one last longing look at the boys' po' boys and then followed Veronica down the hallway. I was starting to worry that I would never get to eat again.

"All right," she said, taking a seat behind her desk, "what do we know?"

I flopped into my usual chair. "That Ivanna was holding poisoned lip gloss she wasn't wearing. And unless she had some sort of lip protectors like Gilligan wore in his spy dream when Ginger kissed him on *Gilligan's Island,* then I seriously doubt that she was planning to wear it to kiss an enemy."

Veronica smirked and turned on her laptop.

"So, the way I see it," I said, kicking my legs over the side of the chair, "we have three possible scenarios. First, Ivanna was planning to poison someone with the lip gloss, but it backfired."

"How?" she asked as she twisted her hair into a knot.

"Maybe the person figured out what she was up to and killed her instead by making her swallow some of the lip gloss."

Veronica worked a pencil into her bun to hold it in place. "That's possible, I suppose."

I crossed my arms and sunk deeper into the chair. "The only problem with that is we don't know how much oleander it would take to kill a woman Ivanna's size. A little bit in some lip gloss may not be enough."

"Good point. I'll send David an email right now asking him to add that to his to-do list," she said, clicking the keys on her keyboard.

As she typed, I casually swiped a lone peppermint from the corner of her desk. I felt it was owed to me since she was delaying my lunch. "We also need to figure out where the poison came from."

Veronica looked up. "You don't think it came from Oleander Place?"

"It depends," I said, quietly unwrapping the peppermint out of view. "We know Ivanna was at the plantation before she was murdered, so maybe she took some oleander leaves. But— and this is my second theory—Adam could have added the oleander to the lip gloss with or without her knowledge. And if that's the case, it could've come from anywhere."

"Why would Adam poison the lip gloss?" she asked, cocking her head.

I discreetly popped the peppermint into my mouth and replied, "Either he was in on Ivanna's poisoning plan, or he wanted to poison Ivanna."

She folded her hands beneath her chin. "It sounds like it's time to have another face-to-face chat with Dr. Geyer."

I nodded, savoring the yummy peppermint flavor.

Veronica resumed typing. "What's your third theory?"

"That whoever killed Ivanna put the lip gloss in her hand to make a statement."

"Such as?" she asked, raising an eyebrow.

I shrugged. "Maybe it's like Delta said about the flower Evangeline was holding. You know, that she was toxic or something."

"Or that her products were."

"I'm not so sure." I blatantly chewed the peppermint and wished it were a po' boy. "Remember, I looked at the ingredients Adam uses, and they're all harmless. Plus, the lip gloss tube didn't have the Lickalicious Lips label."

"So, what are you planning to do?"

"I'm finally going to track down Scarlett," I said, neglecting to mention that I'd be lunching at length first. "Then I'll pay a visit to Adam."

David cleared his throat in the doorway.

"Yes?" Veronica asked.

"The mail just came," he said, depositing several envelopes on her desk. "And I found out that acute oleander poisoning causes cardiac arrest."

I sat up in my chair. "What about respiratory failure?"

"Nope." He consulted the printout he was holding. "It affects the heart, the gastrointestinal system, and the nervous system."

Veronica and I exchanged a look.

"So," he continued, "it could make you puke, give you the runs—"

Veronica held up her hand. "Thank you, David."

"But it wouldn't cause the lungs to fail," I muttered.

"This is getting more and more interesting," Veronica said.

"You mean, confusing." I stared at the pink Post-It notes on Veronica's desk and thought of the diamond. "David, have you ever heard of a nineteenth-century pirate called Beau the Black?"

He scratched his forehead. "I think we studied him in, like, the seventh grade, but I don't remember anything about him."

"His real name was Beauregard Patterson, and he used to be a confederate army soldier. I need you to try to locate any of his descendants. Do you think you can do that?"

"Aye aye, captain," he said with a salute and then limped away like he had a peg leg.

I had to smile at his pirate persona.

Veronica tore open an envelope. "Why do you want to find Beau's relatives?"

"It's time to look into the legend of the pink diamond. Something is off about this case, starting with the cause of death."

"I think you're right." She pulled a card from the envelope and put her hand to her mouth. Then she looked up at me with fear in her eyes.

I glanced at the envelope lying on her desk. Noting the shiny purple of its interior flap, I froze in my chair. I had only one question, "What did Nonna do?"

"Now, stay calm," Veronica said, gripping the sides of the card as though hanging on for dear life. "It's a little thing, really."

I ripped the card from her hand. It was an invitation to a cocktail party celebrating my engagement to "Bradli Artman," the Italian phonetic spelling of "Bradley Hartmann" minus the *h* (which is always silent in the Italian language and never begins a word). My first thought was that maybe the name looked just different enough to convince Bradley that it wasn't actually him I was getting engaged to. But then it occurred to me that another man wouldn't make the outcome any better.

Fueled by a burst of rage that would rival that of Rocky Balboa on steroids, I marched into my office and grabbed my purse and cell phone. Then I pressed my parents' number and headed for the lobby.

"Franki!" Veronica called, her high heels clicking behind me. "What are you going to do?"

"What I do best—fight with my nonna and then stress-eat," I shouted as I stormed from the office. I ran down the stairs two at a time while the phone was ringing. When I got to the parking lot, the answering machine switched on. Certain that Nonna was dodging my call, I climbed into my car and pressed my parents' work number. I was about to start the engine when someone picked up.

"Amato's Deli," my mother responded in a shrill, singsong tone.

To avoid the delay of our usual name game, I blurted out, "Mom, this is Francesca."

"Well, of course it is," she said in an offended tone. "Are you suggesting that I don't know my own daughter's voice?"

So much for saving time. "Mom, I—"

"Well, what else am I supposed to think when you tell me your name, Francesca?"

I sighed and leaned my head against the window. I couldn't win where my family was concerned. "You're right. That was silly of me. Now, can I talk to Dad?"

"He's making Italian sausage, and he's up to his elbows in ground pork."

And I'm knee-deep in poop, I thought. "I need to talk to him about Nonna. It's urgent."

"It's not a good time, dear. Your nonna is here."

My radar went up. There were only three reasons my nonna would ever leave the house: Sunday mass, a papal visit, or a secret mission related to one of her meddling schemes. "What's she doing at the deli?"

"She said she wanted to help your father make the sausage," my mother whispered. "But between you and me, I think she really wanted to get out of the house. Right now she's holding court with Rosalie Artusi, Crispino DiRuggiero from the ceramics store, Agostino Fossati from that new chocolate shop—"

"Okay, Mom?" I interrupted. "I don't need the whole list. Just let me talk to Nonna."

"She's talking to Father Will and Father Roman. I'd hate to disturb them."

"Wait." I paused to collect my thoughts. "Did you say 'Father?'"

"Twice, dear. They're new priests at Holy Rosary Church, and they've become regulars at the deli. They said they've been assigned to teach the marriage preparation classes. Isn't that nice?"

I felt a stabbing sensation in my chest as the reality of what was going on came crashing down on me. *Holy mother of God, Nonna's arranging my wedding.*

"Francesca, are you all right? You sound like you're choking."

"Mom," I said through clenched teeth, "why the hell didn't you tell me Nonna was communing with clergy?"

"You said you didn't want the whole list," she replied, clueless to my priestly plight.

My heart was pounding out the rhythm of *the tarantella.* "Never mind that. Just put her on the phone."

I heard the receiver crash down onto the counter.

"Carmela!" she shouted, even though the tables were all of five feet from the deli's phone. "It's Francesca!"

Next came the usual murmur of the customers, who, upon hearing my name, began asking what I knew to be prying questions about my personal life—questions to which my mother would respond in lavish detail.

"*Pronto,*" Nonna responded with the customary Italian *ready.* And I could tell from her tone that she was indeed ready—for battle.

"Nonna," I rasped, breathless from stress, "I saw the invitation. How could you do this?"

"What's-a the big-a problem?"

I gasped. "The 'big-a problem' is that Bradley hasn't asked me to marry him. And if he sees that invitation, he never will."

"He will-a, he will-a," she reassured. "You leave everything-a to me."

I laughed in disbelief. "If I do that, I'll end up a *zitella* for sure. Now please tell me that you did *not* send him that invitation."

"*Calmati*, Franki," she reassured. "I only send it-a to Veronica."

I bowed my head on the steering wheel and silently thanked God, Jesus, Mary, and Joseph for their divine intervention. But then curiosity got the best of me. "Why did you only send it to her?"

"Because it's-a just a sample, and I want-a her opinion."

"Why *her* opinion?" I asked, admittedly a little put out. After all, it was an invitation to *my* engagement party.

"It's-a simple," she said matter-of-factly. "Veronica's got-a class."

The woman sends out clandestine purple invitations to my non-engagement with the name of my non-fiancé misspelled, and she implies that I'm the one who's unrefined? "Class or no class," I hissed, "there is no engagement. So do not send out any more invitations, *capito?*"

"I can't-a make-a you no guarantees," she replied without missing a beat.

I wanted to scream, but I remained calm because I knew I had Catholicism on my side, er, sort of. "Nonna, even if Bradley and I do decide to get married one day, we can't have a church wedding because he's divorced. If you have any questions about that, I'm sure Father Will and Father Roman would be more than happy to explain the Church's policy regarding divorcees."

She chuckled softly. "It's a like-a we say in Italy, Franki, 'rules are just-a suggestions.'" Then the line went dead.

* * *

"As God is my witness, I'll never be hungry again," I vowed à la Scarlett O'Hara before I popped the last bite of po' boy into my mouth and pulled into the parking lot of Oleander Place. I cut the engine and climbed out of my car, slamming the door as I mentally cursed my nonna. Thanks to her Machiavellian machinations, I'd eaten not one but two po' boys and a whole bag of Spicy Cajun Crawtators—the family size, not the individual serving. But what did it matter? It wasn't like I was watching my figure because that was a full-time job, and I was far too busy for that. And besides, with Nonna in my life, I was destined to grow old alone, anyway.

Speaking of being a zitella, I thought as I walked up the path to the back porch, *I could really go for some baked ziti*. I climbed the steps to the porch and pulled my second-hand Burberry scarf tightly around my neck. The sky was still overcast, and the temperature had dropped by at least twenty degrees. I approached the back door, and the magnolia tree quaked violently in the wind as though warning me not to enter. Shaken from my nonna ruminations, I suddenly realized that the plantation appeared to be deserted. I glanced at the time on my phone. It was only two thirty. But since there was no "closed" sign on the door, I turned the handle and went inside.

"Delta?" I called. I peered into her office, but it was empty.

A pall of silence hung in the air. And for the first time, it occurred to me that the plantation home was actually kind of spooky. Because of the cloudy day, it was particularly gloomy inside. The house smelled of must and decay, and the antique furniture and old family portraits seemed to cast dark, deathly shadows on those who entered, i.e., me.

As I crept down the hallway toward the parlor, I considered going back to the car to retrieve my gun. After all, someone had warned me to stay away from Oleander Place, and that someone might be a plantation employee. But then I told myself to get a grip. I was fairly certain that the noises I was hearing had something to do with Delta or Scarlett, and I definitely didn't believe that the infamous plantation ghosts were responsible. And even if I did, my gun certainly wouldn't stop them.

When I entered the parlor, I gave a start. Beneath the painting of Evangeline, the courter's candle was flickering. *Was this a sign that Evangeline was alive and waiting for her flame?* I shook the thought from my head. No, a spirit hadn't lit that candle, a real live person had. And it looked like they'd done so recently because it was barely burned.

Now that I thought about it, Delta had complained that Scarlett was always lighting the candle. So I assumed that she was in the house somewhere, avoiding me. "Scarlett? It's me, Franki. I have a quick question for you."

I waited for her to reply and heard a loud thump from above. Something had fallen, like a piece of furniture—or a body. Thinking that Scarlett might be hurt, I rushed up the stairs to the second floor. "Scarlett? Are you okay?"

When I reached the landing, there was another thump followed by a scraping noise. It sounded like something was being dragged across the floor above. *Or was it "someone?"* I swallowed nervously as I tried to decide whether to proceed without my weapon. But then I remembered that the third floor was a storage area. Relief flooded through my body when I realized that Delta was probably up there moving things around.

"Delta. I'm here to question Scarlett," I called as I climbed the stairs.

It was noticeably darker on the top floor, but there was a light shining from the doorway on my right. As I approached, I caught a glimpse of a shadow on the wall to my left. It took a moment for my eyes to make out the shape, but when they did, my heart skipped a beat—or several. The shape was that of a man wearing a long coat and a tricorne, the triangular-shaped hat worn by eighteenth-century soldiers and pirates. My mind flashed, terrified, to Beau the Black.

This time, instead of thumping or dragging, I heard the unmistakable metallic sound of a sword being drawn from its sheath.

I took a step backward. *Was it? Could it be?*

"Avast!" a craggy male voice cried. "Or I'll cleave ye to the brisket, I will!"

As a Texas girl, I knew darn good and well what a brisket was. I shielded my chest with my arms and screamed bloody murder.

CHAPTER TWELVE

The sword clattered to the floor as the pirate ghost let out a distinctly unpirate-like—and unghost-like—shriek. I cut my screaming short and peered through the crack between the door and the doorjamb. I saw a nice-looking guy, around twenty-six or so, with sandy blond hair and twinkling blue eyes. Beau the Black he was not.

He stepped into the hallway with his hat in his hands. "Sorry about all of that. I was goofing around with the clothes, and I didn't realize anyone else was in the house." He grinned sheepishly. "We're all kind of jumpy around here these days."

I laughed. "I can understand why. I'm Franki Amato, the PI Delta hired to investigate the murder of Ivanna Jones."

"Troy Wilson," he said as we shook hands. "I'm the Oleander Place historian."

"Great! You're the last staff member I need to interview."

He looked thoughtfully at me. "You know, Delta said she'd hired a private investigator, but..."

"Is something wrong?" I asked.

His face flushed with embarrassment. "It's just that she described you a little differently."

Now my face flushed—with anger. I was sure that Delta's description of me had been less than flattering. "Oh she did, did she? Care to elaborate?"

He shoved his hands into the pockets of his khaki-colored Dockers. "Uh, she made it sound like you were a lot taller." He paused. "And dark."

My lips curled. I was fair-skinned, but because I was Italian, Delta was stereotyping me. "You mean swarthy?"

He smiled. "Delta isn't all bad. She's just a little high strung, as we say down here in the South."

"That's one way to describe her," I said through gritted teeth.

"Do you mind if I put these clothes away?" he asked, gesturing toward the storage room.

"Not at all," I replied. I followed him to the doorway and shivered when I looked inside. It was straight out of a haunted house, with dusty antiques, boxes, clothing dress forms, and porcelain dolls strewn about.

Troy knelt and placed the tricorne into a hatbox inside an old trunk. "So, are you Italian on both sides of your family?"

"Yeah, my mom's maiden name was Pavan."

He rose to his feet and dusted off his pants. "That's from the Veneto region, right?"

I nodded, impressed. Unlike other Italian surnames, those from the Veneto were often missing a final vowel. "How'd you know?"

"I specialized in the Italian Renaissance for my Masters, so I had to study the Venetian Republic. But then I switched to American history."

"What made you change from the Venetian Republic to the Early American Republic?"

He smirked. "The language requirement. To study European History, you have to know two foreign languages, and I only know Greek."

"Greek?" I repeated, surprised. "I thought you'd say Italian."

"My mother is from Greece. Can't you tell?" he asked, shaking his blond hair.

"Honestly, I would have said you were a California beach boy, except for your pirate clothes. Do you always wear a waistcoat?"

"This old thing?" Troy joked as he removed the coat. "It's just a little something I threw on."

I laughed. It was nice to finally meet someone at Oleander Place I could relate to—except for the part about the graduate degree in history, of course.

He wrapped the waistcoat in tissue paper and placed it into the trunk with the hat. "Seriously, though," he continued, "I was doing research for my dissertation."

"Delta said I should ask you about that." I leaned against the doorjamb and crossed my arms. "What are you studying?"

He smiled. "Plantation chic."

I blinked. "You mean, plantation fashion?"

"That's right. What we wear influences the way we perceive ourselves, so it says a lot about who we are and what we value. You know the old saying "Clothes make the man"? And Oleander Place is a veritable treasure trove of information. Or should I say 'treasure chest'?"

I smiled. "Definitely the latter."

Troy locked the trunk and dragged it to the back wall. Then he hoisted it onto another trunk.

That explains the thump and the dragging sounds, I thought.

"Shall we go downstairs?" he asked as he brushed off his shirt.

"Please," I replied. "It's creepy up here."

"This whole place is creepy," he began with an exaggerated shudder, "especially now that there's been a murder in the pink room."

I followed Troy downstairs to the first floor.

"Let's go into the dining room," he said, ushering me into an elegant, marble-floored space. "Would you like something to drink?"

What I wanted was a shot of Pepto-Bismol to counteract the effects of those po' boys. But instead I said, "A glass of water would be nice."

I took a seat at the mahogany table. While I waited, I counted fourteen place settings with polished silverware, cornflower blue and white china, and fluted crystal goblets. On one side of the table, a rope was hanging. I looked up and saw that it was connected to a contraption that was shaped like an upside down lyre and had a panel of rich red velvet trimmed in gold fringe attached.

"That's a fan," Troy said, handing me my water. "While the family and guests dined, a slave would pull the cord to make the fan sway back and forth for the duration of the dinner. Wretched life, eh?"

I nodded. "Speaking of wretched lives, what can you tell me about the murder victim, Ivanna Jones?"

"Not much," he replied, taking a seat beside me. "I was at a graduate student conference in Nashville that day."

I took a sip of water. "When did you get back?"

"I drove home on Saturday night, and I got in around ten thirty. So I missed all the drama. But Delta showed me her photos of the crime scene when I came to work on Monday."

"Had you ever seen Ivanna before?"

"Based on the photos, it's hard to say." He straightened the silverware at his place setting. "She might have taken one of my tours of the grounds, but I can't be sure. Up until the time of the murder, we had as many as three hundred visitors per day."

I thought about Troy's expertise as a historian and wondered whether he had any special insight about the crime scene. "Did anything about the pictures strike you?"

"There were so many similarities to the death of Evangeline Lacour, the room, the dress, the bed, the position of the body. Even Ivanna's hair was the arranged the same way. The only thing we don't know is whether she was poisoned by oleander."

I couldn't disclose the presence of the oleander in the lip gloss because the police hadn't released that information. But I needed to know whether the poison had come from the plantation. "During your ground tours, did you happen to notice whether any of the oleander bushes had been tampered with?"

He shook his head. "I only focus on the lives of the slaves, so I don't really pay attention to the plants. Our groundskeeper, Miles McCarthy, would be the one to ask about that, but he's already left for the day."

"That reminds me, do you know where Scarlett is? Delta said that her last tour would end at three o'clock."

Troy furrowed his brow. "That's weird. Scarlett told me her last tour ended at noon."

"*Cavolo*," I muttered.

"Pardon?"

"Oh, it means 'cabbage.'" I gave a wry smile. "Italians use it like we use 'crap' or 'dang.'"

"If it's any consolation," he began, leaning back in his chair, "I don't think you would have gotten much out of Scarlett today. She was really upset about something."

I leaned forward. "Do you know why?"

"I asked, but she wouldn't say." He shrugged. "She was on edge the whole morning, though. It was like she couldn't wait to get out of here. But who can blame her after everything that's happened?"

I nodded, but I wondered whether her behavior had anything to do with Miles or her warning to me.

Troy glanced at his watch. "Listen, if you don't have any other questions, I need to get back to my research." He sighed. "Unfortunately, that dissertation isn't going to write itself."

I smiled. "Thanks for your help. I'll let you know if I need anything else."

After Troy left, I debated whether to phone Scarlett. But I decided she would be more likely to cooperate if I respected her request not to call her. I would just have to try to talk to her the following morning when I returned with Chandra.

As I stood up to leave, I remembered the courter's candle. I went into the parlor and saw that it had been extinguished. I assumed that Troy had put it out moments before, but something prompted me to touch the wick. It was cold, as was the wax. Someone had put out the flame while we were upstairs. But who?

* * *

I reclined on the chaise lounge in my living room and counted the shiny gold *fleurs-de-lis* on my fuzzy, blood-red wallpaper while I waited for Adam to answer the phone. It was the second time I'd tried to call since leaving Oleander Place an hour and a half before, but not even his voice mail was responding. I pressed *end* and tossed my phone to my side, narrowly missing Napoleon.

He leapt to the floor as though I'd thrown it straight at him.

"Napoleon, I did *not* try to hit you with my phone," I chided. "I'm the one who just came home early to let you out, remember?"

He shot me a "whatever" look before settling on the bearskin rug and resting his chin on his front paws. That was his pensive pose.

"So that's the thanks I get? For the record, I should be on my way to Lickalicious Lips right now trying to locate a possible lip gloss poisoner."

Napoleon sighed through his nose.

"And you're not the only one who feels like they're under attack, you know. A psycho-killer sent me a death threat yesterday—okay, so they didn't threaten to *kill* me, but that's beside the point. Meanwhile, Nonna is threatening to send invitations to my non-engagement to Bradley, and Pauline is threatening to tell him about it so she can steal him from me."

Wait. Bradley! I bolted upright. *Was tonight the night we were having dinner?*

I sent a quick text to his cell and then stared at my jagged fingernails and hairy legs. With Pauline lurking in the periphery, I had to go big—not broken and bushy—or go home.

My text tone sounded. *Late meeting. See you at Antoine's in the Quarter at 7? xoxo, B*

I looked at the time—five o'clock. I fired off a confirmation reply and fled to my bathroom in a panic.

Two hours and a flurry of plucking, polishing, painting, preening, and perfuming later, I exited my apartment in a fitted (read *unintentionally tight*) red dress and turned to lock the front door.

"Va-va-voom!" Glenda shouted from behind me. "That's some get-up you've got on there, Miss Franki."

I turned and saw Glenda and Veronica walking up the sidewalk. "Speaking of get-ups," I began, noticing that they were both wearing yellow, "you two look like twins." *Albeit in a Danny DeVito-Arnold Schwarzenegger way.*

Veronica was beaming with a post-shopping-spree glow. "To celebrate spring, we bought matching sundresses."

"Um, yeah," I said as I tried but failed to see the similarities between the two dresses beyond their color.

Veronica's was a sleeveless Diane von Fürstenberg, while Glenda's was more like a crotchless Dita Von Teese. And there was no way to compare the plunging neckline of Glenda's dress to Veronica's V-neck, unless the *v* stood for "vagina."

"How did it go today?" Veronica asked.

"Well, I'm pretty sure Scarlett and Adam are avoiding me, but I finally managed to question Troy, the historian tour guide."

Upon hearing the word *historian,* Glenda yawned in mock boredom and began admiring the live yellow roses inside the clear plastic soles of her stripper shoes.

"What was he like?" Veronica asked, brushing a lock of hair from her eyes.

I raised my hands like a director framing a scene. "Think smart California surfer."

Veronica nodded, but Glenda's foot popped like Mia's did when she kissed Michael in *The Princess Diaries*. It was like a divining rod, only instead of water, it sensed men.

"If I'm right in thinking that this case involves Obsessive Love Disorder, then Troy might be able to help us understand Ivanna's appearance."

Veronica twisted her mouth to one side. "But he's a historian, not a psychologist."

"Yes, but he studies the social meaning of clothing from the plantation era. In fact, he was wearing a pirate outfit when I met him."

"There's a surfer pirate at that plantation?" Glenda whispered to no one in particular.

"Oh, wow," Veronica said. "So he might be able to shed some light on Evangeline's pink dress."

I gave a satisfied smile. "And why Ivanna was found wearing it."

Glenda took a drag from her yellow cigarette holder and exhaled slowly. "I just might have to take a tour of Oleander Place. I've got a yearning for some California-flavored pirate booty."

"Speaking of booty," I said with a wink, "I need to get going, or I'll be late for my date."

* * *

At six forty, I was driving down Canal Street on my way to the French Quarter when I noticed that the lights were on in Ponchartrain Bank. Because the bank closes at six, I assumed that Bradley was still inside. Thinking that we could go to the restaurant in one car, I pulled into a parking space and headed for the main door.

"Bradley?" I called as I entered the lobby.

There was no answer. I walked to his office to see whether he was still in his meeting. I was surprised to find that the lights were out and it was locked. Bewildered, I looked around at the other offices, but they were dark too. The only explanation I could think of was that the last employee to leave had forgotten to lock up.

I was about to call Bradley to inform him of the situation when an Italian expression popped into my head. *Prima il dovere, poi il piacere*, which means "Duty before pleasure." I needed to get my hands on the bank security tapes for Corinne's case, and what better opportunity than this?

I turned and looked at the unmarked metal door next to Bradley's office. As I debated what to do, the strains of Elvis Presley's "It's Now or Never" infiltrated my brain. It was as though the King was guiding me. With a trembling hand, I reached for the handle and turned. The door was unlocked.

I felt a rush of excitement as I entered the room and closed the door behind me. Not only was the computer screen lit up, but a folder with the video files for April was open. Someone had recently been working with the files.

With my heart in my throat, I quickly scanned the files for April 12th and 16th, the days that Corinne was missing money from her drawer. They were right where they should be, by order of date.

I rummaged around in a desk drawer and found a flash drive. I plugged it into the USB port and copied the two files. Then I glanced at the clock. It was ten to seven, which meant I had just enough time to get to Antoine's.

"It's like it was meant to be," I whispered as I ejected the flash drive and put it in my silver clutch.

I stood up to leave and heard a key being inserted into the lock. I froze as the realization of what had just occurred struck me like a club. Someone had locked me into the security room.

I tried the doorknob—it didn't budge. My first instinct was to beat on the door, but I held back. If Bradley had been the one to lock the door, I certainly didn't want him to unlock it and find me on the other side. But when I thought about missing our dinner and spending the night in the bank, I began pounding on the door. "Bradley! It's me, Franki! Let me out!"

He didn't come. *Surely he heard me*, I thought. *Why isn't he letting me out? To teach me a lesson?*

As I was contemplating my next move, the scent of Pure Poison wafted into the room—like a noxious gas. *Pauline!* She was in charge of the security room, and she'd probably been working with the files when I came into the bank. I smacked myself in the forehead with the butt of my hand. The Italian word *scema*, or *fool*, came to mind, and then I smacked myself again because Italian is what had gotten me into this mess in the first pace. "Duty before pleasure!" I scoffed. "Why would anyone in their right mind live by that credo?"

I mentally ran through the techniques I'd learned at the police academy for escaping from a locked room, but none of them applied. I didn't have the strength to break down a metal security door, and I couldn't pick the lock thanks to the protection plate covering the latch. And there was no point in calling Veronica because I was convinced that Pauline had left and locked the main door good and tight behind her. "Oh, God," I whined. "What am I going to do?"

But deep down I knew there was only one thing I could do—call Bradley.

While I pondered what to tell him, I tried to calm my nerves with a breathing method I'd learned the time I took yoga. I inhaled for three counts and exhaled for six, but my heart was still racing like I'd just run a marathon. *Okay, forget yoga breathing*, I thought. *This is going to take Lamaze.*

I pulled my phone from my clutch. But before I could dial the number, I heard a sound I knew all too well, a police siren.

"Oh no, she didn't," I breathed.

The siren stopped in front of the bank.

"Oh yes she did." I started the Lamaze breathing.

Within a matter of seconds, there were excited voices in the lobby. They were coming toward the security room.

"New Orleans Police!" a gruff male voice cried.

Following police procedure, I shouted, "I'm unarmed, and I'm an ex-cop." Then I held my hands in the air.

"Franki?" Bradley asked in an incredulous tone.

I stopped breathing.

The door opened.

I gave a wan smile and a little wave—and tried to look incredibly hot in my red dress. "Yeah, it's me."

Bradley's jaw contracted as his mouth drew into a thin line, and his eyes narrowed into slits.

The ruddy-faced officer scrutinized me through gold, wire-rimmed glasses and then turned to Bradley. "Do you know this woman?"

"I'm afraid I do, John," he ground out through clenched teeth. "Can I talk to you in my office for a minute?"

"Sure," the officer replied.

Bradley turned to me. "Don't move a muscle," he said, pointing his finger at my chest. "Not even to blink. Do you understand?"

I nodded and watched as Bradley and the officer went into his office and shut the door.

I'd never seen Bradley this angry before, not even after I'd punched him in the face and kicked him in the *coglioni* (that's Italian for...well, you know), which I still say was perfectly justified given that he'd kissed me while he was married to his ex. I simply had to think of some way to justify my presence at the bank both to Bradley and the police without betraying Corinne's confidence.

Bradley marched out of his office and right up to my face. "As a personal favor to me," he said in a dangerously low tone, "Officer Quincy is going to forget he saw you here."

"Oh, thank God," I gushed. "Why don't we just go to Antoine's, and I'll explain..."

"We're not going to Antoine's, and you're not going to

explain because I don't want to hear it. Now, I don't know where you're going when you leave here tonight, but I can tell you this—you'll stay far from this bank."

"But—"

"No buts," he said, raising his hand.

I took a step backward, just in case.

"Officer Quincy may be willing to forget you were here," he continued, "but I still have to deal with the anonymous tip to the police. Management will expect a detailed explanation as to why someone saw an intruder in the bank after hours. So if I were you, I would get going before I change my mind about asking Officer Quincy not to arrest you."

I looked searchingly in his eyes and then stalked out of the bank. I was angry with him for not letting me explain, but I was also mad at myself for being so careless. Oh, and at Pauline for being so evil. I didn't know what was going to happen between Bradley and me, but I knew one thing for sure. The fact that Pauline had made an anonymous call to the police told me that she had something serious to hide. And I was going to make it my duty to expose her. Make that my pleasure.

CHAPTER THIRTEEN

———

I placed my "Italians Drink It Better" cappuccino mug on the kitchen counter and glanced at the microwave clock. It was nine a.m., which meant Veronica would be expecting me at the office any minute. But the last way I wanted to start my day was by telling my employer that I'd almost gotten arrested for burglary of a bank. So instead, I flopped down at the kitchen table and opened the bakery box in front of me.

Bradley might not have known where I would go when I left the bank last night, but I sure did—to Bittersweet Confections on Magazine Street. It was closed by the time I got there, but luckily the night baker let me in when she saw my frantic face and fancy attire. Naturally, I bought the peanut butter–banana Elvis cupcake to wolf down in the car and the decadently chocolate Bittersweet Cake to scarf up at home. The King was indirectly responsible for me entering that security room, after all, and a cake eaten following a fight with one's boyfriend can only be bittersweet.

I picked up a knife and scraped the sludgy remains of the cake bottom from the box. As I slid the yummy goo into my mouth, I remembered how angry Bradley had been. I definitely had some 'splainin' to do, but I couldn't figure out what I was going to say. As far as he was concerned, Pauline was a dedicated professional, and I was just a jealous girlfriend. (Okay, the last part was true, but only partially.) To add insult to injury, I'd promised to get along with her—the mere thought of which almost made the cake come back up—so I could hardly tell him my suspicions. No, I needed hard, cold evidence before I talked to Bradley, and I planned to get it.

I polished off the last of the cake sludge and dialed the office. While the line was ringing, something bumped against the back door. Napoleon was out like a light on the chaise lounge, so I knew it wasn't him trying to get in. Worried that it might be my aggressor coming to peel me like a pineapple, I opened the gold velour curtains of the window beside my kitchen table and peered into the backyard. Fortunately, I didn't see anyone.

"Private Chicks, Incorporated," David answered in a clipped, professional voice. "If you give us the time, we'll solve your crime."

"I'm so glad you're there," I breathed. "Have you been able to do that background check on Pauline?"

"I just finished it. She's clean."

I don't know how when she's so dirty, I thought. "Listen, if I bring in some video files from a security camera, will you be able to tell whether they've been tampered with?"

"Uh, it kinda depends on what they did to the file. My vassal could for sure do it, though. He's a total video pro."

I vaguely remembered the vassal saying something about wanting to study film. "That's fine with me, but I thought he only had to serve you for one day."

"For that one entire day," David clarified. "But he *gets* to do whatever my fraternity brothers and I tell him all year long. It's one of the privileges of rushing a frat."

"Uh-huh," I agreed skeptically. "So, if I bring the files to the office this morning, could you take them to him?"

"Sure. I'll see him in algorithms class this afternoon."

I shuddered. I couldn't think of a more boring way to spend my time. "How fast do you think he could analyze the video?"

"I dunno, but he's throwing a party for his comp sci buddies at his dorm tomorrow. He could do it then, I bet. Wanna come?"

Now I could think of a more boring way to spend my time. For me, computer science parties conjured up mental images of Lord of the Rings posters, Star Wars action figures, comic books, and unwashed males unfamiliar with the female gender. But I was willing to do whatever it took to out Pauline to Bradley, even if that meant spending my Saturday night with a bunch of leering freshman nerds playing video games. "Count me in."

"Solid," he said in college-ese. "I'll pick you up tomorrow at two."

"In the morning?" I asked, shocked.

"No, the afternoon. The vassal likes to be in bed by nine," he explained in a matter-of-fact tone.

That vassal is a real party animal. "Okay. Is Veronica there?"

"Yeah. One sec."

As I waited for Veronica to pick up, I saw something move in the backyard. I jumped up and stood to one side of the window. When I peeked out, I spotted Glenda watering her plants in nothing but six-inch heels and a smile (her robe was so sheer it couldn't be considered clothing). I pulled down the blind *and* closed the curtains.

"Hey!" Veronica answered. "How'd your date go last night? I'll bet you really wowed Bradley with that racy red dress."

"I wowed him, all right," I said, collapsing back into my chair. "But it had nothing to do with my dress."

She paused. "Uh-oh."

"Look, I'll spare you the undignified details, but last night I snuck into the security room at the bank, and Pauline tipped off the police anonymously."

An awkward silence followed, and I knew that the attorney in Veronica was running down a mental list of Private Chicks' potential liabilities.

"Everything is fine," I added to ease her concern. "And I think I've figured out why Pauline didn't seize the opportunity to rat me out personally to Bradley."

"Why's that?"

"I can't prove it yet," I began, as I picked up the cake knife and scrutinized it for more sludge, "but I think she's stealing from Ponchartrain Bank."

"You're talking about the money from Corinne's teller drawer, right?"

I snorted. "Trust me, Pauline's not the type to content herself with a lousy thousand dollars. I have a hunch she's planning to steal a lot more than that, if she hasn't already. And by taking money from Corinne's drawer, she's setting her up to look like the thief."

"So, what are you going to do?" she asked, her liability anxiety no doubt approaching a critical level.

"I'm going to research everything I can about the New York branch of Brehman Bank until I find the name of a manager who knew her." I scratched a speck of sludge from the knife and popped it into my mouth. "I'm telling you, there's a reason she left that bank off her resume."

Veronica let out a long slow exhale. "Just be careful, Franki. If she *is* stealing from the bank, it sounds like she could be dangerous if you back her into a corner."

"Don't worry. I won't fall into one of her traps again," I said, and I meant it. Now that I had an idea of how far Pauline would go to get me out of the picture, I would be sure to keep my guard up. "Speaking of being trapped, I'm taking Chandra to the plantation today, and I could use a buffer during the car ride. In addition to her psychic ability, that woman's also got the gift of gab."

"Sorry. I have a packed schedule."

"Oh." I swallowed my disappointment. As much as I loved being the lead on a case, I missed having my best friend fighting crime by my side.

"I have an idea," she exclaimed. "Since tomorrow's Saturday, why don't we have brunch at Atchafalaya and stuff our faces? My treat."

I put the knife back into the empty cake box. Between last night and this morning, I'd consumed enough calories to keep a platoon of soldiers alive during a weeklong survival-training course. "I don't know…"

"They have a make-your-own-bloody-mary bar," she intoned.

"I'm in," I gushed. After all, empty calories weren't as bad as full ones, right?

"Good. Then it's a date."

"Yeah, and let's drop by Lickalicious Lips afterward. Adam won't be expecting us on a weekend."

She cleared her throat. "I can't. I need to be somewhere at noon."

"I guess I'll see you tomorrow then," I said and closed the call. I wondered whether Veronica was avoiding me, but I dismissed the idea since she'd just invited me out to eat. Whatever was going on, I intended to get to the bottom of it at brunch.

* * *

I switched the windshield wipers to high and strained to see the turnoff to River Road. Even though it was only eleven a.m., the sky was as black as night, and the torrential downpour wasn't helping visibility. I glanced at Chandra snoozing in the passenger seat. Her head was pressed against the window, and drool was dripping from her open mouth.

As it turns out, I hadn't needed a buffer from her babbling but rather from her snoring. She'd nodded off before we even got to Private Chicks to drop off the flash drive. And she'd snored the entire way to the plantation. In fact, sometimes it was hard to tell whether thunder was rumbling or Chandra was sawing logs.

Now that I thought about it, I realized that the weather turned every time I was around her. I debated whether this was proof that she really was cosmically connected to the universe. If it was, I decided that it might not be such a swell sign that storms followed her wherever she went. But then it occurred to me that the bad weather might not be a reflection on Chandra but on me. *Was I living under a dark cloud—literally and figuratively?*

I was mulling over this possibility as I pulled into the Oleander Place parking lot. The second I shut off the engine, Chandra shot up in her seat.

"Oh God, are we at the plantation?" she shouted, already in the clutches of her phasmophobia. Then she grabbed her head. "Owww. I shouldn't have let Lou talk me into that third beer sampler last night at the Crescent City Brewhouse."

My first thought was, *Does Chandra ever go anywhere or do anything that doesn't have a moon-related theme?* Next I wondered whether bringing a hungover psychic with a fear of ghosts to a haunted plantation was a good idea. I was about to suggest that she stay in the car when I saw Miles heading toward the parking lot from the direction of the little mill. "I need to talk to this guy real quick," I said, motioning toward him. "I'll be right back."

Chandra followed my gesture and perked right up when she saw Miles. "I'll come with you," she offered as she smoothed her hair, which was shaped like a cone after being pressed against the window. "I need to stretch my legs."

I gave her a sidelong glance. It figured that a Boston native would be attracted to a big Irishman. When I turned to exit the car, I found Miles looking into my window. I rolled it down a crack. "Hi, Miles."

"Mornin', Miss Franki," he said.

Chandra practically threw herself across my lap. "I'm Chandra Toccato, the Crescent City Medium."

I gripped the steering wheel and moved forward in my seat in an effort to block her from his view. "Do you have a minute?"

"I was fixin' to run to de hardware store, but I always have time to talk to two beautiful ladies," he said staring at Chandra, who was batting her eyelashes so fast she looked like a crazed cupie doll.

"Great," I said in a flat tone, trying to discourage any further flattery. "Listen, have you noticed anything unusual on the grounds in recent weeks? Like, any changes in the plants?"

"De plants?" he repeated, scratching his head.

"Well, the oleander bushes," I clarified.

Chandra sighed. "I just *adore* oleanders."

I spun around and shot her a cool-it look.

"All de oleanders are doin' jus' fine, Miss Franki." He looked at the sky. "Dey're sure lovin' dis rain."

"I wasn't talking about their health. What I need to know is whether any of the bushes have been altered. You know, like maybe someone picked a bunch of flowers or cut off some branches?"

His nostrils flared, and I knew that something about my question had angered him.

He forced a smile. "I can't say as dey have."

I looked into his eyes to see whether he would avoid my gaze, but he met it straight on. I knew there was no point in pressing him further. "Interesting," I said in an intentionally suspicious tone. "Have you seen Scarlett today?"

His face relaxed. "I saw her goin' into de main house dis mornin', but I haven't seen her since."

"Thanks," I said, still scrutinizing his face.

"Anytime, Miss Franki." He nodded at Chandra. "You ladies have a lovely day at Oleander Place."

"Oh, we will," Chandra replied before kicking off another round of eyelash batting. "I've just been *dying* to see the house."

I rolled my eyes and rolled up the window before their coquetry could continue. Then I watched in my rearview mirror as Miles got into his car. He was looking in our direction, which meant that either Chandra had made an impression on him or my question had. Something told me it was the latter. I was positive he was hiding something. What I didn't know was whether it concerned only the oleanders or Ivanna's murder too.

Chandra sighed. "It looks like the rain is letting up. I guess it's time to get this reading over with."

"Yeah, let's make a run for it," I said, grabbing my keys.

As we ran to the back entrance, I outpaced her three-to-one—not so much because of the difference in our strides but because of the difference in our shoes. Ever since Delta's dog-sharks had feasted on my feet, I'd worn riding boots to the plantation. But Chandra was in four-inch platform stilettos with lace ankle socks. *Definitely not standard Ghostbusters issue*, I thought as I watched her hop like a bumbling bunny across the soaked lawn.

When she reached the porch, she followed me inside with eyes as big as, well, two moons.

"First, I'll introduce you to Delta," I said in an effort to steady her nerves. "Then while I'm questioning the tour guide, Scarlett, I'd like for you to do readings in the pink room and on the balcony."

She didn't respond.

I turned and saw that she looked kind of green, or maybe lunar blue. Either way, I wasn't sure if it was because of the

Oleander Place spirits or those three samplers. "Are you okay?"

She bobbed her head up and down and began what sounded like a series of sighs.

"Um, is that a psychic technique?" I asked, more than a little concerned about her mental state.

"It's a stress-reliever," she replied, staring at me like *I* was the crazy one.

I shrugged and tried the handle of the office door. It was locked. "Delta must have stepped out. I'll take you to see the painting of Evangeline before we go upstairs."

We'd just started down the hallway when Chandra began making suction noises.

I stopped and stared at her. "*What* are you doing *now*?"

"Nothing," she said defensively. "My socks got wet."

I took a deep breath and headed for the parlor as she sighed and squished along behind me. Apart from the racket she was making and the intermittent rumbling of thunder, the house was ominously silent. And dark.

"Sweet Jesus!" Chandra shrieked as her hands clamped onto my triceps like lobster pinschers. "Is that a ghost?"

I clenched my teeth and wrenched free of her grip. Then I looked down the hallway and saw a flickering light coming from the parlor. *The courter's candle!*

I rushed into the room with Chandra practically attached to my back. The entire parlor had been turned into a shrine to Evangeline. Coral-pink tulle was draped over her painting, and dozens of oleander bouquets filled the room. The courter's candle, which was once again alight on the mantle, cast an eerie glow over the scene. Even more haunting, all the windows were open, causing the white sheers to flail like frenzied spirits in the storm winds.

I stood there open-mouthed until a crash of thunder shook me from my stupor. I went to close the windows, and as I latched the last one, the door shut behind me.

"Someone locked us in!" Chandra shrieked. Then she leapt on me, piggyback-style.

"Get off me," I ground out as I pried her legs one-by-one from my waist.

"We've got to get out of this place," she wailed.

"You've got to stay calm," I snapped as I walked to the door. I grasped the doorknob, and it fell into my hand. The part of the knob that attached to the door had a round opening, and the knob itself was hollow inside. I got down on my knees and inspected the doorplate. There was a rod protruding that was connected to the doorknob on the opposite side. After I'd reinserted the rod into the knob, the door opened on its own. "See?" I turned to Chandra, who was standing all of two inches from me. "No one locked us in."

"Do you think the wind closed it?" she whispered.

"Maybe," I replied. Although I wasn't convinced since the door opened into the hallway. The more likely scenario was that Scarlett had closed the door so that she could slip past me.

I walked to the window. Her truck was in the parking lot, so I knew she was around somewhere.

"What's the matter?" Chandra asked, raising her hands to her mouth.

"Scarlett's avoiding me, but I have to question her before she leaves today," I explained. "Do you want to go wait in the car while I look for her?"

She scowled and put her hands on her hips. "Oh, no. You're not leaving me alone on this ghost trap of a plantation!"

Things psychics should never say, I thought.

We searched the first floor, but Scarlett was nowhere to be seen. Chandra stuck to me like glue until I headed up the stairs, and then she started to drop back. She was no longer sighing and squishing, just huffing and puffing. As I approached the second-floor landing, she'd only made it halfway up the staircase. I looked back at her. "Are you sensing any spirit activity yet?"

She shook her head. "They're (huff) laying (puff) like (huff) broccoli (puff)."

"You mean, being still like vegetables?" I joked, paraphrasing from *Pretty Woman*.

She didn't laugh.

She's probably saving her breath, I thought. *Because that was funny.*

When I reached the second floor and looked in the direction of the pink room, I jumped from fright. There was a tall figure looming in front of the French doors. I couldn't make out who it was in the semi-darkness, but I could see the outline of a crinoline dress. It was a woman, and she was moving slightly—actually, floating. *Like a ghost.*

"H-hello?" I stammered. I felt my knees start to buckle and grabbed the stair rail for support. *Was I seeing the spirit of Evangeline Lacour?*

Chandra arrived at the top of the stairs. "Did (huff) you (puff) find (huff) Scarlett (puff)?"

A flash of lightening illuminated the figure, and I immediately recognized the red fabric of the dress.

"Yes, I did," I whispered as Chandra let out a hair-raising scream and fell to the floor.

I knelt down and checked her pulse. Then I looked up at Scarlett.

And I wondered how long she'd been hanging.

CHAPTER FOURTEEN

———

I sat on one of the canopied beds in the children's room and put my head between my legs. Six hours had passed since I'd found Scarlett's lifeless body, but I still felt dizzy and nauseated. I was convinced that she hadn't committed suicide, because there was nothing on the floor below that she could have used to reach the noose. Someone had hanged her like she was a worthless rag doll, and I couldn't stop wondering whether there was something I could've done to save her. Maybe I should have insisted that she go to the authorities or at least tell me what she knew.

Overwhelmed by a wave of guilt, I sat up and looked enviously at Chandra dozing on the opposite bed. When she'd regained consciousness and learned that the looming figure in front of the French doors hadn't been a ghoulish ghost but rather a mundane murder victim, she'd returned to her serene, sleepy self. In fact, after the St. James Parish PD had asked us to wait in the children's bedroom while they completed their preliminary investigation, she'd flopped onto the two-hundred-something-year-old bed and started snoring.

Footsteps pounded up the stairs as the responding officers returned from the makeshift command post they'd set up outside.

The sound awoke Chandra, who sat up and stretched. "I'm sheets!"

"Where'd you find liquor?" I asked. Now I was really envious.

She fluffed her bed-head hair with her fingernails. "Who said anything about alcohol?"

"You said you were 'sheets.' You know, as in 'three sheets to the wind?'" I mimicked a drunk chugging a drink.

She gave an exasperated sigh. "'I'm sheets' is a Boston expression for 'I'm tired.'"

"Too bad." I walked over to the window. "I could use a drink."

"Right?" She stood up and tugged at her miniskirt. "We've already told the police everything we know. When are they going to let us go?"

I pulled the curtain to one side and saw the CSI unit van in the parking lot. "After they've secured the crime scene and questioned the staff."

The door opened and Delta entered. Her hair was spikier than usual, and with her black jeans, smudged white work shirt, and red neckerchief, she looked like a cowgirl Cruella. She furrowed her brow and gave Chandra the once over. "Are you one of those police psychics?"

Chandra put her hand to her chest. "I *am* a medium. How did you know?"

"Just a lucky guess," Delta drawled.

I repressed a laugh. It didn't take a psychic to figure out that Chandra was a psychic. She was covered in stars and moons, and her T-shirt said, "I talk to dead people." I cleared my throat. "Sorry, Delta. I didn't even think to introduce you after what happened. This is Chandra Toccato."

"Charmed, I'm sure," Delta replied dryly.

Chandra's face beamed like a full moon. "I believe you are."

"Well, apparently you're not, because you didn't look into your crystal ball and see this disaster coming," Delta snapped.

The glow on Chandra's face waned as Delta's dubious charm wore off.

"For that matter," Delta continued, "neither did you, Miss PI."

I sighed. "No one saw this coming, not even the police."

"Well, that's why I hired you, isn't it?" she asked, pointing her finger at my chest like a gun. "To figure out the things the police couldn't?"

I held up my hands in surrender. "Scarlett refused to cooperate with me, so there was nothing I could do. But speaking of doing my job, I have a few questions for you, starting with where you, Miles, and Troy were when Scarlett was killed."

Delta glared at me and began pacing, as though agitated by the mention of Scarlett's death. "We were in the little mill pulling artifacts for a photo shoot. *Southern Living* magazine contacted me last month about doing a feature on plantation life in the Old South. It's scheduled for tomorrow—that is, if it's still going to happen."

Out of the corner of my eye, I saw Chandra handling items in a curio cabinet. I moved to block her from Delta's view. "How long had you been there?"

"Since eight this morning," she said, massaging the back of her neck as she paced.

"Did any of you leave the mill?"

She stopped and put her hand on her cheek. "Just Miles, when I sent him to the hardware store for rust remover. That was around ten forty-five or eleven."

Fifteen minutes could have been enough time for Miles to go to the house and kill Scarlet before I saw him in the parking lot at eleven. But he'd been coming from the little mill, and I wasn't sure that he could have committed a murder and then returned to the mill in that time frame. Also, I couldn't understand why he wouldn't have gone straight from the house to the hardware store. "Did Miles come back to the mill for any reason before he left?"

Delta shrugged. "He may have, but Troy and I didn't see him. We were in the back of the mill."

I chewed my thumbnail. I couldn't rule Miles out as Scarlett's killer. But if he wasn't the culprit, then the only other suspect I knew of was Adam. The problem was that I had no way to connect him to her. "Do you know what Scarlett was doing in the house?"

"She had a tour booked for one o'clock, but she came early to do her cleaning," she replied, twisting the tips of her neckerchief. "Miles saw her arrive at around nine thirty."

"Wait." I scratched my head. "How did he see her if none of you left the mill?"

She wrinkled her mouth into a smirk. "One of the mill windows overlooks the parking lot. That Miles is always watching the goings-on at the plantation."

"Oh, right." I remembered her mentioning that before. I was also reminded of the day Scarlett had seen him looking in the window when she was cleaning in her corset and petticoat, and then a thought occurred to me. "Did Scarlett usually clean in her costume?"

"Of course not," she said with a wave of her hand. "Corsets and crinoline dresses are uncomfortable as hell, and they're expensive too. Even if she'd wanted to wear her costume to clean, I wouldn't have allowed it."

"And yet she was hanged in her red crinoline dress," I observed.

"Odd, isn't it?" she asked. "You might want to talk to Troy about those dresses. He's spent a lot of time studying them, from what I understand."

I nodded. Delta had a point. It was possible that the killer attached some sort of significance to Scarlett's red dress, as with Ivanna's pink one, and Troy's historical knowledge of plantation chic might offer some clues.

Chandra gave a sonorous yawn and plopped down on the bed.

Delta spun around to face her. "What do you think you're doing? That bed is almost three hundred years old."

"Someone has a brown aura," Chandra muttered. Then she shielded her lips from Delta's eyes and mouthed the word *greedy* to me.

Delta grabbed a giant rolling pin from the foot of the other bed. "Well, someone is going to have a black and blue aura if they don't get off my antique furniture."

"There's no need for violence," I said, extending my hand to stop her. "Why don't you give that to me, and I'll take it down to the kitchen?"

"It doesn't belong there," she snapped. "In the Old South, it was used for smoothing moss mattresses." She looked pointedly at Chandra. "But nowadays it's used for smacking mouthy mediums."

Chandra slid her "aura" off the bed and rushed to my side, just in case.

There was a knock at the door.

Delta threw the rolling pin onto the mattress. "Come in."

I stifled a gasp when the policeman entered. It was Officer Quincy from the bank.

"Oh, John. Thank God you're here!" Delta exclaimed. "It's so nice to have a friend from the New Orleans PD by my side at a time like this."

"I came as soon as I heard," he said, smoothing his gray-blond comb over.

At the sound of his voice, Delta forgot all about her furniture and collapsed onto a pink cushioned armchair near an antique crib. "I'm ruined, John!" She buried her face in her hands. "Over two centuries of my family's legacy down the drain."

"Now calm down, Delta." He placed a hand on her shoulder.

"How can I?" she wailed. "I was planning to turn the plantation into a bed and breakfast, but no one will stay here now."

"You're right about that," Chandra agreed, taking cover behind my back.

I turned and gave her a dirty look. "You never know," I said, feigning an optimism I didn't feel. "The guests may return in time."

Officer Quincy lowered his glasses on his hawk-like nose and narrowed his piercing blue eyes at me. Then he looked down at Delta. "Do you know this woman?"

She looked at me and frowned. "This is Franki Amato, the private investigator I hired to look into the Jones murder. A lot of damn good it did."

"Oh, I know Miss Amato." He sneered. "I had the pleasure of making her acquaintance the night before last."

"At my boyfriend's bank," I hurried to add. Then I shot him a pleading look. If Delta found out I'd burgled a bank, I could kiss this case *arrivederci*.

He opened his mouth to speak, but my phone began to ring.

I answered before he could say a word. "Hello?"

"Franki," Nonna began, "we need-a to talk."

Surrounded by the enemy, I thought. "Just a minute, Nonna."

I looked at Officer Quincy. "It's my grandmother—a family emergency," I said, which was never a lie where my nonna was concerned. "Can I take this in the hall?"

"Don't you contaminate that crime scene, you hear?" he growled. "You stay just outside that door."

I gave him a blank stare before escaping into the hallway, careful to shield my eyes from Scarlett's body. "Okay, Nonna." I sighed. "I'm at work, so please make this quick."

"Your mamma told-a me that-a your new-a case is at a *piantagione*."

"Plantation," I corrected. "And yes, I'm there now. Working."

"Is it a big-a place?"

I nodded in greeting at a crime scene investigator as he passed by with a camera. "It's three stories, maybe forty thousand square feet. Why?"

"The Internet-a say it's-a fifty-five-a thousand."

I leaned against the door in shock. The last time I was home, my nonna couldn't turn on a TV, much less surf the net. "You know how to use a computer?"

"I'm-a chock-a full of surprises," she replied, dead-pan.

Don't I know it. I heard the clicking of the crime scene investigator's camera behind me, and then something clicked in my head. "So, why are you looking up information on Oleander Place?"

"It's-a really interesting," she said with no enthusiasm whatsoever. "We don't have-a no plantations in *Sicilia*."

The only things my nonna had ever expressed an interest in were *ragù*, babies, and my marital prospects, so now I knew she was up to something. But I decided to play dumb. "Sicily might not have plantations, but it does have noble palaces that are older and far more luxurious, like the one you took me to in Palermo when I was little."

"You mean-a *Palazzo Ajutamicristo*?"

The palazzo was named after a sixteenth-century baron whose surname meant *Help me Christ*, which is exactly what I was thinking in that moment. "That's the one."

"It's-a too far away."

Here we go, I thought. "Too far away for what?"

"I'm-a thinking about-a having a *festa*."

I clenched my teeth and started to respond, but the door behind me opened without warning, and I had to grab the doorjamb to keep from falling flat on my rear end. Officer Quincy escorted Delta out, scowling over his shoulder at me as they descended the stairs. "What kind of party would that be?"

"Eh, for the *famiglia*."

Chandra popped her head into the hallway.

I turned my back to her. I wasn't equipped to deal with the medium and the meddler at the same time. "Nonna, you and I both know that this is for me and Bradley. But since we're not engaged, drop the party plan, and *pronto*."

"Maybe if-a he knows you can-a get a discount on the plantation, he'll ask-a you to marry him."

I laughed incredulously. "Why? Because I'm frugal?"

"*Sì*. It's a fine-a quality in a woman."

I closed my eyes and ground out, "I'm not going to book the plantation for my engagement party. Not now, not ever."

"Why-a not?" she asked in a perplexed tone. "Now that there's-a been a murder, you can get a real-a deal-a."

I felt my whole body tense. I didn't dare tell her that there'd been two murders, otherwise she'd want me to reserve the plantation for my wedding reception too.

"Your grandmother's right, you know," Chandra whispered from behind me. "After today, you could rent this place for a song."

I turned and pushed Chandra by the forehead back into the children's room and pulled the door closed. "Nonna, I'm only going to tell you this once. Stop trying to marry me off to Bradley because we're not getting married." I should've stopped there, but my anger got the best of me. "We're just going to live in sin."

She let out a combined gasp-gag—the kind of sound you'd expect from an elderly Sicilian woman who believes that her only granddaughter has just been possessed by the devil.

"*Ciao ciao*," I intoned and closed the call.

I leaned the back of my head against the door. A wedding-planning call from my nonna was the last thing I'd needed today. Not only were Bradley and I not getting married, we weren't going to live together either. And after he'd found me in the bank security room, I was pretty sure we weren't going to be doing anymore sinning. But I couldn't think about that now. I had another murder to solve, and this one was personal.

Chandra knocked on the other side of the door.

"Come out," I called.

She pulled open the door. "I think they forgot about us. And if I don't feed Lou dinner soon, he's likely to pass out."

And if I don't let Napoleon out soon, he's likely to p—.

"Um, I'll find the detective in charge and ask if we're free to go."

Her saucer-sized eyes grew to the size of plates. "And leave me alone in here?"

"This place is crawling with cops," I said, putting my hand on my hip. "The killer won't come after anyone now."

Chandra folded her hands in front of her mouth. "It's not the killer I'm afraid of."

"Ghosts are afraid of cops too," I said as I patted her on the shoulder and pushed her back into the room. "I know because they never show up at crime scenes."

"If you say so," she said uncertainly.

"I do." I closed the door and hurried downstairs. As I made my way outside, I put in a call to Adam to find out whether he had an alibi for that morning, but I got his voice mail. I hung up and headed for the command post, which had been set up in one of the cabins in the slave quarters. When I approached the doorway, Troy stepped out, looking pale and slightly dazed. "How are you holding up?"

"It's rough," he began, running his hand through his hair, "but I'll deal."

I nodded. "Listen, have you seen Detective Sims?"

Troy shoved his hands into his pockets. "You just missed him. The district attorney and the medical examiner pulled up a few minutes ago, so he went to meet them."

I would kill to be a fly on the wall during that conversation, I thought. "Do you have a minute?"

"Sure." He gestured toward the doorway. "Let's sit inside."

I entered the cabin and sat at the crude wooden table. "I wanted to ask you about crinoline."

He looked surprised. "You mean, the historical significance?"

I crossed my arms on the table. "That and whether you think it has a connection to the murders."

Troy furrowed his brow and stared at the table. "I guess it's possible. Crinoline has certainly been controversial among historians, so I suppose it could evoke some sort of emotion in the killer."

I leaned forward, intrigued. "How so?"

"Well, according to feminist historiography, the crinoline dress functioned as a female prison, which turned women of the Victorian era into quote 'exquisite slaves,'" he said, making quotation marks with his fingers.

"That's ironic considering the plantation context," I remarked.

"Right, but the opposing view maintains that women who wore crinoline weren't slaves at all. They were actually asserting their independence."

I blinked. "How does wearing a huge dress qualify as asserting your independence?"

He smiled. "That's the point. The dresses were so big that they emphasized women's presence in the patriarchal society. Women were no longer content to be wallflowers. Instead, they were literally filling rooms with their crinoline dresses, and in the process they were violating social norms by taking center stage."

I thought about how Scarlett O'Hara's dresses had been considered scandalous in *Gone with the Wind* and how she'd used her clothing to flout social expectations to get what she wanted—and then I made a mental note to get myself a poofy dress. "So, women derived power from wearing crinoline."

"And narcissistic pleasure," he added. "But of course, the feminists say that it's inappropriate to speak of female pleasure since men used the dresses to domestically enslave women."

I glanced out the window and saw the detective and two men entering the house. "There's Detective Sims. Sorry to run, but I need to ask him something."

"No problem," he said, rising to his feet.

I sprinted across the lawn to the house and crept up the stairs with the stealth of a ninja, er, nonna. Silence had never been my thing.

Before stepping onto the landing, I peeked through the railing and saw Detective Sims flanked by a man in a three-piece suit, who I presumed to be the district attorney, and the medical examiner. They were looking up at the noose around Scarlett's neck, so I seized the moment to slip into the children's room unobserved.

"Well?" Chandra huffed, hands on hips. "Can we go, or what?"

"Shhh!" I waved my arms to quiet her and then peered around the doorjamb.

Detective Sims turned to the medical examiner. "Any chance poisoning could be at work here?"

"The discoloration and swelling is consistent with hanging," the medical examiner replied, pointing to Scarlett's face. "I'll have to run a Mass spec. to tell whether any poison was involved."

"Can you hear anything?" Chandra whisper-shouted into my ear.

I glowered at her, and she took a step backwards.

"The previous victim died from oleander poisoning, right?" the D.A. asked.

"That's what we thought initially," Detective Sims replied. "But this morning there was a toxicology hit for belladonna."

Belladonna? I thought, stunned. Was this what the spirit had meant when she'd said not to trust the oleander flowers? The hair stood up on my arms, and I glanced back at Chandra. Maybe she was better at this psychic stuff than I'd thought.

The D.A. stroked his chin. "Was it ingested or injected?"

The medical examiner put his hands on his hips. "Probably ingested. There were no needle marks on the body, but there was no food in her stomach, either."

"Adding eavesdropping to your criminal repertoire, Miss Amato?" Officer Quincy snarled.

I leapt at least a foot in the air and then acted like I was just doing a combined ballet-yoga stretch. "Actually, I was waiting to ask Detective Sims if we could leave."

He removed his glasses and rubbed his forehead. "This is a complicated and dangerous case that's best left to police professionals."

"I think he's right," Chandra said softly.

I allowed myself a moment to fantasize about beating her with the bed roller, and then I said, "I used to be a police officer, so I can handle this case just fine."

He narrowed his watery blue eyes. "I want you to listen and listen good," he said in a menacing tone. "If I catch you interfering in this investigation again, I'll have the two of you locked up before you can say 'hard time.'"

I clenched my fists. "On what grounds?"

"I'll make some up," he said, raising his chin. "Now beat it before I make good on my threat."

Chandra, despite her platform stilettos, ran down the stairs and to the car like Florence Griffith Joyner on speed.

For the sake of my dignity, I exited the house with my head held high, but inside I was anything but poised. Scarlett was dead, and I felt semi-responsible. And now I knew I'd been dead wrong about the poison that had killed Ivanna Jones.

No matter how hard I tried, I couldn't understand why Ivanna would have been killed with belladonna when she had oleander-laced lip gloss in her hand. But I was starting to think that she'd known about the poison in the lip gloss. And if she had, I figured that she'd been coming to the plantation either to get the oleander or to give the lip gloss to an enemy. Of course, she could have been making trips to Oleander Place for some other reason. But what?

Once again my thoughts drifted to the pink diamond.

CHAPTER FIFTEEN

———

The busty blonde waitress literally bounced up to the table with a pot of coffee in hand. "Can I get y'all anything else this mornin'?"

"I'm good," I said from beneath her bulky breasts. Then I realized how that sounded under the, um, circumstances. "I mean, nothing for me thanks."

Veronica gave a wan smile and shook her head.

The waitress flashed a toothy grin. "Be right back with your check."

"Sorry if I've been a boring brunch date," Veronica said, staring at her mimosa glass as she twisted it in circles on the wooden table. "I just can't believe Scarlett's dead."

"I know." I looked at my half-eaten plate of Eggs Louisianne. "I woke up this morning thinking that it had all been a nightmare, but then reality hit me like a baseball bat. I can't help but feel partly responsible."

She glanced up at me. "You shouldn't, Franki. Scarlett was either involved in the murder or she knew who did it, and it was her responsibility to do the right thing. You reached out to her, but she made it clear she didn't want your help."

"I guess," I said, picking at my poached eggs with my fork.

"Do you think she was poisoned too?" she asked and then tossed a popcorn crawfish into her mouth.

"I doubt it." I rested my elbows on the table and clasped my hands. "This wasn't like Ivanna's murder. Whoever killed Scarlett did it to shut her up."

"Are you sure it wasn't some sort of ritualistic thing? After all, you did see that shrine."

"Yeah," I began, shifting in my chair, "but because the shrine was to Evangeline, it tells me that Obsessive Love Disorder was a factor in Ivanna's killing. My guess is that when Scarlett went to work early yesterday, she surprised the killer while he was worshipping Evangeline."

"That's so disturbing." She drained the last of her drink. "Who do you think did it?"

"Well, Miles might have had time to kill her before he left for the hardware store." I glanced at the wall of old wooden window frames that separated the dining area of Atchafalaya from the lobby. "But if I'm right about my altar theory, he couldn't have been inside the house when Scarlett came to work because he was looking out a window in the sugar mill when she arrived. And now that we know about the belladonna, I think Adam is a possibility. As a chemist, he'd have access to all kinds of poison."

She drummed her fingers on the table. "I still don't get why the killer would've put Scarlett in her crinoline."

"Remember, we don't know why she was wearing that dress." I popped the last of my crab cake into my mouth and licked creole hollandaise sauce from my fingers. "She could have put it on herself for some reason."

"But if she didn't?" She took a bite of her Eggs Treme.

"Then I might know why she was wearing it," I said, wiping my hands. "Ivanna too, for that matter."

"Why?" she pressed, leaning forward in anticipation.

"Troy said that crinoline literally gave women a larger presence in Victorian society and that it had an erotic aspect. And if you think about it, all of that fits with Obsessive Love Disorder. The killer transferred his obsession for Evangeline and her pink crinoline dress to Ivanna. But at some point, Ivanna crossed a line, so he put her in her place. As for Scarlett, she overstepped her bounds, so she got her comeuppance too."

Veronica nodded. "It makes sense, I suppose. But why the belladonna?"

I shrugged. "That's the part I don't get."

"Do you think the name is significant?" She cut into a boudin cake. "It does mean 'beautiful woman.'"

"I thought about that," I replied, stirring my green tomato bloody mary with the pickled green bean garnish. "My laptop is at the office, but I used my phone to look up belladonna on a poison control website. It didn't mention anything about the origin or history of the drug, but it listed some fascinating symptoms."

"Such as?" Veronica smiled at the waitress as she placed the check on our table.

I took a sip of my drink. "Well, it causes respiratory failure, for one thing. But it also causes blurred vision, blindness, and hallucinations."

"Well, aside from the respiratory failure, we don't have any evidence that Ivanna experienced those other symptoms," she said as she examined the bill.

"No, but if she was going blind or hallucinating, she might have been thrashing around the room, and that could account for the torn curtain and the broken perfume bottle." I sucked down the last of my bloody mary. "But then again, maybe she was in a fight for her life with the killer."

Veronica shuddered. "Let's change the subject. Have you heard from Bradley?"

At the mention of Bradley's name, I was filled with longing for another make-your-own-bloody-mary. "I texted him this morning, but he hasn't answered."

"It's only been a couple of days," she said, reaching for her billfold. "Give him a little more time."

"And let Pauline move in for the kill? Uh-uh, no way." I bit angrily into my alligator sausage as I flashed back to that dark day at the swamp. As far as I was concerned, those gators were partially responsible for my current relationship predicament.

Veronica rolled her eyes. "You don't have any proof that Pauline is after Bradley."

I started to tell her about the Three of Cups card, but I bit my tongue. Even I knew that a tarot card didn't exactly constitute hard evidence.

"Besides," she continued, "deep down you know she's not his type."

"I never underestimate the power of an enemy, Veronica, especially not one as pernicious as Pauline." I glanced at my watch and realized that it was almost eleven a.m. "I'm going to call him later, but first I need to find an elusive chemist, and after that I've got a frat party to attend."

"I'll go with you," she said. Then she held up her hand. "But only to Lickalicious Lips."

I looked at her in surprise. "I thought you had something to do."

"It can wait," she said, laying four twenties on the tip tray. "I don't think you should be alone when you question Adam about the belladonna."

I smiled. I was glad to have my partner back. As we left Atchafalaya, I joked, "I can't believe you'd miss the vassal's party. I mean, besides the Rex Ball at Mardi Gras, it's the social event of the season."

* * *

By the time Veronica and I drove from Uptown to the French Quarter, located a parking spot, and made our way through the throngs of Saturday tourists, it was almost noon when we arrived at Lickalicious Lips. As I'd suspected, Adam was there. In fact, he was in the process of locking the front door as he balanced a large cardboard box on his hip.

Given that he'd never bothered to return any of my calls, I dispensed with the friendly greeting and went straight to the point. "Did you resign or something?"

Adam stiffened and then threw his head back and sighed. "If you must know, I've been relieved of my services."

"I'm sorry to hear that," I said. "Does that mean Ivanna's father is in town?"

"Not yet," he said pulling the key from the door and turning to face us. "But his secretary called to let me know that he'll be arriving in New Orleans tomorrow to make funeral arrangements and put the business up for sale."

"Could you please let him know that we'd like to speak with him?" Veronica asked.

He gave a caustic laugh. "His secretary also let me know that the good Dr. Jones would rather not see me—since I'm a suspect in his daughter's death and all."

I could see that Adam was in no mood for questions. But he'd been avoiding me, and I wanted to know why. I also felt now might be my only opportunity to get some answers. So I decided to press. "Speaking of the investigation, I'm sure the police have contacted you about the death of Scarlett Heinz."

"They have indeed," he said as he stepped around Veronica and me and opened the trunk of an orange Corvette parked on the street.

I crossed my arms and shifted my weight to my hip. "Do you mind if I ask whether you have an alibi for yesterday morning?"

"Actually, I do mind." He loaded the box into the trunk and slammed the hood. "But if it'll get you to stop calling me," he began, dusting his hands on his faded jeans, "then I'll gladly tell you that I don't have an alibi because I was here yesterday morning packing up my things."

"No one can vouch for you?" Veronica asked. "You didn't see anyone or make any calls?"

"Look, I said I don't have an alibi, all right?" he yelled.

Adam was starting to try my patience. "Listen, we're just trying to get to the bottom of this case before anyone else is killed. Obviously, you don't have to talk to us because we're not the police. But I can tell you that refusal to cooperate only makes you look like a more appealing suspect."

"That's odd," he said in mock bemusement. "Because I have been cooperating, and yet I seem to be everyone's prime suspect." He yanked open his car door.

"Wait," Veronica said, making a clicking sound as she ran around his car in her heels.

He rested his arm on the car door. "I'm kind of in a hurry."

Using her signature manipulation move that I'd nicknamed the *bat and twirl,* Veronica immediately began batting her eyelashes and twisting a lock of her golden hair around her index finger. "Could we please just ask you one more question?" She stepped closer to him, opened her cornflower-blue eyes extra wide, and gave one last bat. "Pretty please?"

Adam softened like butter on a sweltering summer day. "What do you want to know?"

"Whether you've ever used oleander or belladonna in your products," she replied sweetly.

"Or elsewhere," I hurried to add.

He shook his head in frustration as he looked up at the sky. "They're highly toxic plants that have no use in cosmetics. Now, if you'll excuse me, I have somewhere to be."

Before Veronica or I could respond, Adam got into his Corvette and hit the gas. The car spun toward the curb and ran up on the sidewalk—narrowly missing a bodybuilder with a blond brush cut who was carrying a giant frozen margarita and wearing a wife beater that read "Keep Calm and Carry a Go-Cup"—before righting itself and speeding down St. Peter. The bodybuilder kept on walking, either too drunk or too calm to react.

Veronica removed her Gucci sunglasses. "What do you make of that exit?"

"Well, a) the Corvette is too much car for the chemist, and b) he didn't answer the question."

"He didn't, did he?" She rested the tip of her sunglasses on her lower lip. "Do you think he really had somewhere he needed to go?"

"He just wanted to get away from us," I said, as we began walking up St. Peter. "The question is why."

* * *

I looked at David out of the corner of my eye and smirked. He had a swagger in his step as he strutted down the musty corridor of Monroe Hall, presumably because he was a sophomore in a freshman dorm and because he had an older woman, i.e., me, at his side.

"Yo, Shor-tay!" David cried as he high-fived a skinny, five-foot-tall kid wearing orthodontic headgear.

I held my bag against my chest as we continued down the hall. "Is this the vassal's floor?"

"Someone's ready to party," he observed with a wink.

"Actually, I'm ready to have some answers about Corinne's case," I replied. But that was only partially true. The fact was that walking past the hormonal teenaged males milling in the hallway made me uneasy. Although I was modestly dressed in white Capri pants and a sleeveless turquoise shirt, you'd have thought I was wearing one of Glenda's stripper costumes. Every time I passed a boy, his beady, sex-starved eyes bore into my exposed flesh like lasers, or, given the context, like Star Trek phasers.

David stopped at an open doorway and gave a chivalrous bow. "After you, Ms. Amato."

When I entered the vassal's room, I expected to see a dorm-sized version of the set of "The Big Bang Theory." But the small space was so jam-packed with electronics that it looked more like the inside of a Best Buy, and it had that same plastic, new technology smell too. I glanced at a group of gamers gathered around a video console. "Where's the vassal?"

No sooner had I asked than the bathroom door opened and the vassal emerged. He was in full party mode—the top button of his plaid shirt was undone, and his bangs were hanging loose on his forehead. "Welcome," he said with a casual nod. "Can I get you a drink from the cooler?"

I eyed a nearby ice chest full of Mountain Dew Game Fuel. "Um, I really don't have much time. I'd rather just get to the video, if you don't mind."

"Not at all." He took a seat in the replica of Emperor Palpatine's throne that was facing his computer. "Give me a minute to pull it up."

While the vassal searched for the file, I studied a silver, crystal-studded sword mounted on the brick wall above his computer. "Is that from *Game of Thrones*?"

David's jaw dropped.

"Harry Potter," the vassal corrected in a hushed tone. "It's an authentic recreation of Godric Gryffindor's sword."

I rested my hand on his shoulder. "You *do* know that there was no Godric Gryffindor, don't you?"

The vassal scrutinized me with his slack-jawed stare. Then he turned away and cleared his throat. "So, both of the video files were altered."

I felt like I'd just won the lottery. "How do you know?"

He pointed to the bottom right on the screen. "You can tell by looking at the time stamp." He clicked the play arrow. "But first, just watch this clip from April 12th."

I leaned in and saw Corinne standing at her teller station. She handed a customer some cash and a receipt and then turned to look at the female teller at the next station, which was about three feet to her right. The teller said something, and Corinne walked over to her.

"Is there audio?" David asked.

The vassal shook his head. "But I think the woman is saying that something's wrong with her computer."

I watched as Corinne and the woman knelt down and pulled a tower computer from beneath the counter. Corinne jiggled one of the computer cables, and then she stood up and smiled before returning to her own station.

The vassal clicked pause.

I frowned. "I didn't see anything unusual in that clip."

"That's because whoever edited the video made clean cuts," he explained. "Now I'm going to slow it down, and I want you to watch the last two digits on the time stamp. They represent the seconds."

I nodded. The time stamp read 11:32:01 AM when the vassal clicked play. I kept my eyes glued to the *seconds* column.

"There!" David shouted. "Dude, it jumped by like thirty seconds."

"I saw it too," I said, struggling to contain my excitement. "At 11:32:19 AM, when Corinne was checking the cable, the time jumped to 11:32:49 AM."

"Right," the vassal said. "So your friend was probably at the woman's computer for another thirty seconds before she got up and walked back to her station."

"Which was enough time for someone to grab some cash from her drawer," I concluded. "What about the video from April 16th?"

"Same thing," the vassal replied. He opened the file and clicked play. "Someone edited out twenty-five seconds."

In the next clip, Corinne again went over to the teller station on her right, this time to see a customer's baby. I watched as she, the other teller, and the proud mother smiled and cooed at the infant. And then I saw another woman appear briefly in the bottom left corner of the screen. "Stop the video!"

The vassal jumped so high that his head hit the curved roof of his throne.

"What did you see?" David asked.

I motioned for him to wait. "Replay that, please, and slowly."

The vassal rubbed his head as he restarted the video.

I held my breath as I squinted at the screen. About thirty seconds into the clip, I saw Pauline's long, silky hair obscuring her face as she straightened some magazines in a waiting area near the teller stations. She glanced furtively through her hair toward Corinne and the others and then disappeared from view. "Did you see that woman?"

Both David and the vassal nodded, their tongues practically hanging out of their mouths.

"Never mind," I said with an eye roll. There was no point in discussing what I'd seen with the boys. I had what I needed, sort of. I could now go to Corinne and show her when the money was taken from her drawer, I just couldn't identify who did it.

Of course, I knew that Pauline was the culprit, especially after seeing her pretending to tidy up the waiting area in the second clip—something I was quite sure she would never lower herself to do without an ulterior motive. But there was no way I could prove it to anyone, and especially not to Bradley. He didn't want anything to do with me, much less with video I'd stolen from his bank. And even if I did summon up the courage to show him the clips, I wouldn't put it past Pauline to accuse Corinne of altering them to eliminate herself as a suspect.

The time had come to get someone at Brehman Bank to talk to me about Pauline, and by any means necessary. Because I was no longer dealing with a hard-hearted hussy—I had a cold-blooded criminal on my hands.

CHAPTER SIXTEEN

——————

At four o'clock on the dot, I pushed open the door to Private Chicks and marched into my office. It was bad enough that I was working on a Saturday, but because David had driven me to the party, I'd lost precious Pauline investigation time while I waited for him and the vassal to finish a very un-rousing game of Scrabble—played entirely in Klingon, I might add. To add insult to injury, Bradley still hadn't returned my text. So, I was probably going to be working a lot more Saturdays unless I could prove that his super secretary was a stellar stealer, which is precisely what I was going to do.

I woke up my computer and set about tracking down a Brehman Bank manager. I couldn't find the name of a single employee on the website. Then I did a Google search and found several of the managers' profiles on LinkedIn. I wanted to send them an InMail, but I could hardly tell them that I was a PI investigating a possible embezzler. I tapped my Leaning Tower of Pisa necklace charm on my teeth as I pondered how to proceed.

My best option, I reasoned, was to make myself look like an enticing client. Because PIs were notoriously cash poor, I changed my LinkedIn job profile to *finance entrepreneur*. It wasn't a total lie since I was always trying to come up with creative ways to manage my money (around two hundred dollars) and my credit (ahem, debt). Then I sent each of the managers a message saying that I had questions about investment funds, omitting the minor detail that I wanted to know whether one of their former employees had ever stolen said funds.

Feeling rather pleased with my progress, I texted Corinne and asked her to call me when she had a minute.

Next, I switched gears and googled belladonna. A Wikipedia reference popped up first, but I wanted something academic. I scanned the search results and was surprised to see belladonna listed on a botany site, since the name had a synthetic ring to it, like *ecstasy* or *spice*. I clicked the link and saw an image of a plant with purple bell-shaped flowers and blueberry-like berries that was labeled *atropa belladonna*. According to the article, this plant was one of the most toxic in the world.

"Just like oleander," I observed.

I resumed reading and learned that belladonna was a shade plant native to parts of Europe, North Africa, and Asia, but it was naturalized to moist climates in North America.

"New Orleans is nothing if not moist," I muttered. And then I bolted upright in my chair. What if belladonna was being grown at Oleander Place? If so, that would point the finger away from Adam and squarely at Miles.

I was going to have to pay an early evening visit to the plantation to look for the plant away from Miles' prying eyes. But even if I did find it on the grounds, that wouldn't tell me why it was used to kill Ivanna. Oleander made a kind of sick sense given the killer's obvious obsession with Evangeline. But belladonna?

I looked back at the article, and a sentence got my attention. *Belladonna has a long history of use as a medicine, cosmetic, and poison.*

"A cosmetic," I breathed. The medical examiner had reported that Ivanna was healthy at the time of her death, so I could rule out the medicinal use of belladonna. And given Ivanna's education and line of work, I knew she wouldn't be caught dead—pardon the expression—using makeup that would kill her. But what if the killer had used a cosmetic to kill the cosmetics CEO? It would make sense, and it would also point the finger right at Adam.

Or maybe at Ruth? No, she was so blunt she would've called me and told me she'd murdered Ivanna. And then she would've called the police and demanded to know why they were taking so long to arrest her.

I rested my elbows on the desk and massaged my temples. Until I found the source of the belladonna, I was at a standstill in this case.

My "Baby Got Back" ringtone sounded from inside my bag. Hoping it was Bradley, I grabbed my phone and looked at the display. "Hey, Corinne," I answered, deflated. "Thanks for calling."

"But of course," she said. "I am on a break at work, so I do not have much time. Is everysing okay? I haven't seen you at ze bank in a few days."

I couldn't tell her I'd been banned from the premises, because I knew she'd feel responsible when she found out why. "Bradley and I had an argument," I fibbed. And then I added a flat out lie. "I'd rather not see him right now."

"I am sorry, Franki. But if you need to come in, he is not here at ze moment. He just left to take Pauline home."

I felt a pang of jealousy. "What happened to her car?"

"Oh, zey came to work togezer zis morning."

That pang turned into a stab.

"Because zey went to New York yesterday for a meeting," she hurried to add.

And spent the night, I thought as *Psycho*-style stabs pierced my gut. I unclenched my teeth and asked in a forced casual tone, "So, where does Pauline live? I'm just curious."

"In Faubourg Marigny."

"That's the artsy neighborhood below the French Quarter, right?"

"*Oui*, ze locals call it ze Marigny Triangle."

The whooping of a battleship attack alarm sounded as the word *triangle* echoed in my brain. Whether it had anything to do with the Three of Cups card or not, that was one too many triangles for my liking. Pauline was clearly on the offensive. I needed to counterattack, and quick.

"Listen, I'll make this fast," I said, pulling my keys from my bag. "I watched the security tape for the days money was taken from your drawer, and it was definitely tampered with."

She gasped.

"Both times, someone took money when you went to talk to the teller next to you," I continued, "and I have reason to believe it was Pauline."

"I kill her wis my bare hands," Corinne rasped.

I was startled by the Clint Eastwood quality to her typically fairy-like voice. But then I remembered that even the Disney Tinker Bell was vindictive. "Don't do anything rash," I warned, "because I can't prove it yet. Just hold tight, and I'll be in touch."

"Okay," she said. "I wait for your news."

I closed the call and headed for the door. I had a triangle defense to plan before I went to the plantation, and I knew exactly with whom I was going to consult.

* * *

I crammed the last bite of Lucky Dog into my mouth and entered Chandra's office. I started to say hello but began to cough as "Slap Ya Mama" Cajun seasoning stung my throat.

"Would you like some of my Tab?" Chandra asked, holding up a hot pink soft drink can with purple lipstick stains.

I gagged a little, and then I choked out, "I'm fine. I just need your advice."

She wrinkled her mouth. "Okay. Don't eat food from Bourbon Street vendors."

I tossed my purse on the floor and straddled a chair. "I see your psychic powers have returned."

"That has nothing to do with it." She pulled out a box of Sandalwood incense. "You smell like a cheap hot dog."

"Better than smelling like a cheap whore," I quipped.

"No, it isn't." She lit the incense. "Are you here on business?"

"I wanted to ask you about Bradley."

"It's going to—"

"Will forty dollars cover it?" I interrupted, shoving a couple of twenties in her face. Two could play this psychic game.

She tucked the money into her bra. "It depends on the seriousness of the issue."

"It's about that Three of Cups card." I waved a stream of smoke away from my face. "Ever since you told me about it, everything's coming up triangles."

"Triangles?" she echoed.

"You said the upside down card meant that I was in a love triangle, remember?" I huffed.

"Oh." She leaned over and began rummaging around in her giant Chanel bag. "Well that's just one interpretation."

I looked at her from beneath my brow, wavering between hatred and hope.

"It could also represent a separation," she continued, pulling out a rag.

"You mean, like spending time apart?"

Chandra shrugged. "Yeah, or that Bradley's indulging in threesomes."

I hung my head as I tried to maintain my composure. "Meaning aside," I ground out, "is there anything that can undo the Three of Cups card?" I thought of Odette Malveaux, the mambo who'd helped me solve my last case. "Like voodoo?"

"Voodoo?" She scoffed as she dusted her crystal ball. "Don't tell me you believe in that hocus pocus."

About as much as I believe in clairvoyance, I thought.

"There's no easy way out," she said, shaking her dust rag at me. "You're going to have to tackle this problem head on."

So much for that triangle defense, I thought. "I'm already working on it," I said, resting my chin on the back of my chair. "Listen, I also wanted to talk to you about Oleander Place."

She turned up her nose and began wiping incense ashes from the card table. "I'm not going back to that haunted house of horrors, if that's what you want to know."

"I wouldn't ask you to go back after what happened," I said. "I just want to know if you can summon the spirit of Ivanna or Scarlett here in your office."

Her lips thinned. "I don't think so."

I looked her in the eyes. "Because you can't, or because you won't?"

Chandra fingered a charm on her star and moon bracelet. "I don't want anything to do with that place. Those spirits are scary."

I suppressed an eye roll. "Look, I wouldn't ask if it wasn't important. There's been a surprising development in the case," I said, wishing I could tell her about the belladonna. "And I need to make sense of it if I'm going to find the killer. He could strike again, you know."

She sighed. "Even if I wanted to help, I couldn't. Lou has forbidden me from having any more to do with the investigation. I'm sorry." She began dusting a crystal.

Chandra didn't strike me as the type to go against her beloved Lou, so I knew there was no point in pressing further. I picked up my bag and rose to leave.

"Wait. There's something I need to tell you." She put down the crystal. "You know the French doors where we found Scarlett?"

I nodded.

"Something about the door on the right is off."

I sat down and crossed my arms on the back of the chair. "What is it?"

"I'm not sure."

"Is it stuck or something? I mean, maybe that's why you had a vision of the spirit tugging at it."

She shook her head. "That's not it. But I'm positive something about it isn't right."

The door opened and hit me in the behind. I turned and glared at a bug-eyed male in his mid-thirties poking his head into the room.

"I'll be right with you," Chandra said.

Somehow his eyes opened even wider, and then he closed the door.

"Don't your clients knock?" I asked, annoyed.

"It's the lunar eclipse," she said under her breath.

"Ah," I said, instantly visualizing half-men, half-werewolves. "Well, I've got to get out to the plantation, anyway. Let me know if you figure out what's wrong with that door."

"I will," she said in a soft voice. "Be careful out there, Franki."

"You be careful in *here*," I said, thinking of the lunar eclipse loonies. Speaking of which, when I opened the door, Chandra's client was standing to one side gnawing his nails.

Noting tufts of black hair protruding from his collar, I gave him a wide birth as I headed for the exit.

Just before the main door a voodoo doll with long black hair caught my eye. I picked it up and considered buying it. If nothing else, it would feel good to stick a pin in Pauline. Now that I thought about it, I wished I could get a voodoo replica of Oleander Place too. Between Pauline and the plantation, I was nearing my wits' end. As of this moment, I could no more prove that she was a thief—of money and men—than I could identify the killer. And I was starting to question whether I was cut out to be an investigator, lead or otherwise.

Xavier appeared from below the counter. "You git better news this time?"

I looked at him, startled. "Uh, about what?"

He crossed his arms and leaned against the wall. "From your readin'."

"Oh, well, like you said last time, it's a war zone out there." I put the doll back on the stand. "And I'm engaged in more than one battle."

He nodded toward the voodoo doll display. "Black magic ain't gonna do ya no good."

"What about this Pat O'Brien's Hurricane cocktail mix?" I joked, holding up a package.

He jutted out his bottom lip. "Spirits neither. You just need to remember that the situation ain't never as bad as you think it is. Nine times out o' ten, the solution's starin' ya right in the face."

"Thanks. I really hope you're right," I said and then headed out onto Bourbon Street.

As I began weaving through the throngs of tanked tourists, I wondered whether there was some truth to what Xavier had said. I mean, I did have a tendency to exaggerate— but just the teensiest, weensiest little bit. Maybe it was time to consider the possibility that I'd been overthinking one or both of my cases.

* * *

I pulled into the Oleander Place parking lot at six thirty and switched off the engine. As I'd anticipated, the plantation was deserted, and there was still plenty of light for a plant hunt.

I started to get out of the car but then stopped. Chandra was right. It was time to take the bull by the horns, or the boyfriend by the hairs, as it were, and confront Bradley. Otherwise, I was going to stay in this miserable state of limbo.

I dialed Bradley's number and waited with baited breath.

"Hello," he answered flatly.

Following his lead, I kept it emotionless—that is, on the surface. "We need to talk about what happened at the bank. Can you meet me later?"

There was an awkward pause. "I'm sorry, but I can't. I'm in the middle of some critical negotiations here at the office."

My heart sank. "You can't spare fifteen minutes to talk about us?"

He sighed. "Franki, please understand. Some big changes are underway for the bank, and all of us in management are working twenty-four seven. We're meeting literally throughout the night. I can't just leave."

"So, what does this mean?"

"It means I need some time."

Tears stung my eyes. "I can give you all the time you need."

Without another word, I hung up and leaned my head against the headrest. I wasn't sure what was happening with Bradley and me, but I knew it wasn't good. I could understand that he was upset about finding me locked in the security room, but he was more distant every time I talked to him. I wondered whether Pauline had finally told him that my nonna was planning our engagement.

I shook my head to rid my mind of the thought. I couldn't go there, not now. Just like my pride, daylight was burning. I had to look for the belladonna plant.

I dragged myself from the car and headed for the back porch. Because the plantation had grown sugar cane, there were few opportunities for shade on the grounds. I started by making a round of the house and then searching a pecan grove behind the slave quarters. Next, I checked the area around the restaurant and headed for the little sugar mill.

When I rounded the back of the building, I noticed that sod grass had been laid out in a two-foot area against the wall. I crouched and lifted one of the squares and saw that the ground had been tilled. Of course, it was difficult to grow grass in shade. But because grass was growing along the remainder of the wall, I had to question whether something else had been planted previously in that spot. Like belladonna.

"Evenin', Miss Franki."

My head jerked up as my heart jumped in my throat. "Miles!" I exclaimed, dropping the sod square. "Wh-what are you doing here so late?"

"I'm gettin' de big mill ready for a photo shoot," he replied. He was holding what appeared to be two giant soup ladles, and he looked like he had a bad taste in his mouth.

I glanced up at the ladles from my crouched position, suddenly painfully aware that I was alone on the plantation with a potential killer. I rose to my feet and casually took a step backward, trying my best to remain calm. "I didn't see your car in the parking lot."

"Dat's because I parked 'round back o' de big mill." He swung the ladles over his shoulder.

"Ah," I said, struck by the effortlessness with which he'd swung the heavy-looking objects.

Miles narrowed his eyes. "What was you doin' wit' dat patch o' grass?"

"Oh, that." I forced a laugh. "I've never seen grass planted like that before," I replied, realizing how suspicious that must have sounded. I couldn't let him know I suspected him of anything, so I had to keep talking to put him at ease. "Whatcha got there?"

"Dese are old cane syrup ladles for de kettles. We store all de old artifacts in de little mill."

"Delta said something about that," I remarked, stalling for time. I had to figure out how to ask about the belladonna, because the police still hadn't released that information. "She also said that's where you keep the Greek Revival accents that were stripped from the exterior of the house."

"And some things from inside de house, like de original windows and French doors. Dey was gettin' ruint on account o' de humidity from de rivah."

"Yeah, with the Mississippi right in front of the property, the plantation feels like a tropical rain forest." This was a perfect segue into belladonna, so I decided to go for broke. "Do you ever try to grow any exotic plants out here?"

Miles scratched his head. "Such as?"

"I don't know, like belladonna or...venus flytraps." I mentally cursed myself for that last one, but it was the only other exotic plant I knew. Could I help it if I wasn't a botanist?

He furrowed his brow and frowned. "Nevah heard of 'em."

"Too bad. I mean, okay," I fumbled. "Anyway, I really should get going," I said. Then, as a safety precaution, I lied, "My boyfriend's waiting for me."

He nodded, stonefaced. "Have a nice evenin'."

I smiled and headed for the parking lot, half-convinced that Miles was going to launch a ladle at the back of my head. I glanced over my shoulder, and of course he was staring right at me. He looked angry too. The second I rounded the corner of the mill, I hoofed it to my car and hightailed it home.

* * *

When I pulled into my driveway an hour later, I gave a sigh of relief. After my unsettling encounter with Miles, all I wanted was to spend the night curled up safely in my apartment with Napoleon. But as I walked up the sidewalk, my stomach fell. There was a brown cardboard box beside my front door, and it was just like the one that had contained the portentous pineapple.

I took a step back and debated whether to open it. After all, it could have been a bomb or a severed head. But on the off chance it was an apology gift from Bradley, I wanted it—and how.

I grabbed a stick from the yard and pried the flaps open. Then I peered into the box. As I'd feared, this was no gift. It was a courter's candle that had been burned down to a stump. And just like last time, there was a note. But I knew what this one said before I'd even read it.

Your time is up, Miss Franki.

CHAPTER SEVENTEEN

A loud blast rang out, like a gunshot.

In one fluid motion, I leapt from a supine sleeping position into a combat shooting stance with my knees bent and my gun drawn. Actually, after I'd had a second to wake up, I realized I was gripping my phone. Napoleon had assumed my same crouch only he'd drawn his lips.

I took a step backwards to retrieve my Ruger from beneath my pillow when another bang sounded. Then my whole body went slack. It was just Glenda slamming doors in her apartment upstairs.

I looked at the ceiling and gave a long exhale. "All clear, little buddy."

Napoleon relaxed and jumped onto the bed.

"Good idea," I said, nestling back into my pillows. But there was no way I was going to let myself fall sleep again with a death threat hanging over my head. I glanced at my phone display and was shocked to see that it was almost one o'clock. I'd been awake until sunrise, and then I must have drifted off.

"I need a double espresso to deal with my double threat," I muttered as I checked my voice mail. David had tried to call me, but there was nothing from Veronica. And given that I'd knocked on her door and texted her at least ten times since finding that creepy candle, I was starting to get worried. Then a sickening thought occurred to me—*what if my aggressor had done something to Veronica?*

I held my breath as I dialed David's number.

"Yo," he answered.

"Hey, have you seen Veronica this morning?" I gushed in a single breath.

"Yup."

"Yay," I snarked in keeping with the one-word *y*-theme. "Where the hell has she been? I've been trying to get hold of her since yesterday to tell her I got another death threat."

A paper bag crinkled on the other end of the line.

"Oh wow," he said, chewing what sounded like a mighty mouthful. "Like, are you all right?"

"Yes," I muttered, unintentionally continuing the theme. "But do you know why Veronica hasn't called me back?"

"Uh-huh." He swallowed loudly. "She lost her phone while we were staking out this lady's cheating husband at The Roosevelt Hotel. We were there until like eleven this morning, and then she had to meet the lady for brunch at The Veranda."

I was glad I'd escaped that lengthy assignment. But still, I was kind of offended that Veronica had asked David to be her partner and not me. "What are you eating, anyway?"

"Uh, Veronica bought me a bag of beignets."

Another knife to the gut, I thought as my hand drifted to my empty belly. She never bought me any beignets after a stakeout. "So, what are you doing working on a Sunday if you've been up all night? You need to get some rest."

"Can't." He made finger-licking noises. "I have to make up some hours. Besides, I'm all right. After I dropped you off yesterday, I went back to the vassal's and *shut that party doooown*."

Of course, for most college students, staying until the end of a party would mean that they were hung over. But I knew David was jacked up on that hyper-caffeinated gamer drink. "Dude, you need to lay off The Dew. Otherwise, you seriously might not sleep again until you graduate from college. Now, why did you call me earlier?"

There was another telltale crinkle of the beignet bag.

"I tracked down a descendent of Beau Patterson on ancestry.com. Her name is Kristy Patterson, and luckily for us, she hasn't set many of her privacy settings on Facebook."

"What did you find out?"

"On Thursday she posted that she's in town this week for Shore Leave."

"That's fantastic," I enthused, referring both to Kristy and to the notion of thousands of muscle-bound sailors in uniform flooding the streets of New Orleans. "I guess she's with the Navy?"

"Uh," he began through a bite of beignet, "her profile says she's a jeweler in New York City."

"A jeweler? Then what's she doing on shore leave? Trying to find herself a sailor?" *Not that there was anything wrong with that.*

He cleared his throat. "Oh, it's not for sailors. Shore Leave is, like, a four-day pirate festival in the French Quarter. It's run by this group of women called the NOLA Wenches."

Well that stood to reason. Any women who would invite thousands of men in velvet and feathers with fake pirate accents to flood the streets where I worked were wenches in my book. "When does it end?"

"Today's the last day."

"Hm." I wrinkled my mouth. "That doesn't give me much time to find her, but I'll see what I can do. If all else fails, I'll Facebook her."

"I tried that. But if you're not her friend, the message goes to her 'Other' folder. So I doubt she'll get it."

"Okay. Is there a good picture of her on the page, at least?"

"Lots of them. She looks like she's really short, maybe in her thirties. And she's wearing something you'll be interested to see."

I sighed. "Please tell me it's not pirate garb."

"Nope," he said with a lip smack. "It's an emerald-cut pink diamond ring."

I bolted upright in bed. That *was* something I wanted to see.

* * *

After a double espresso, a double-decker sandwich, and some Double Stuf Oreos—I was big into themes today—I peeked out the front window and spotted Veronica's car in the driveway. I dialed her number in case she'd found her phone, but the call went to voice mail.

I chewed on my pinky nail. It was two o'clock, so I figured that Veronica was out like a light after her all-night stakeout. But I had to warn her about the threat. I scribbled a quick note about my ordeal and slipped out front, keeping my eyes peeled for a killer. I pounded on Veronica's door and waited.

The door of Glenda's apartment flew open, and I caught sight of black thigh-high boots descending the stairs. Once I saw the rest of Glenda, I averted my eyes. Aside from the boots, she had a black patch on her eye, a stuffed parrot on her shoulder, and not much else.

"*What* is all the racket about, Miss Franki?" she asked.

"I need to talk to Veronica," I said, pretending to be engrossed in my phone. "Besides, I could ask you the same thing. Your door slamming woke me up."

"Well, I couldn't find my skull and crossbones pasties."

"I see you found them," I said, keeping my eyes glued to my phone. "You wouldn't, by any chance, be going to Shore Leave, would you?"

"When the Quarter is filled with pirates, sugar, I plunder."

I looked up—and winced. "I'm on my way there now for that case I've been working on."

Glenda eye's lit up like a lighthouse. "Oh, a treasure hunt," she squealed, wiggling her hips. "Can I help you look for the pink diamond?"

My initial thought was that I'd rather be in Davie Jones' locker than at a pirate party with Glenda. But I had to admit that it made sense to go with her. She'd know the popular pirate hangouts, which could narrow down my search. "Okay, but let's take my car."

"Not until we get you a costume," she said, tightening the knot on the transparent scarf that served as her skirt. "I've got a reputation to protect. I don't want pirates to think I rent to a landlubber." She pointed her cigarette holder at me. "Come."

I slid the note under Veronica's door and followed Glenda upstairs with a mixture of dread and anticipation. I was anything but eager to let her dress me, but I was excited to finally see her apartment. Judging from the Red Light District décor of my place, I figured hers would look something like the set of the film *Moulin Rouge* or maybe the Louisiana version of *The Best Little Whorehouse in Texas*. But when I entered the all-white fur, feather, and leather living room, I didn't see any stripper poles or sex swings. In fact, there wasn't even a sofa. Just a six-foot tall champagne glass. "Wow," I remarked, impressed. "Is that one of those champagne Jacuzzis like they have at that resort in the Poconos?"

"Bite your tongue, sugar," Glenda spat. "Under no circumstances do you fill a champagne glass with *water*." She grabbed a key from a hook on the wall. "Now let's go find you something suitable to wear."

We went to the apartment next door to hers, which held her infamous stripper costume collection. I'd expected to see racks overflowing with gowns, but instead they were thick with thongs, packets of pasties, tiny strips of cloth and various, um, accessories.

"Of course, none of my pirate corsets will fit you," she said, exhaling a cloud of smoke. "But I have a Southern belle costume that should work." She began rummaging in a closet and emerged with a dome-shaped metal contraption the size of a children's playscape.

Before I could protest—after all, I wasn't *that* much bigger than Glenda—she'd stripped me down and dressed me up faster than a wardrobe changer at a fashion show. After a few twists of a curling iron, she led me to a standing mirror. "What do you think, Miss Franki? It's a replica of Scarlett O'Hara's white ruffled prayer dress from the opening scene of *Gone with the Wind*."

I stared at my ringleted reflection in shock. Troy had been right about crinoline dresses. In fact, I was larger than "larger than life." Only, unlike Scarlett O'Hara, there was no chance in hell I was going to church in Glenda's version of the getup since it had a tear-away bodice and peepholes beneath the ruffles. "Frankly, I think it gives a whole new meaning to the phrase *tent dress*. You could put an entire pack of Boy Scouts under here."

"Not the Boy Scouts, sugar, the Scoutmasters," she said with a saucy wink. "Speaking of the opposite sex, the dress has a pull-cord."

I had no idea what she was talking about, but it didn't sound good.

"It's here on your right," she continued, grasping a silk cord at my waist. "If you pull it down, it'll raise the skirt so you can flash your man."

I stared at her, open-mouthed.

"What did you expect?" she asked with a shrug. "It's a stripper costume."

Out of curiosity, I gave a slight tug on the cord. The force of the metal cage beneath the dress was so powerful that it knocked the mirror against the wall.

"Whoa!" Glenda shouted as she stood the mirror upright. "This dress wasn't made for the boxing ring—it was designed for the stripping stage. You've got to make sure the object of your affection is standing at a distance before you raise that thing."

I looked at my reflection again. My skirt might be the size of the Superdome, but now that I knew it could take down a persistent pirate—or a potential perpetrator—it was really starting to grow on me.

* * *

I bent over and examined the huge hole that Glenda's cigarette had burned into my skirt. "I told you that you shouldn't smoke in a convertible! Now there's an extra peephole in this dress, and it's right at crotch level."

Glenda took a drag off the offending instrument and narrowed her eyes. "Personally, I think it's an improvement on the design."

"Maybe if I was in a strip club, but I'm on Bourbon Street," I huffed as I did my best to arrange the sash to cover the hole.

"Same difference, sugar," she said, stubbing out her cigarette with her boot toe. "Now, who or what are we looking for?"

"Kristy Patterson." I showed Glenda a picture of the petite brunette from my phone. "She's a descendent of Beau the Black, and she may be wearing a pink diamond ring."

Glenda blinked. "*The* pink diamond?"

"That's one of the things I need to find out," I replied, stuffing my phone in my bodice.

"Well, if she's descended from a pirate, then we need to check Jean Lafitte's."

"Sounds good to me," I said. "I could go for a purple voodoo." I didn't usually drink on the job, but I could use a little relief from driving this dress.

"Not the Blacksmith Shop, sugar," she said with a frustrated flip of her hair. "I mean Jean Lafitte's Old Absinthe House. All the real pirates go there to partake of the so-called green fairy."

"A little green voodoo will work too."

As we set off down the center of the street, the crowd parted like the Red Sea did for Moses. But it wasn't to make room for my dress—it was to make way for Glenda. She was in stripper-strut mode, and with her dyed platinum hair swaying in rhythm with her breasts, she was quite the sight.

"Begad!" a pirate cried. "It be Gunpowder Glenda!"

"Good ol' Gunpowder!" another yelled.

Glenda gave a satisfied smirk and kept strutting.

I kicked my Keds into gear and maneuvered myself to her side. "Why are they calling you 'gunpowder'?"

She gave a throaty laugh. "Because when you load my cannon, Miss Franki, it goes off with a bang!"

I dropped back behind, sorry I'd asked.

When we arrived at the Old Absinthe House, I navigated the entryway with a shove from behind from Glenda.

I flailed my arms to regain my balance. Once I was steady on my feet, I couldn't believe my eyes. Drunken swashbucklers and their women, er, wenches, were singing the predictable "Fifteen Men on a Dead Man's Chest" shanty as they sloshed mugs of beer and grog. It was like a tavern scene straight out of *Pirates of the Caribbean*. The only thing missing was Johnny Depp, and trust me when I say that his absence was felt.

My impromptu Depp daydream was rudely interrupted when a doppelganger for Peter Ustinov in *Blackbeard's Ghost* approached us.

"Gunpowder Glenda?" he asked, wide-eyed. "Well blow me down!" And then he gave a hearty laugh and slapped his knee. "Or just blow me!"

Glenda put a hand on her hip. "You old scallywag!" she exclaimed with a bat of her eyelashes. "Is that a hornpipe in your pocket? Or are you just happy to see me?"

I rolled my eyes. If this went on much longer, I was going to find a plank and walk it.

I left Glenda to cavort with her pirate and began scanning the room for Kristy Patterson. After only a few minutes, I was starting to get discouraged. I didn't think she was at the bar, and I was overwhelmed at the thought of searching the entire French Quarter.

On a hunch, I pulled my phone from my bodice and checked Kristy's Facebook page. I was relieved to see that she'd updated her location at two forty-five. According to her post, she was going to be sampling rum for an hour or so at Pirate's Alley Café and Olde Absinthe House, which was located on a narrow street known as Pirate's Alley about a half mile away. It was three thirty now, so that gave me fifteen minutes, give or take, to walk there.

I shoved my phone into my bra and realized that Captain Hook's real-life twin was checking me out, or rather, the burn in my skirt.

He gave me a lusty wink. "Mind if I fire me cannon through yer porthole?"

I arched a brow and considered pulling the cord. But instead I heaved my hulking skirt to one side, stepped around him, and then let it rip, so to speak. Next I heard the sounds of shattering glass and a table overturning. *Time to set sail.*

I scoured the motley crew for Glenda.

"Put me down!" Glenda mock-protested.

I looked up and saw her grinning from ear to ear as a brawny buccaneer hoisted her onto his shoulder. "Hey Glenda, we need to leave," I shouted. "Kristy's at another bar, and I might have just maimed a guy with your dress."

"Oh, sugar," she whined as she slid languidly down the length of the buccaneer's body to the floor. "It's just starting to get fun."

"Why don't you stay here?" I asked with a little too much hope in my voice. "I'll be back in an hour or so."

Glenda looked not-so-coyly at her boisterous buccaneer. "Wanna drop anchor in my lagoon?"

On that sour note, I hiked up my hoop skirt and fled. I took the exit at a run, so I was able to get out of Jean Lafitte's unassisted. Once outside, I tried to jog—okay, speed walk—the distance to Pirate's Alley, but my dress was literally dragging me down.

When I got to the café fifteen minutes later, I was out of steam and, I feared, out of time.

Grasping either side of the entrance doorjamb, I catapulted myself inside, knocking a woman flat on her back in the process. "Hey! Why don't you watch where you're going in that thing?"

"I'm so sorry," I said, reaching over my skirt to help her up. "This costume should be a registered weapon."

She picked up her tricorne and brushed her long brown hair from her eyes.

I recognized her face immediately—that and the coral-pink, emerald-cut diamond ring on her right hand. "Kristy Patterson?"

She jutted out her chin. "Who wants to know?"

Spoken like a true rogue, I thought. *Or a New Yorker.* "I'm Franki Amato," I said, extracting a business card from my bra à la Chandra. "I'm investigating two murders that took place at the Oleander Place plantation, and I'd like to ask you some questions, if you don't mind."

"Dammit!" she yelled, kicking the wall. "I knew I shouldn't have come back to NOLA."

A thirty-something male in a velvet waistcoat and foppish feather hat walked up behind her. "What happened?"

Her face hardened. "Delta Dupré gave my name to the cops. You *know* she told them that I single-handedly killed those women."

"No," I objected, stunned to learn that Delta and Kristy had a history. "You're not a police suspect in the murders as far as I know. I just want to talk to you about the pink diamond that your ancestor Beau gave to Evangeline Lacour. I think it might be key to the investigation."

"All right," she began as she put her pirate hat on her head, "but let's grab a seat at the bar. I'm going to need another drink to rehash this sordid story."

CHAPTER EIGHTEEN

———

"We need a round of absinthe over here," Kristy called, waving at a bartender.

My eyes zeroed in on the pink diamond as it reflected the lights that adorned the miniature pirate ship above the bar. "First I have to ask the obvious question—is that the Lacour diamond?"

She looked at her ring. "Don't I wish. Beau bought this to remember Evangeline by after she died."

That was quite a romantic gesture for a ruthless pirate. Maybe I had the swashbuckling types figured all wrong. "What do you think happened to the original?"

Kristy placed her tricorne on the counter. "My family and I are positive that it's still in Evangeline's hiding place, wherever that is."

I glanced at a skull perched on a wine rack. "What makes you so sure? A hundred seventy-seven years is a long time for a precious gem to stay hidden."

"Well," she began, crossing her black leather–clad legs, "we have Evangeline's last letter to Beau. She told him that she'd hidden the diamond in the house and that no one knew the location but her."

"I don't know," I said, rubbing my eye. "It just seems like someone would have found it by now, maybe even on accident."

"Some days, I'm inclined to agree with you. But if someone did find the diamond, I really think that we would have heard about it by now."

I wasn't convinced. There were too many cases of famous jewels and paintings that had been "missing" for decades, even centuries, only to turn up in the hands of private collectors.

"Here ye go, me hearties," the bartender boomed as he put two glasses of absinthe in front of Kristy and me.

I watched, fascinated as he placed a slotted spoon with a sugar cube on top over the mouth of each glass, set the cubes on fire, and opened the spigots of an antique water fountain that dripped water on the cubes until they dissolved into the green liquid below. "You know, I probably shouldn't drink on an empty stomach," I said, eyeing the now murky yellow contents of the glass with concern. "Could I get some rum cake to go with that?"

"Aye, aye." He brushed my cheek with his finger. "A wench after me own heart."

I blushed as red as the scarf knotted around his head and turned away to face Kristy. "Did your family ever try to look for the diamond?"

She took a long drink. "To my knowledge, not a one of Beau's descendants has ever made it past the front door of Oleander Place, except for my dad and me."

"Why not?" I asked, stirring the sugar granules in my drink.

She crossed her arms in a defensive posture. "Beau wasn't just the black sheep of his and Knox's family. He's the black sheep of the entire Patterson ancestral line. Knox's people didn't and don't want Beau's people to have anything to do with the plantation or its contents."

"So, how did you and your dad get in?"

"About five years ago, we went out to the plantation to ask Delta if we could help search for the diamond. We made it clear to her that we weren't trying to claim it. We just wanted it to be found for historical record."

"How did Delta react?" I took a swig of the absinthe and grimaced at the taste of anise.

"In a surprise move, she let us search the house. And then the next thing we knew, the police had arrived, and she fabricated this whole story saying that we'd stolen items from the house."

My eyes opened wide. That was a bold move, even for Delta.

"Then, out of nowhere, a cop produced a warrant to search my purse. And surprise, surprise, there were plantation knick knacks in there that I'd never even seen before, much less stolen."

I gasped. Until that moment I had no idea just how far Delta would go to protect her beloved Oleander Place.

"Just wait," Kristy said, touching my arm. "It gets worse."

I couldn't imagine how.

"Delta also claimed that my dad and I had threatened to hurt her if she reported us to the police for stealing. So, on top of two years of probation, we got restraining orders slapped on us."

"And the police never questioned any of it."

"Of course not." Kristy arched an eyebrow. "You know she has police connections through her late husband, right?"

"All too well." I took another sip of my drink, this time grimacing at the memory of Officer Quincy rather than the anise. "So, that's what you meant when you said you knew you shouldn't have come back here."

"Exactly." She tipped her head back and drank all but one sip of her absinthe.

The bartender placed my rum cake in front of me with a saucy wink.

I averted my eyes and cut into my dessert. "What's the Lacour family's involvement in all this? If anyone can claim ownership of that diamond, it's them."

"Well, Evangeline was an only child, and she never had children. So, she doesn't have any direct descendants. To my knowledge, no one from her family has ever come forward."

I swallowed a glob of gooey cake and cut myself another bite. "I wonder how many times Delta has searched the plantation for that diamond."

"Honestly, I wouldn't be surprised if she never has. Delta doesn't want the diamond to be found."

I stopped in mid-chew. "Why do you say that?"

Kristy shrugged. "Because it adds mystique to the plantation, and where there's mystique, there's money." She took the last gulp of her drink and wiped her lips with the back of her hand. "Delta herself said that a lot of tourists go out there hoping to find the diamond."

"That's interesting," I said, drumming my fingers on the bar. "She never mentioned that to me." I thought about Ivanna and wondered if she were one of those very tourists. "Did Delta happen to mention whether she'd ever caught a tourist looking for it?"

"Not to me, she didn't." She placed her tricorne on her head. "But I can tell you this—I wouldn't want to be that poor bastard."

"Neither would I." I drained the last of my drink. Maybe it was my conversation with Xavier the day before, or maybe it was the alleged mind-altering effect of the absinthe, but whatever it was, I realized that I needed to shift my focus. Instead of trying to verify that Ivanna was after the diamond, I started to consider how Delta would have reacted if she'd perceived Ivanna as a threat to her plantation's main attraction.

* * *

When I left Pirate's Alley Café for Jean Lafitte's, I decided to walk up Chartres Street to avoid the partying pirates on Bourbon. Even though it was only five o'clock, I was hoping to convince Glenda to leave soon. I wanted to get out of the Quarter before the marauding turned to mutiny.

After a couple of blocks, I ran into Blackbeard's Ghost and his pirate posse.

"Why look, mateys!" he exclaimed. "It's Gunpowder Glenda's fair friend, the plantation owner's daughter."

Jeez, these pirates are pests, I thought as I gave a wan smile and walked past them. *If only I had some Britney Spears music to drive them away.*

"Would ye like to join me for a glass of rum, me beauty?" he boomed. "I'll show ye why me Roger is so Jolly!"

Resisting the urge to dust him with my dress, I shot him a shut-your-bung-hole look and crossed to the opposite side of the street.

There was a buzz inside my bodice. I pulled out my phone and looked at the display. Veronica.

"I see you found your phone," I answered. "Have you been sleeping all this time?"

Veronica yawned. "You make it sound like I've been asleep for hours."

"Well, I've been trying to get hold of you for forever," I said accusatorially.

"Um, we had brunch together yesterday."

"Well, a lot has happened since then," I chided.

"Are you actually mad at me for not calling you last night?" she asked in a bewildered tone.

I sniffed. "Kind of. I did get another death threat, after all."

"I can't believe this," she muttered under her breath. "How could I have known about the threat when I didn't have my cell?"

"This isn't just about last night," I snapped. "You've been late, distracted, or MIA for weeks."

Veronica said something, but I didn't hear her because a steaming plate of shrimp pistolettes was beckoning to me from a window at the Original Pierre Maspero's.

"Franki, are you even listening to me?" she demanded.

"I'm sorry, what?" I asked, tearing myself away from the savory beignets.

"I said," she began tersely, "you haven't been around much either, you know."

"Me?" I was taken aback. "I can't believe you would say that when I've been slaving away on the Jones case."

She snorted. "You mean, when you've been slaving away on the Pauline case."

I gasped. "Veronica, you know Corinne hired me to investigate the thefts at the bank."

"And I also know you've seized on that as an excuse to investigate the personal life of your romantic rival."

"Wait," I said, screeching to a halt in my skirt. "So, now you think that Pauline really is my competition?"

"Gah! You see?" she marveled. "In the middle of an argument, your insecurity about Pauline rears its ugly head. It's like you're obsessed with her or something."

"That's not true." *Somewhat preoccupied, maybe, but not obsessed.*

"If you're not going to be honest about this, Franki, then I don't see how we can work through it."

I was stunned by that last remark. Was Veronica talking about our friendship or work or both?

As I stormed down the street searching for the right thing to say, the door of K-Paul's Louisiana Kitchen swung closed and caught the back of my dress. I turned to free my skirt and saw Bradley sitting at a table. I couldn't make out who he was with, but I could see that he was gazing at his companion from beneath his brow. And he had a playful smile on his lips that I recognized all too well. I hurried to a window and peered inside. He was dining with Pauline.

I clenched my jaw, my fists, and anything else that would clench. *Working "twenty-four seven" at the bank, eh? "Can't just leave"' you say?*

"Veronica, something's come up," I said, fuming like a downed ship. "I need to let you go."

"Hold on," she ordered. "I know that voice. What happened?"

Against my better judgment, I decided to tell her. I mean, Veronica is my best friend, right? I took a deep breath. "I'm at K-Paul's, and Bradley is here having dinner with Pauline."

She let out an incredulous laugh. "You're kidding me, right? I'm trying to talk to you about your problem with Pauline, and you tell me you've got to go because of Pauline."

I tried to put my hand on my hip, but I couldn't find it because of my skirt. I settled for my waist. "Do I need to remind you that I have a responsibility toward my client to investigate this situation?"

"Of course not," she replied, her voice dripping with sarcasm. "Because what Bradley is eating and who he's eating it with are completely relevant to Corinne's missing money."

"That was a low blow, Veronica," I said as I glanced into the window and saw Bradley hand the check to the waiter.

"You're right. I'm sorry. But I'd like you to remember that while you're working your two cases, I'm juggling six."

"Oh, so are you implying that I'm lazy now? Because if you are, then I'd like *you* to remember that I'm working seven days a week."

She sighed. "I wasn't implying anything. All I was trying to say is that I'm drowning in work, and I could use a little understanding and support from you too."

"Okay, okay," I said. "We'll talk about this later. I really have to go."

I closed the call and shoved my phone into my bodice. I felt bad cutting Veronica off like that, but I had a full-fledged crisis on my hands, and I needed to concentrate.

I zoomed in on Bradley and Pauline's table, looking for clues that this dinner was strictly business. There was nothing to indicate otherwise, unless you counted the candles, the empty bottle of Dom Perignon, and the crème brûlée they were sharing.

Bradley raised a spoonful of the creamy mixture to Pauline's lips, and she licked the spoon with her tongue.

I stood back and blinked hard, just in case the absinthe had caused me to hallucinate that little scene.

"Hey, can I bum a cigarette?" a guy standing next to me asked.

When I turned and saw that he was wearing a swamp creature costume for Shore Leave, I knew I hadn't hallucinated Bradley's romantic gesture. This was just an average day in New Orleans. "Sorry, I don't smoke," I replied. Then I gave Pauline a hard stare. *At least not inanimate objects.*

I began pacing in a circle—I couldn't go back and forth because my dress would get ahead of me. I only had a few minutes to decide whether to confront them or leave. But that only took a second since I'm hardly the go-quietly type. The real issue was *how* to confront them. Let them see my pain and hurt? Or inflict pain and hurt on them?

"Blimey! Who do we have here?" the exact voice of *Spongebob's* Patchy the Pirate exclaimed. He pointed his fake hook hand at the hole in my skirt. "Little Bo-Peep?"

Arrgh! Not another perverted pirate, I thought. "Well, you got the 'peep' part right, Patchy. Now beat it."

"Come again?" he asked, dropping the pirate parley.

"You heard me—scram, *smamma*, as they say in Italy. Or I'll sick my dress on you." I tugged just enough on the cord to raise the dress by a foot.

He looked at me like I was the swamp creature and split.

I turned back to the window and saw Bradley place his hand on Pauline's bare back as he pulled out her chair. *The inflict-pain-and-hurt option it is*, I muttered.

Bradley, oblivious to my presence, opened the restaurant door for Pauline as she made a triumphant exit.

She took one look at me and burst out laughing.

Bradley stepped away from the door and stopped dead in his tracks. I wasn't sure whether it was from the shock of seeing me or my dress.

"I've always questioned your taste in clothing, Franki," Pauline sneered. "But super-sized Shirley Temple? Really?"

Ignoring her taunt, I searched Bradley's face for a reaction. I saw nothing but surprise.

"What are you doing here?" he asked, still frozen in place.

"Actually, that's what I was going to ask you," I said, my voice barely above a whisper. "I thought you had to work all weekend long."

"We *are* working," he insisted. "Pauline and I were just taking a break from the office."

I glanced at Pauline, who was staring stone-faced at Bradley. Apparently, she didn't view their dinner as a break from the office but rather as a break from me. "Some break," I said, "especially considering that you couldn't even spare fifteen minutes for me."

Bradley held out his hand. "Look, Franki—"

"I wonder," I interrupted, putting my hand to my cheek in mock reflection, "were the two of you discussing business when you spoon fed each other that crème brûlée?"

He looked at me with a blank stare. "Can I call you later so we can talk?"

Pauline shot daggers at Bradley and crossed her arms. "What are you waiting for?" she hissed. "Tell her!"

"Tell me what?" I asked, looking from Pauline to Bradley. Although I had a feeling I already knew the answer.

Bradley opened his mouth to speak, but nothing came out.

"For crying out loud!" Pauline exclaimed, turning to face me. "You might as well know. I mean, it had to come out sooner or later." She put her hands on her hips. "Bradley and I have feelings for one another."

Bradley stood as still as a statue.

"Is that true, Bradley?" I asked softly. "Do you have feelings for her?"

He exhaled a long, slow breath and looked at the ground. "Yes."

I felt like a cannon ball had just been fired through my stomach, and I wanted to drop to my knees from the pain. But I stood firm. "And this is how I find out?" I demanded, my voice no longer anything even approaching soft. "You didn't have the decency to tell me in private?"

A couple stepped out of the restaurant and briefly looked at us before walking away.

"Oh, stop your sniveling," Pauline snapped. "You're causing a scene."

"Pauline," Bradley intervened, putting a hand on her arm.

She shrugged him off. "From the moment I met you, you've done nothing but drag Bradley down with your jealous antics—spying on him, breaking into his bank."

When she put it that way, even I had to admit that I sounded like a less-than-ideal girlfriend.

"It's time for you to face it," she continued, getting right in my face. "A man in his position needs to be with a woman of class and distinction, and not with—"

"That's enough, Pauline," Bradley interrupted, grabbing her roughly by both arms. "It's time to go."

"No, let her finish," I said with surprising calm. My eyes narrowed. "Go on, Pauline. And not with what?"

She sneered. "And not with a trashy Texan guidette like you."

The definition of *guidette* flashed before my eyes: n. (derived from 'Guido') *A loud, promiscuous, overly made up Italian-American party girl from the North with a fake tan, a fake rack, and an all-too-real nose.* And that's when I finally pulled the cord.

* * *

I dragged myself out of Jean Lafitte's and leaned against the wall. Glenda was nowhere to be found, and I was sorely tempted to drive home—to Houston, that is. Bradley and I were over, Veronica and I were on the outs, and my cases were at a standstill. Suddenly, living and working in New Orleans didn't seem like such a good idea anymore. But I knew what my mom would say to me if I showed up on her doorstep. "Francesca Lucia Amato, I did not raise you to be a quitter."

I sighed and dialed Glenda's number. As I waited for her to answer, I watched a parade float, designed to look like The Black Pearl, making its way down Bourbon Street.

"Ahoy thar, Miss Franki!" Glenda called.

I squinted at the float and saw her. She was standing up top in the crow's nest waving a spyglass.

"Wanna party on the poop deck?" she shouted.

I considered the prospect of going back to my apartment and spending the evening sulking about Bradley while being stalked by a killer. It didn't sound at all appealing.

I walked over to the massive float.

"Need a lift, lassie?" a pirate with a fake peg leg asked as he clung to a rope, extending his hand. "Long John Silver, at your service."

Why not? I thought as I let Long John lift me onto the ship. For tonight, at least, it was a pirate's life for me.

CHAPTER NINETEEN

My eyes popped open. It was dark, and I wasn't in my bed. I was curled up in a fetal position inside a cramped space, and I felt like I'd been hit over the head. I held out my hand and touched the cool, slick side of my enclosure with a rising sense of panic. *Had the killer knocked me out and dumped me in his bathtub?*

No, wait. There was something furry beneath me, and the ceiling was way too close to my face. I sat up and looked around. And then I held out my arms for balance. I was inside Glenda's giant champagne glass.

It was bad enough to wake up with a hangover, but waking up in a glass was a new low.

I massaged my temples as the events of the previous night came flooding back to me. After weighing anchor with Glenda's merry band of men, we went to John Lafitte's Blacksmith Shop where I followed up my green fairy with a purple voodoo, courtesy of the swamp creature. Then I discovered that when you mix green and purple you get brown, so Glenda and the pirates took me home—by car, not by ship. When I drunkenly babbled that I was afraid to go inside because a killer was after me, Glenda hid me in her champagne glass while the pirates raided my apartment for my necessities— pajamas, a toothbrush, a jar of Nutella, and Napoleon.

Napoleon! I peered over the edge of the glass.

He was staring up at me with narrowed eyes. Clearly he hadn't enjoyed his stay in the pirate den.

"I'll be right down, boy," I fibbed. I didn't know how I'd gotten into the glass, much less how I was going to get out. And I didn't want to disturb Glenda, because if I recalled correctly, she had a gentleman pirate caller—or two. Best to let sleeping sea dogs lie.

Realizing that the only way to get out of the glass was to jump, I stood up with the precision of a surfer on a surfboard and threw myself onto a pile of pillows below. When I landed, the whole house shook. And then it kept shaking. I was well aware that I was no petite flower, but this was just insulting.

"Bury your treasure deeper, Quartermaster!" Glenda shouted from her boudoir.

Oh, I thought wryly. *So that's the cause of the quake.*

I scooped up my belongings and dashed downstairs with Napoleon. I cautiously entered the apartment, and we checked each room—me with my Ruger, Napoleon with his food bowl.

"All clear," I said, removing the bowl from his mouth. "Let's get some grub."

I grabbed my laptop from the living room and headed for the kitchen where I was relieved to discover that it was only eight a.m. I needed time to pull myself together before facing Veronica at the office.

I fed Napoleon and then looked in the pantry. I was craving Cap'n Crunch but had to settle for cold pizza from the fridge. As I chewed my pepperoni and sausage slice, I wondered whether Pauline had been right about me being a guidette. In less than twenty-four hours, I'd gotten into a cat fight (or, at least my dress had), partied with pirates, and woken up in a champagne glass. And now I was eating Italian food for breakfast.

"Better a guidette than a thief," I muttered as I opened my computer. I checked my LinkedIn page, but none of the Brehman Bank managers had responded to my InMail. Of course, it was just after nine in New York, but I couldn't wait any longer. Pauline had already stolen Bradley—I would be damned if I was going to let her steal more money from Corinne.

I went to the bank's home page and dialed the main number, setting the call to speaker.

"Brehman Bank," a youthful-sounding male answered. "How may I direct your call?"

Reading the first name from the LinkedIn list, I replied, "Steve MacDonell, please."

"One moment."

I picked at my purple nail polish as I waited for Mr. MacDonell's secretary to answer.

"This is Steve," a tired voice replied.

I wasn't prepared to get him on the first try. "Uh, my name is Franki Amato."

"How can I help you, Ms. Amato?"

Now what? For lack of a better plan, I went with honesty. "I'm calling about a woman who used to work for your bank. Her name is Pauline Violette."

There was silence on the other end of the line, which told me that he recognized the name.

"If this is regarding a reference check," he began in a stiff tone, "you'll have to contact our Human Resources department."

"It has nothing to do with a reference," I said. "I'm a private investigator, and I've been contracted to look into whether she's embezzling money from a bank in Louisiana."

He snorted. "I can't—"

"She may be stealing from a charity for children," I interrupted. "So if you know anything that could help—"

"Good day, Ms. Amato."

The line went dead.

"*Mannaggia,*" I cursed. *"Damn" indeed.* I was sure he knew something about Pauline, and now I was going to have to call all the managers on LinkedIn.

I decided to target the women first since they might be more empathetic to a case involving theft from children. As I was scanning the list, my phone rang. I didn't recognize the number, but I knew the 212 area code was from New York. "Hello?"

"Franki, this is Steve MacDonell," he said in a low voice. "I'm calling from my personal cell. I could lose my job for this, so I need to make it quick."

My stomach was in knots. "I'm listening."

"The woman you mentioned, Pauline Violette? Well, her full name is Pauline Violette Malaspina, and she was terminated in December of 2012."

I was stunned. That explained why she had a nonna and why she'd been such a pain in my behind—her last name was Italian for *bad thorn*. "Why was she fired?"

"She was the assistant of a manager who's serving time for embezzling from a charity our bank was representing. She was in on his scheme, but she got total immunity in exchange for information. I can't tell you any more."

"I really appreciate you sticking your neck out to help me."

"Yeah, well, I've got kids, so it's the least I could do," he grumbled. "Don't call again, though."

"I won't," I said. But he'd already hung up.

So, I was right. Pauline had a past and probably a present. Of course, embezzling from a Brehman Bank charity didn't prove that she was stealing from Corinne, but it sure made her a suspect. It also raised serious concerns about her involvement in the Shoot for the Moon charity event. The only problem was that I didn't know what to do with the information. I couldn't go to the police because I didn't have any evidence against her. The main person this news would be of interest to would be the president of Ponchartrain Bank. One Bradley Hartmann. But chances weren't good that he'd listen to me, not now that he was Pauline's prey. Nevertheless, I had to tell him. Somehow.

* * *

As I climbed the stairs to Private Chicks an hour and a half later, I felt like I had a marching band in my head and a majorette in my stomach. The four aspirin I'd taken had done nothing for my hangover, and I was nervous about facing Veronica after our fight. I knew she'd be upset that I'd cut her off on the phone, so I had no idea what she'd do when I asked her for advice on how to handle the latest Pauline bombshell.

I entered the lobby and stopped short.

Veronica was sitting on the couch across from an elegant older male with a full head of gray hair and an expensive-looking black suit. She rose to her feet. "Franki Amato, this is Dr. Liam Jones, Ivanna's father.

My stomach felt like the majorette had just dropped her baton. "Pleased to meet you." I reached over the coffee table to shake his hand as he rose. "I guess Dr. Geyer told you we wanted to talk to you?"

"No, that was Mrs. Dupré," he replied, settling back in his seat. "I went to the plantation yesterday to speak with her and see the crime scene."

I noticed that he avoided referring to the plantation as the site of Ivanna's death. And despite his serene demeanor, the sadness in his deep blue eyes told me that he was grieving.

Veronica cleared her throat. "Liam was just saying that the police have given him permission to bury Ivanna."

I was so surprised to find him at the office that I'd forgotten my manners. "I'm sorry for your loss. You must have been so proud of your daughter. She was obviously a smart, successful, and beautiful woman."

He smiled. "I like to think that she got her mother's good looks and my head for business," he said. Then he looked down at his hands. "Unfortunately, it wasn't enough for her."

I cocked my head. "What do you mean?"

"Ivanna lost her mother, Rosa, when she was sixteen. And she was never the same after that."

"That's terrible," Veronica said. "How did Rosa die?"

"Heart failure," he replied in a quiet tone. "But Ivanna was convinced that she'd died of a broken heart, and she blamed me."

Veronica and I remained silent.

He sighed. "You see, because of the nature of my work I was away for long periods. And I worked very closely with another doctor. A woman," he stressed as his neck flushed from embarrassment. "Rosa found out about us. She didn't want a divorce because of her Catholic faith, but she returned to her hometown in Italy and took Ivanna with her. She died a short time later."

His story left a bad taste in my mouth. And I couldn't help but wonder whether this woman had seduced him like Pauline had Bradley.

Veronica glanced at me, no doubt sensing my discomfort. "Where was Rosa from?"

"Treviso, in the Veneto region."

The same region my mother is from, I thought. "How did Ivanna change after Rosa died?"

"I was getting to that." He grimaced. "Her opinion of me and all men, I'm afraid, changed."

Understandable, I almost said under my breath.

"From that point on, men were just a means to an end for Ivanna. And I played along by trying to buy back her affection. So when she approached me about starting her cosmetics company, I was all too happy to fund it. She'd always been obsessed with makeup." He looked down and laughed. "When she was a little girl, she used to crush up berries and flowers from our yard and make her own. Rosa and I were afraid she was going to poison herself."

A heavy silence fell over the room.

"Do you think she did?" Veronica ventured. "Poison herself, I mean?"

"Impossible," he said with a wave of his hand. "I don't know how the belladonna got into her system, but I can assure you she wasn't responsible. Ivanna loved life, and she knew all about the potential hazards of cosmetics. She wouldn't have poisoned herself on purpose or by accident."

"But there was oleander in the lip gloss she was holding," I said. "So, either she was making poison lip gloss or someone gave it to her."

"I don't know anything about that lip gloss," he said. "But I know it wasn't the reason she was at Oleander Place."

I glanced at Veronica. "Go on."

He closed his eyes and squeezed the bridge of his nose. "As I said, she changed after her mother's death, but it wasn't just in her attitude about men." His eyes opened. "She also became more focused, driven. But not for the right reasons. She was determined to right past wrongs, particularly those that pertained to her mother. And as far as she was concerned, Oleander Place had wronged Rosa."

I leaned forward in my seat. "What did her mother have to do with the plantation?"

"Well, Rosa must have sensed her health was failing, because right before she died she started telling Ivanna her family history. And, she told her that she was a descendent of Danielle Benazet."

Veronica wrinkled her brow. "I'm sorry, but I don't recognize the name."

"Right, forgive me," he said, holding up his hand. "Benazet was Danielle's married name. Her maiden name was Lacour, and she was Evangeline Lacour's paternal aunt."

The silence was so thick that you could have heard a pink diamond drop.

"So, she *was* looking for the diamond," I said.

He nodded. "I'm sure of it. She would've wanted to find the diamond to honor her mother's memory. Apparently, Rosa had written to Mrs. Dupré some years before, asserting a claim to the diamond if it were ever found."

I flashed back to my conversation with Kristy Patterson about Delta's protectiveness of her plantation. "How did Delta respond?"

"She didn't. When I spoke to her about it yesterday, she said she'd never received the letter."

A convenient excuse, I thought. "Then, Delta didn't know that Ivanna was related to Evangeline?"

"She said she had no idea."

I had my doubts about that. Delta was too shrewd not to suspect a link between Evangeline and a modern-day look-alike who was poking around her plantation.

Liam rubbed his forehead and rose to stand. "Please don't think I'm being rude, but it was a long, difficult trip, and I still have to make arrangements for Ivanna's burial."

"Of course," Veronica said as she escorted him to the door.

He handed her his card. "If you have more questions, please call. I'm so grateful for your efforts on behalf of my daughter."

"Thank you," Veronica said, putting a hand on his arm. "We'll do everything in our power to find the killer." She closed the door behind him and turned to me. "Can you believe Ivanna is a Lacour?"

"No, and yet it was staring us right in the face." I crossed my arms and kicked my feet up on the coffee table. "How crazy is it that she looked just like Evangeline after who knows how many generations?"

"It's pretty bizarre," Veronica said, sitting on the arm of the couch. "But at least one mystery is solved."

"Yeah, but so many remain."

She patted my shoulder and stood up. "You'll figure it all out. I know it."

"I hope so," I muttered as she headed back to her office. But I wasn't too confident. Because I had the funny feeling that there was something about Liam's conversation that I was missing—some detail, some connection. I just couldn't put my finger on what that was.

* * *

I added the last of Liam's information to the Jones case file and leaned back in my desk chair. I kept thinking about his recollection of a young Ivanna mixing makeup with plants from their yard. If she'd used flowers to produce makeup before, then there was every reason to believe she'd done it again with flowers from Oleander Place.

I quickly formulated a plan and then located Adam Geyer in my phone contact list. I pressed his name and waited.

"Yes," he answered.

He sounded annoyed. And based on our previous phone history, I was surprised he bothered to answer at all. "I met with Ivanna's father today."

"Oh?" His voice oozed sarcasm. "And how is the good doctor?"

I could tell he'd been drinking for a while, and it was only ten thirty in the morning. "As well as can be expected under the circumstances. He did lose his only child."

"I'm well aware of that, thank you," he growled.

I sighed. "Listen, I didn't call to upset you. I have a cosmetics question related to something Dr. Jones said."

"All right," he said warily.

"Would crushed pink oleander flowers turn a clear lip gloss solution pink?"

He paused. "It would turn the color of the flowers, yes."

Time to go in for the kill, I thought. "So, when you made the lip gloss Ivanna was holding, you used crushed flowers from Oleander Place."

"I don't know what you're talking about," he spat.

"Actually, you do," I insisted. "And it would behoove you to tell me where you got those flowers. Because if I tell the police that you got them from Oleander Place, then that puts you at the plantation, and hence, at the scene of the crime."

It was silent on the line except for the sound of his jagged breathing.

"It's time to tell the truth, Adam," I pressed. "It will help you in the long run, trust me."

"Ivanna gave me powdered oleander," he said.

I bowed my head into my hand.

"But I didn't think anything of it. The plan was to use the flowers to produce a prototype. We would have never sold a toxic lip gloss to the public. You have to believe me."

"I do," I said, moved by the desperation in his voice. "I just wish you would've told me this sooner."

"I didn't kill her, Franki." He choked back a sob. "I loved Ivanna, and I'm going to find out who did this to her."

I started to reply, but the line went dead.

I stared at the phone as I tried to sort through my muddled thoughts. This was a side of Adam I hadn't seen before. There was so much conviction in his voice. I wanted to believe him, but he'd lied on so many occasions. I couldn't be sure he was telling the truth now.

"Did I hear you talking to Adam?" Veronica asked, appearing in the doorway. She was balancing her compact mirror and blush in one hand as she stroked her blush brush across her cheek with the other.

"He just admitted that he and Ivanna made the lip gloss with flowers from Oleander Place."

Veronica's head jerked up from her compact. "He did?" she asked as her blush fell to the floor. She knelt down. "Oh, darn it."

I looked at the pile of pink powder on my floor and said, "I'll go get the vacuum." I headed for the door and stopped. "Oh my God. Miles!"

"What about him?" she asked, rising to her feet.

"That day we went to question him," I gushed. "He was vacuuming up pink powder in the sugar mill!"

"So?"

"He told me it was rat poison, but it wasn't. Adam said Ivanna gave him powdered oleander. Don't you see? Miles was in on it! He dried the flowers and ground them into a powder for Ivanna."

Veronica put her hand to her mouth. "Oh, Franki. Are you sure?"

"Yes! It explains why he was so nervous that day, and why he was so upset when I asked whether any of the oleander bushes had been tampered with." I grabbed my phone from my desk and dialed the plantation. "Plus, it fits with Liam's remark that Ivanna used men for her own purposes."

She took a seat in front of my desk. "Are you calling him now?"

I shook my head. "Delta."

The phone went to voice mail, but I hung up and tried again. I certainly couldn't leave this kind of information in a message.

"Oleander Place," Delta answered.

"Delta, this is Franki," I replied. "I just figured out that Miles knew Ivanna."

"We just figured that out too," she snapped.

Something was wrong—I could feel it. I collapsed into my desk chair. "You knew he was helping her make that lip gloss?"

"All I know is that this morning Troy found Miles inside one of the sugar cane kettles." She paused. "He's been murdered."

CHAPTER TWENTY

———

Hoping to stay below Delta's radar, I drove past the plantation and parked at the swamp. The second I got out of the car, the sight and smell of the fetid water brought me back to that fateful day with Bradley and Pauline. *If I'd known then what I know now*, I thought, kicking my car door closed, *I might've let those gators gobble them up.*

I still couldn't believe Bradley had left me for Pauline. It seemed so out of character for him, and yet I'd seen them together with my own two eyes. He was a lying cheat like all the other men I'd dated, a true *truffatore*.

I shook my head in an attempt to force him from my thoughts. Now wasn't the time to lament another lousy love. I had to keep my mind on the Jones case. My life literally depended on it.

As I made my way along the shore to Oleander Place, I almost wished a gator would pull a Jaws and swallow *me* whole. At least then I could be sure that I wouldn't run into Delta. Because, at this point, I figured she was either going to fire me or kill me. And the latter option seemed particularly likely given that the suspects in the Jones case were dropping like characters in an Agatha Christie novel—specifically, *And Then There Were None*.

All jokes aside, my gut told me that Delta was more than capable of murder. But I didn't think she was the killer. Oleander Place wasn't just her livelihood, it was her legacy, and she'd demonstrated in more ways than one that she was fiercely proud and protective of it. Even if her business was in trouble, I couldn't imagine her sullying the name of her beloved plantation—not on purpose, anyway. Besides, if she'd known who Ivanna was and what she was after, she would've slapped a restraining order on her like she'd done to Kristy Patterson and her father. Problem solved.

No, Delta didn't fit the profile, but Adam was a different story. He had a motive to kill. According to Ruth, he was an alcoholic on the edge who'd worshipped Ivanna, and she'd repaid his devotion by threatening to ruin him. Then she turned to a plantation groundskeeper for help making her lip gloss. So, Adam could have viewed Miles as a threat to his job or even his relationship with Ivanna and killed them both for their betrayal.

Another possible scenario was that Adam murdered Miles, believing him to be responsible for Ivanna's death. After all, he *had* vowed to find the person responsible for her murder.

But Scarlett? As hard as I tried, I couldn't come up with a reason for Adam or Miles to kill her. Yet I knew her horrific hanging had everything to do with whatever it was she'd warned me I was "messing with."

As I crept along behind the hedge separating the border of the property from the swamp, I wondered for the thousandth time just what the hell I'd gotten myself into. And I wished Veronica were here with me, helping me get to the bottom of these awful crimes. When this was all over, I intended to talk to her about the way we work our cases—that is, if the killer didn't do me in first.

Halfway down the hedge, I arrived at the back of the slave quarters. I assumed that the police were keeping Troy there or at the big mill where he'd found Miles' body. I dashed to the command post window and peered inside. Troy was sitting at the table with a blanket around his shoulders. His face looked ashen, like a man who'd just seen a ghost. Or a corpse.

An officer passed by the window, so I ducked down. I heard him say something to Troy, and then he exited the building.

I waited until I saw the officer enter the house and then slipped inside the command post. "Troy! Are you okay?"

He blinked a few times as though struggling to recognize me. "I guess."

I glanced back toward the door. "Listen, where's Delta?"

"She's with Officer Quincy in her office." His voice was monotone, like he'd been sedated.

Hopefully they stay there, I thought. I had neither the time nor the inclination to get thrown in jail by Officer Quincy. "Good. I was hoping to talk to you alone. I'm trying to make sense of what happened to Miles."

Troy met my gaze, and his blue eyes looked as though their usual sparkle had been extinguished. "I got a call from Delta Sunday morning. She was in a panic because Miles hadn't shown up for the photo shoot, so she asked me to sub for him."

"I take it he never came."

He shook his head. "But during the shoot, I found his car parked behind the big mill. Delta was worried that he might be injured somewhere on the grounds, so we started searching."

"Whose idea was it to look in the kettles?" I asked. It was well known in police circles that the person who found the body was often the prime suspect.

"No one's." His speech had dropped to almost a whisper. "After we'd looked everywhere we could think of, we were on the back porch trying to figure out what to do next when we saw Delta's dogs circling the *grande* kettle."

Like little vultures moving in for the kill, I thought.

"So I offered to go take a look," Troy continued. "He was hit over the head with a cane syrup ladle, maybe more than once." He swallowed and averted his eyes. "The ladle was in the kettle with him, covered in blood."

I grimaced and put my hand on his forearm. "Who do you think is behind these murders?"

He stared at his coffee. His face was as blank as the plain white mug he held between his trembling hands. "When I was little, my *ya-ya* told me that the three Fates determined life and death. Clotho spun the thread of life on her spindle, Lachesis measured its length, and Atropos cut it short with her horrible shears."

Now was clearly not the time to press Troy for details. He was in shock. "You've been through a traumatic event. Have you thought about seeing a doctor?"

"I can't." He placed his mug on the table, taking care to center it on the coaster. "I have to help Delta tomorrow."

I recoiled at his comment. "You're going to keep working here after everything that's happened?"

"I couldn't even if I wanted to. Delta's closing Oleander Place tomorrow."

Now that was news. "Permanently?"

"Until they catch the killer," he replied.

That was a good plan. If she'd shut down the plantation earlier, Scarlett and Miles might still be alive. "Are you planning to come back to work when it reopens?"

He looked away. "It's a great job for a grad student."

It was hard for me to believe that anyone would describe working for Delta as *great*, but I kept my feelings to myself. "I guess you have to do what you think is best," I said, rising to my feet. "Anyway, I need to get going before Officer Quincy catches me here. Take care, Troy. And be careful."

I dashed from the room.

"Franki?" he called.

I ran back to the doorway, and I was struck by the intensity in his eyes.

"Stay away from Oleander Place," he said in his strange, flat tone. "It's not safe."

The understatement of the century, I thought as I darted for cover in the hedge.

* * *

I walked across the street to Thibodeaux's, shielding my eyes from the cemetery. I'd had enough death for one day. I pushed open the door and saw Veronica and Glenda sitting at the bar and watching the evening news on a flat screen TV.

"Hey." I tossed my bag on the barstool next to Veronica and began digging for my wallet. Despite a persistent hangover, I was ready for happy hour.

"I ordered you an absinthe," Veronica said.

My head shot up.

She pressed her fingers to her lips, repressing a smile. "Glenda told me about your escapades at Shore Leave, so I thought I'd order you a cocktail worthy of a corsair."

I sealed my lips tight. I wasn't going to say a word in case there was something about last night I didn't know and didn't want everyone at the tavern to know either.

Phillip approached and placed a fluted glass on the bar napkin in front of me. "Here's your Prosecco."

I smirked at Veronica and slid onto my stool.

Glenda lowered her metallic gold bifocals, which matched her one-legged catsuit to a T. "Miss Ronnie hornswaggled you, sugar."

I took a long sip of my drink. "If the two of you don't mind, I'd like to put my pirating days behind me. Besides, I'm not really in the mood for jokes."

The smile faded from Veronica's lips. "We know you're taking this case really hard, Franki. We were only trying to cheer you up."

"That's nice of you, but I'm past that point." I looked at Glenda. "I suppose you told her about Bradley and Pauline too?"

Glenda tossed back a shot of tequila. "Just the lowlights, sugar."

Veronica put her hand on mine. "I'm so sorry this happened."

I sighed. "Honestly, with all the murders and the death threat, my relationship with Bradley doesn't seem that important right now."

Veronica nodded and tucked her hair behind her ear. "What did you find out at the plantation?"

I crossed my elbows on the bar. "Basically, that I'm a failure as a PI."

Glenda slammed her second shot glass onto the bar. "Now why in heaven's name would you think that?"

"Because my suspects are dropping like flies, and I don't have a clue who's killing them," I replied, waving my arms like an orchestra conductor.

Veronica gave a frustrated flip of her hair. "Franki, you were a cop, so you of all people should know that there are countless homicide cases that even the best detectives can't solve."

"Take me, for example," Glenda said. "Back in the day, I was the hottest strip act in the South, and I do mean hot." She put a finger to her lone, nude butt cheek and made a sizzling sound. "And yet I can't whip a bunch of newbie dancers into shape."

"What do you mean?" I asked, failing to see the connection between me, her behind, and her stripper students.

"After almost two weeks, my boot camp is still nothing but a booty camp. Thanks to rap music, girls these days think the only thing to stripping is butt work, and the ones I'm training can't even do that well. Yesterday one of them was supposed to twerk, but she booty popped instead."

"So?" I was more bewildered than before. "What difference does it make?"

Glenda pointed a gold-gloved finger at me. "I'll tell you what difference it makes. The popper knocked her unsuspecting partner off the damn stage and dislocated the girl's shoulder."

"That's a serious mistake," Veronica said, her eyes wide.

"You're telling me." Glenda shook her head. "Try as I might, I do *not* understand why we can't attract quality girls to the stripping profession."

Try as *I* might, I couldn't understand what Glenda's booty-camp misadventures had to do with my misinvestigation. But I appreciated that she was trying to help.

Veronica patted my thigh. "You see? Sometimes even the best in the business have no control over a situation."

"I guess," I replied, grabbing my glass. "But I feel like there's something I'm missing. Like if I had this one piece of information, the puzzle would be complete." I took a sip of my Prosecco and watched as Phillip put whipped cream on a strawberry daiquiri. "And I still want to know what flavor of alcohol is pink."

Glenda looked at my glass. "The nectar of the Gods comes in pink."

"Ambrosia?" I asked, confused.

"*Champagne*, sugar," she replied in a bite-your-tongue tone. "Your Prosecco comes in pink too."

I felt a jolt go through my body. Ivanna's mother, Rosa, was from the region where Prosecco was made, and her name was Italian for "pink." And now that I thought about it, the Lacour diamond was alleged to be the very same shade as the Prosecco—coral pink. That's why Ivanna was so obsessed with getting the color of the lip gloss just right! It wasn't just her perfectionism at play—it was her desire to memorialize her mother.

I hopped off my barstool and grabbed my phone. "Glenda, you might've just solved one of the mysteries of this case. I'll be right back."

"Where are you going?" Veronica asked, her brows knitted in concern.

"Outside to call Ivanna's father. I can't hear over the TV." I rushed out the door and held my breath as I dialed the number.

"Hello?" Liam's tone was pleasant but tinged with sadness.

"This is Franki Amato," I said. "Do you have a moment to talk?"

"Yes," he replied. "How can I help you?"

I sat on the curb, resting my elbows on my knees. "I've been thinking about the lip gloss Ivanna was holding, and I was wondering if you knew whether Rosa liked pink Prosecco."

"It was her favorite drink," he replied with a note of surprise in his voice. "It's made in the town of Monteforte d'Alpone where she grew up."

I was so excited I did a fist pump. "Did Ivanna know that?"

"Oh, yes. From the time she was eight or nine years old, Rosa would let her have a small glass—mixed with water, of course. You know how Europeans are about alcohol." He chuckled. "Ivanna would complain every time Rosa added the water."

"Because it diluted the alcohol?" I mean, I would have been disappointed too.

"Because it changed the color," he replied. "Ivanna was always particular about her colors."

Indeed she was, I thought. *So much so that she was willing to use poisonous oleander flowers to get the right shade for her lip gloss.* "Liam, I think that lip gloss was for Rosa. I can't prove it, but I'd be willing to bet that Ivanna was planning to call it 'Prosecco Pink.'"

"That sounds like a product she would've had in her line," he said. "And I know she wanted to honor her mother."

"I'm sure she would have, too, if she'd had the chance."

Liam was silent for a moment. "Do you have any news about the death of the groundskeeper?"

I sighed. "Not yet. But you'll be the first person I call when I do."

"I would appreciate that. And thank you for telling me about the lip gloss. It's good to have at least one answer in this case."

"I couldn't agree more. Bye now."

I closed the call and immediately thought of Chandra. The day I met her, she said that the ghost who'd gotten me in this mess had done something bad, and it involved a relative. If Chandra was for real, then that spirit was Ivanna, not Evangeline. Did that mean Ivanna was the spirit pulling the handle of the French door? If so, why? Was she in danger and trying to get out? Or was there some other reason?

"Pff!" I exclaimed as I stood up. The ghost angle was too absurd to even think about. I brushed off the seat of my jeans and went back inside Thibodeaux's.

Glenda and Veronica were again fixated on the TV. But so was everyone else in the bar.

I slid onto my barstool and gazed at the screen. "What's going on?"

Veronica's mouth was set in a grim line. "Adam was arrested for the murders a little while ago."

I felt like I'd turned to stone. But on the inside, emotions were coursing through my body like liquid fire. Sadness, guilt, and relief flooded through me at the same time. Yet for some reason, I was anxious too. I could tell that Veronica was waiting for me to react, so I blurted out, "Then the case is solved."

"It looks that way." She put her hand on my back. "Franki, an entire police team was working the case, but there was only one of you. So, don't beat yourself up about this. Okay?"

"Yeah, just look at the positive side," Glenda said, jumping off her barstool. "You don't need pirate protection anymore."

"Right!" Veronica nodded with way too much enthusiasm.

"But now that I think about it, sugar," Glenda added, pulling her catsuit out of her crotch, "that's the *negative* side." She cackled and slapped her bare leg.

I said nothing and turned my attention to the news coverage. As I watched a ragged-looking Adam being lead into the police station in handcuffs, I felt a growing sense of apprehension. I'd suspected him of the killings as recently as this morning, and yet his arrest didn't sit right with me.

My phone began to vibrate in my hand, startling me from my stupor. Ruth Walker's name was on the display.

I stood up and headed for the door. "This is Franki."

"I thought you'd have called me by now," she barked.

"I just saw the news a few seconds ago," I protested as I exited the bar. I don't know why Ruth persisted in thinking that I should report to her.

"Well, I, for one, am not buying this arrest nonsense."

I stopped short. "What? You were so sure that Adam was involved in Ivanna's murder."

"Yes, but the police are saying that he had belladonna at the lab. And that's utter hogwash."

"How can you be sure? Adam *is* a chemist."

"Because I drove by Lickalicious Lips this morning and found Ivanna's father there. He was kind enough to let me help myself to anything in the office since he's shutting down the business. So, I went through the place with a fine-tooth comb, and there was no poison there."

Although I was quite sure that Ruth had impeccable strip-the-office-clean skills, I had my doubts about the absence of the poison. "Maybe he hid it in the ceiling or something."

She snorted. "Trust me, I know all the places the man stashed his liquor, and they were empty."

This from a woman who claimed not to drink.

"Now I know I said he was capable of killing Ivanna," she continued, "but something is rotten in the state of Denmark."

"Are you suggesting that the police planted the belladonna?"

There was a pause, and I heard what sounded like the tinkling of ice in a rocks glass followed by a loud slurping sound.

"Not necessarily," she replied a bit out of breath.

"Then who do you think did?"

Ruth harrumphed. "That's your problem."

"Thanks," I said under my breath.

"You're welcome," she was quick to reply. "I'll thank *you* the day you find the killer," she added, crunching an ice cube. "I'm on pins and needles here wondering if I'm his next victim."

"I know the feeling," I muttered. "But now that there's been an arrest in the case, my client's going to terminate my contract."

"Then you'll have to go it alone," she said. "I'll talk to you soon."

As I shoved my phone into my back pocket, Ruth's words weighed on my mind. I already felt like I *was* going it alone, but at least I was getting paid. I wondered whether I could afford to continue investigating the case for free, even though I already knew I had no choice. If Adam wasn't guilty, I had to keep looking for the killer—for my own safety and everyone else's.

The real question was whether there was a chance that Adam was guilty. I flashed back to the day Veronica and I had seen him packing the trunk of his Corvette. He was upset, and I was positive he'd been drinking. And while it was certainly possible that he'd left evidence behind, I didn't think it likely. Careless, forgetful types didn't earn PhDs in chemistry.

But if he didn't leave the belladonna in the lab, then who put it there? Delta?

Or was it Dr. Jones?

CHAPTER TWENTY-ONE

———

After what seemed like an eternity, the toaster finally popped. I grabbed the hot waffles with the tips of my fingers and tossed them into a bowl. Yes, a bowl. My plan was to drown my sorrows in waffles drowning in syrup because nothing had turned out like I'd hoped—not the Jones case, not the Pauline case, not my job with Veronica, and certainly not my relationship with Bradley.

"Breakfast is ready!" I called.

Napoleon jumped off the chaise lounge and sped into the kitchen.

I broke off a piece of waffle for him and added a dash of syrup. He was the one constant in my life right now, so he deserved a special treat. I ruffled the fur on his head and handed him the bite. "There you go, boy."

Next, I squeezed a cup or two of syrup onto my waffles and grabbed a spoon. Yes, a spoon. It's the only way to eat waffles swimming in syrup. Then I flopped down at the kitchen table.

As I spooned the waffle-syrup soup into my mouth, I expected the warm gooey sweetness to soothe the ache in my soul. But it didn't. And I knew it had nothing to do with feeling sorry for myself—it was because there was something important I still had to do.

I grabbed my phone and pressed Bradley's number, taking deep breaths between rings. My stomach lurched when I heard him pick up.

"Franki." His voice was soft but practically screamed surprise.

Drawing courage from his docile demeanor, I announced, "This is a business call, so I'd appreciate it if you kept our personal affairs out of this." Oh, and I made sure to stress the word *affairs,* the lousy cheat.

"Listen," he began in a remorseful tone, "if this about me banning you from the bank—"

"It's not," I interrupted. I wished I could tell him that I was working for Corinne. But Bradley wasn't the man I'd thought he was, so I couldn't take the chance that he'd fire her for hiring me.

"Okay." He paused. "What's this about?"

"I can't go into the details of why I have this information, but Pauline omitted her real last name from the résumé she submitted to you, not to mention a bank she worked for in New York."

"How'd you get her resume?" he asked, bewildered.

"That's beside the point," I snapped. "What matters is that Ms. Pauline Violette Malaspina got off scot-free after embezzling from a charity managed by Brehman Bank, and you've put her in charge of a charity for children."

A stony silence ensued.

"Now, I expect you to put your, uh, *feelings* for Pauline aside and look into the probability that she's stealing from your bank. Because if you don't, I'll have to take the evidence I've acquired to the police," I bluffed.

"Franki, what goes on at Ponchartrain Bank is none of your concern," he said through clenched teeth. "Stay out of this."

I was taken aback by his command. "You lost the right to have a say in my life when you hooked up with the embezzler."

He let out a long sigh. "Look, I can't get into the specifics right now, but things aren't what they seem. You've got to trust me on this."

I gave a laugh that was somewhere between incredulous and outraged. "You've got some nerve, Bradley Hartmann."

I hung up and angrily wiped a tear from my cheek. I refused to cry over a bum like that.

My phone rang, and I was positive it was Bradley calling me back. I responded with a resounding, "Go to hell!"

"I'd really rather not," a surprised-sounding male replied.

I gasped. "I'm *so* sorry! I thought you were someone else."

"Well, that's a relief." He chuckled. "The clergy are often unpopular, but that was a little harsh."

Oh God, did I just tell a priest to go to hell? I gulped. "Um, you're with the Church?"

"Yes, my name is Father Roman," he boomed. "I'm a neophyte at Holy Rosary Church."

Did he just say nymphet? I wondered as I nervously scratched my neck and ran down a mental list of the sins I'd committed since the last time I'd set foot in a church. "The name of your church sounds familiar, but I can't place it."

"We're located in downtown Houston."

Now I knew where I'd heard the name before—my mother. "Does this have anything to do with marriage classes, Father?"

"Actually, I've been asked to speak to you about another matter—your plans to cohabitate with your boyfriend?"

"Nonna!" I exclaimed Seinfeld-style.

"Your grandmother's not the only one who's worried about you," he clarified.

"Oh, I'm quite sure my parents are in on this too," I said, squirming with embarrassment.

"And some of the regulars here at the deli," he added. "You have a whole community of people here who love you, Francesca."

I rested my forehead on the kitchen table. From the sound of things, my nonna had told everyone at Amato's Deli that I was planning to shack up in sin. "I appreciate your concern, Father. But I only told my nonna that I was going to live with a man to get her to stop pre-planning my wedding. And the fact is, my boyfriend has started seeing another woman."

"*Madonna santa!*" my nonna exclaimed from out of nowhere.

I bolted from my chair. "Father, is my nonna on this call too?"

"I'm afraid she leaned in to the receiver just now," he replied. "Excuse me for a moment."

He covered the phone with his hand, and then I heard the muffled sounds of his speech and my nonna's shrieks. I was sure he was trying to calm her down from a conniption fit she was having over the news that I was single again.

Father Roman uncovered the receiver. "I'm afraid we have a little misunderstanding here about your living situation."

"What is it?" I asked. But I didn't have to wait for an answer.

"Franki's-a living with-a Bradley and another woman!" my nonna shouted *a squarciagola*, an Italian phrase which is often translated as "at the top of one's lungs" but actually means that someone is screaming so loudly that it's ripping their throat.

"Are you saying Franki's a polygamist, Carmela?" a scandalized-sounding customer asked.

"Well it sure sounds like an episode of *Sister Wives* to me!" another exclaimed.

"But don't you worry, Francesca," Father Roman continued in a harried tone, "I'll set everyone straight."

"Thank you, Father," I whispered. Then I hung up and took a much-needed swig of syrup.

* * *

When I let the door to Private Chicks slam shut behind me, David's head shot up from his desk.

"Whoa!" He wiped drool from the corner of his mouth with his sleeve. "I can't believe I fell asleep."

I smirked. "I guess you're finally coming down from all that game fuel you drank at the vassal's."

Veronica entered the lobby in a smart-looking navy blazer and white skirt. "I was hoping that was you, Franki. Delta is on her way here to settle up what she owes us. Can you give me the total number of hours you've worked?"

"Actually, I wanted to talk to you about that," I said, shoving my sunglasses into my purse. "What time's she coming?"

"Ten o'clock." She looked at her watch. "And it's five till, so you'd better make it quick."

"Okay," I said with a nod. "Will you come with me while I grab a cup of coffee?"

"Sure," she replied as she followed me down the hallway.

When I entered the kitchen, I was thrilled to see a fresh pot of French Press. I pulled my mug from the cabinet and got straight to the point. "Veronica, I don't believe that Adam committed the murders."

She leaned against the counter and crossed her arms. "Well, the police certainly do. Why don't you think he's guilty?"

I grabbed the carafe and poured some coffee into my cup. "Because I know he wouldn't have been stupid enough to leave belladonna in his lab."

She frowned. "That's hardly proof of innocence."

"There's more," I said, pulling my Bailey's Sweet Italian Biscotti Coffee Creamer from the fridge. "Ruth Walker told me that Liam was at Lickalicious Lips right before the police came and searched the premises."

"So?"

"So," I began, pouring a cup of the creamer into my mug, "he could have planted the belladonna on the premises to frame Adam."

"Hold on a second," she said, holding up her hand. "You can't possibly think that a nice man like Liam Jones killed his own daughter."

"His daughter, no. But I can't rule out the others." I said, stirring my cookie-creamer coffee. "Think about it. We don't know for certain that he was out of the country when they were murdered. I mean, we haven't checked the flight records."

"True." She twirled a lock of blonde hair around her finger. "But what motive would he have had to kill Scarlett and Miles?"

I shrugged and took a sip of my coffee. "Maybe he thought they killed Ivanna."

"And then he framed Adam for his crimes?" She tossed the lock of hair over her shoulder. "This is too far-fetched."

"Just hear me out, okay?" I took a seat at the table. "I don't believe that Liam killed anyone either. But I have this nagging feeling that he's behind Adam's arrest. I mean, Adam told us himself that Liam doesn't like him, so much so that he had his secretary tell Adam to clear out before he came to town. Remember?"

She nodded, staring down at her shoes.

"So obviously there's bad blood there, and it has to have something to do with Adam's belligerent relationship with Ivanna."

She pursed her lips. "Apparently, he does have some harsh feelings toward Adam, but that's a far cry from framing him for murder."

"It gives him a motive, though," I said, raising my index finger. "And if Liam thinks that Adam killed Ivanna, he could have planted the belladonna to make sure that he went to prison for the crime."

Veronica pulled out a chair and took a seat. "You know this is all highly speculative. Without any evidence, I can't ask Delta to let you continue investigating the case."

"Yes, you can!" I pressed my hands together in a pleading gesture. "All I need is a few more days."

She shook her head. "Based on my conversation with her this morning, she's convinced that the police have the right person in custody. So as of right now, the case is closed."

The lobby bell sounded before I could say another word.

"That must be Delta," Veronica said as she stood up and adjusted the white belt around her blazer. "I'm sorry, Franki."

I hung my head as she headed for the lobby. I was disappointed, but I understood her point. She couldn't ask clients to pay us without proof.

David popped his head into the doorway. "Uh, mind if I hide out in your office?"

"Be my guest." I was tempted to hide out with him and avoid the inevitable dressing-down from Delta, but I knew that Veronica expected me to be professional, regardless of how unprofessional the client. I took a gulp from my mug, fervently wishing that the Baileys' creamer line wasn't non-alcoholic. Then I dragged myself down the hallway to my doom.

Despite the fact that it was seventy-five degrees outside, Delta was sitting on the couch in a full-length red fox coat. She tore a check from her checkbook and handed it to Veronica. "This should more than cover Ms. Amaro's investigative *efforts*."

I suppressed a snort—not because of her emphasis on my so-called "efforts," but because of the particular way she butchered my last name. *Amaro* was Italian for "bitter," and I was definitely that.

"Hello, Delta," I said as I made my entrance.

She sniffed and looked down her nose. "Nice of you to say hello considering that you couldn't be bothered when you came to the plantation yesterday. But then I guess you had investigating to do, what with a third murder and all."

"Now, Delta," Veronica intervened, "Franki did her best to find the culprit. And don't forget that the police were on the case too."

"Thank goodness they were!" she exclaimed with her hand on her chest. "Otherwise, that belladonna might not have been found, and I could've been next on Adam's list."

I rolled my eyes. She hadn't been at all pleased with the police the day she'd come to Private Chicks looking for a PI. "Actually, I have a few questions about Adam's arrest."

Delta stared at me through half-lidded eyes. "Don't you think it's a little late for questions? The case is solved."

"I'm not so sure," I said as I eased onto the couch across from her.

Delta's eyes widened—then she turned to Veronica. "What's going on here?"

Veronica angled an annoyed glance in my direction. "Well, Franki was just telling me that she thinks the police may have rushed to judgment where Adam is concerned."

"That's preposterous," she declared with a shooing motion of her hand. "The police found the murder weapon in his laboratory."

I leveled a glare at Delta. "Someone could have planted it there."

She clutched her pearls and began to laugh. "My, you're quite the sleuth, aren't you?"

My Italian blood was getting hot, but I couldn't let it reach the boiling point. If I did, it could cost Veronica that check she was holding, and we needed to get paid. "One thing I am is cautious," I replied with a pointed look. "Because I know that if the wrong man is behind bars, someone else could be killed. And since I'm the only one who's received a bona fide death threat in this case, that someone would most likely be me."

Delta sighed. "What do you want to know?"

I repressed a satisfied smile. "Has Adam actually confessed to the murders?"

"He's lawyered up, which says to me he's guilty."

"It says to me he's smart," I retorted. "Especially if he's being set up, which brings me to my next question. Do you know where, exactly, the police found the belladonna?"

Delta crossed her arms. "I'm not privy to that information."

I found that hard to believe since she'd been privy to every detail of the case until now. She was either really eager to see an end to this case, or she was hiding something. "Did they ever determine how the belladonna got in Ivanna's system?"

"No idea," she said with a shrug. "Maybe the killer made her drink it or put it in her eyes or something."

"Put it in her eyes?" I repeated. That was an awfully specific answer from someone who claimed to have no inside knowledge of the manner of death. "Why would you say that?"

"I must've read it somewhere," she said, grabbing the handle of her Louis Vuitton. "Now, are you almost through? Because I have an appointment with a public relations firm in less than an hour."

I glanced at Veronica, who was willing me to put a lid on it with her eyes. "Just one more question," I replied, since I'd never been good at keeping my mouth shut, not even when explicitly asked to do so. "Were you aware that Ivanna was descended from the Lacour family?"

She narrowed her eyes and fingered her Baron Samedi brooch. "Like I said to her father," she began in a soft but defiant tone, "I didn't have the faintest idea."

I could tell that I'd upset her, and I didn't think it was because I'd offended her Southern honor.

"If you don't mind, I'll be on my way." Delta rose to her feet. "I've got a company to rebuild."

"Thank you for so much doing business with us," Veronica said, following her to the door.

Delta grasped the doorknob and locked eyes with me. "I'd like to say it was a pleasure," she drawled, "but it wasn't."

I leapt off the couch as she exited in a swirl of red fur.

Veronica blocked the doorway, extending her arms to either side of the frame. "No you don't, Franki."

"Just give me one minute in the parking lot with her," I breathed. "That's all I need."

"Sit," she ordered, pointing to the couch. "You know she'd have you arrested if you so much as looked at her the wrong way."

I slunk back to my seat with Veronica running defense behind me. "I'm so sick of her hateful attitude that it would almost be worth a trip to the slammer."

"Well, you don't have to deal with her ever again," she said, hands on hips. "Now why don't you take the rest of the day off? I can handle things around here."

Some time to decompress did sound nice. "Are you sure? I know you need help with your caseload."

"I am." She patted my arm. "Now scram."

I looked up at her. "I'm sorry about the way this case turned out."

"Don't be. There are going to be lots of other cases we can't solve. It's the nature of the business." She smiled. "See you tomorrow."

I watched her walk down the hallway and noticed David poking his head out of my office.

"Is the coast clear?" he asked.

Even though I was miserable, I had to laugh. "Yes, the pestilence has passed."

He wrapped his arms around his chest and shuddered. "That lady freaks me out, man."

"Don't I know it," I muttered. "But thankfully, we've seen the last of her."

"Yeah," he said, returning to his workstation, "Veronica said that Adam guy had belladonna at his lab."

The mention of belladonna reminded me of Delta's bizarre comment. "David, I'm curious about something. Would you do me a favor and google *belladonna* and *eyes*"?

He nodded and keyed in the search. "Okay, so that pulled up *atropa belladonna*. Is that right?"

"I guess that's the scientific name," I replied, thinking it sounded familiar. "Do you see anything about using it in the eyes?"

He scanned the page. "Well, ophthalmologists dilate eyes with it."

I chewed my fingernail. "Anything else?"

"Hang on." He paused. "It says the ladies of the Venetian Court, whatever that is, used a tincture of belladonna eye drops because they thought dilated pupils made them look seductive."

My stomach contracted like someone had attached a vice grip to it. I rushed to his computer. "Where did you read that?"

"It's toward the end of the second paragraph," he said, pointing to the text on the screen.

The second I looked at the passage, one sentence jumped out at me as though it had been highlighted in boldface.

The genus name Atropa *comes from Atropos, one of the three Fates in Greek mythology.*

Finally, all the pieces fell into place—the belladonna, the Venetian Court, the three Fates. And the whole horrible reality of what had happened at Oleander Place came crashing down on me like a *grande* sugar cane kettle.

"Oh my God." I whispered, putting my hand on David's shoulder for support.

"Troy!"

CHAPTER TWENTY-TWO

———

David looked up at me, his forehead wrinkled with concern. "What about Troy?"

"Oh, I just remembered that I promised to read his master's thesis," I fibbed. I hated lying to David, but Veronica had taken me off the Jones case in no uncertain terms. If I was going to go rogue, I couldn't drag him into it. "That reminds me, do you know whether Tulane publishes its students' theses online?"

He tapped his fingers on his mouth. "Let me check the library catalog."

While David clicked away on his keyboard, I thought back to my various interactions with Troy. Things I hadn't thought about at the time took on new meaning for me now. In some ways, he fit the obsessive profile. There weren't many people who loved plantation clothes so much that they planned to devote their entire careers to them. Plus, I'd noticed that he was extremely meticulous—in the careful way he'd wrapped the pirate clothes, straightened the silverware in the dining room, placed his mug in the exact center of the coaster—a quality that would lend itself well to the staging of a dead body. But on the other hand, he was a personable, down-to-earth guy, and I hadn't seen any signs of mental instability.

"So, the theses and the dissertations are online," David said, disrupting my thoughts. "Want me to email you the link?"

"That would be great," I said as I headed for the hallway. "I'll go pull it up now."

To avoid arousing Veronica's suspicions, I tiptoed into my office and sunk quietly into my chair. Then I opened David's email and clicked the link. Within a second of entering Troy's name in the advanced search field, his thesis title popped up on the screen. *Poison and Poisoning in the Venetian Republic*. And I gave myself a good, swift, mental kick for not looking up his research sooner.

It didn't take long to find what I was looking for. As I'd suspected, there was a section in the paper that described the cosmetic use of belladonna among Venetian courtesans—and its fatal effects from misuse.

I chewed my thumbnail while I pondered the ramifications of Troy's thesis. The focus on belladonna looked bad, but it didn't prove anything. I had to have more evidence. Specifically, I needed to find out whether he had a history of mental illness. Of course, if he did have any mental health records on file, they wouldn't be available to the public. So I had to find someone who knew him well, someone other than Delta. The only other person I could think of was his dissertation advisor, but Troy had never mentioned his name.

"I thought you were leaving for the day!" Veronica exclaimed.

I jumped at least a foot—the guilty kind of jump, not the startled one.

"I didn't mean to scare you," she said, sashaying up to my desk. "I came for the Jones file. I want to get this case wrapped up ASAP."

"Sure," I replied, feigning nonchalance. I reached into my lower right drawer and pulled out a manila folder.

Veronica took the file from my hand and sat in front of my desk. "You know, we really haven't had a chance to talk about Bradley."

"What's there to say?" I asked, unprepared for this line of questioning.

"Oh, I don't know," she replied as she straightened a bent corner of the file. "I just thought you might want to vent."

Of course, I wasn't one to be short on opinions. But the shock of Bradley's betrayal had left me kind of numb. And now wasn't the time to try to open that wound, not when I had a killer to catch. "Honestly, I haven't had time to process what happened. But even if I had, I don't think I'd have much to say about it."

She tilted her head. "Why's that?"

"Because it was so unexpected and yet so utterly predictable," I retorted. "Even though I didn't trust Pauline, I never really believed that Bradley would leave me for her. But then, I have such a dismal history where men are concerned, so why should I be surprised?"

"Has he ever given you an explanation for why he did this?"

"Well, when I called him about Corinne's case this morning, he tried to tell me that things weren't what they seemed."

She flinched. "Did he explain what he meant by that?"

"No, and I didn't ask," I replied, picking at my chipped purple nail polish.

"Aren't you the least bit curious?" she pressed. "That's a pretty provocative statement under the circumstances."

"I saw them spoon-feeding each other over candle light, Veronica. Do you think I'm going to believe a word he says?" I shook my head. "Uh-uh. I'm through with that guy."

"I suppose you know what's best," she replied, rising to her feet.

That was highly debatable, but I kept my mouth shut. This conversation needed to end—because I was through discussing Bradley and because I had to track down Troy's dissertation advisor before it was too late.

"Anyway, you'd better get going," she ordered, shaking the folder at me, "or I might change my mind and put you to work."

I managed a weak smile. "Then I'm leaving now."

As soon as I heard Veronica enter her office, I googled the Tulane Department of History and scanned the list of faculty members. Only one specialized in the Antebellum Era, a Professor Claude Miller, and his office hours were from two until five. Since it was only eleven, I had plenty of time to run some errands and grab lunch before heading to Tulane.

On my way out of my office, I saw a photo from the case file on the floor. It was the close up of Ivanna on her deathbed.

I picked up the picture and stared at Ivanna's image, marveling once again at her fairy-tale-like beauty—her rose-red lips, her porcelain skin, the fair hair that framed her face like a golden fleece. And I was reminded of something Troy had said the first day I met him, that Ivanna's hair had been arranged exactly like Evangeline's. It occurred to me that since there were no known photographs of Evangeline in life or in death, the only way he could have known what her hair had looked like on the day of her murder was if he'd scoured over the historical records of the crime scene. Like a man obsessed.

I laid the photo on my desk. I'd return it to the Jones file tomorrow. Right now I had the rest of the day off—to find Troy's dissertation advisor.

* * *

As I walked through the first floor of Tulane's Hebert Hall, I hoped that the twenty or so students sitting cross-legged at the end of the corridor weren't camped outside Professor Miller's office. But no such luck.

I approached a geeky-looking kid at the end of the line. His pasty, acne-spotted skin practically exuded panic, along with copious amounts of oil. "Are all of you waiting to see Dr. Miller?"

He nodded. "We've got an essay exam tomorrow on colonization," he replied, glancing at the professor's door. "It's worth forty percent of our grade."

I slid my back down the wall as I eased onto the tile floor beside him. Thinking of the lengthy wait that lay ahead of me and not the lopsided grade breakdown, I said, "That sucks."

"Right?" he commiserated, clutching a notebook to his "I know H.T.M.L. (How to Meet Ladies)" T-shirt. "Especially since we lost our teaching assistant like a month after class started."

I told myself not to take the bait because I didn't want to spend the next hour or so listening to history department gossip. But I'd just polished off a huge plate of chicken Tchoupitoulas at Coop's Place and was in serious danger of falling asleep. "So, why'd you lose your TA?"

"He dropped out of school," he muttered. "I guess he finally realized there was no future in a PhD in plantation chic."

The bottom dropped out of my stomach. Even though I knew who he was talking about, I had to ask. "Was his name Troy Wilson, by any chance?"

The geek's jaw dropped. "How'd you know?"

"I met him around once or twice."

"Well, if you see him again," he began, cocking a brow high on his greasy forehead, "tell him Cody Putfark said 'thanks for nothing.'"

"I will," I promised in an appropriately solemn tone. Then I leaned my head against the wall and thought back to all the times Troy—and Delta, for that matter—had mentioned that he was actively pursuing a PhD. Now that I knew he'd been lying, my anxiety level was starting to rise. In the back of my mind I'd been hoping that I was wrong about what was going on at Oleander Place. But it looked like Chandra's colleague, Xavier, was right—the solution had been right in front of me all along.

My "Baby Got Back" ringtone sounded, and a couple of students snickered. I looked at the display and wondered what they would do if they knew my psychic sidekick was calling.

"Hi, Chandra," I answered.

"Hey girl," she replied with an unexpected show of intimacy. "Lou and I were watching the news this morning, and we saw that the Oleander Place murders have been solved."

"Yeah, the police got their man," I said, careful not to emphasize the word *their*.

"You must be so relieved," she said, pronouncing *relieved* with an ear-splitting squeal. "Now you won't have to go to that awful plantation anymore or deal with that horrible woman. And you'll have more time to work on your relationship with your honeykins."

I cringed at the reference to Bradley (and at the word *honeykins*). I had no idea why everyone suddenly wanted to talk to me about him, but I wanted it to stop. "Um, we're not together anymore."

"No!" she cried with such emotion that it set her jewelry to jingling. "What happened?"

Chandra was starting to stress me out. I mean, she of all people could use her psychic skills to get the scoop and spare me the painful rehash. "Turns out that Three of Cups card you dealt me was right on the money. There *was* a third person in our relationship—his secretary."

"I'm surprised to hear that," she said in a faraway tone. "I didn't get the impression that the third wheel was a love interest."

Now I was really getting annoyed. I'd paid her for that tarot card reading, and now she was admitting that she'd held out on me? "Well, I don't know what made you think that, but I hope it wasn't your psychic intuition."

She sniffed. "I'll have you know that I'm never wrong about these things."

"Whatever," I said, standing up to relieve my aching behind. I'd originally thought the floor was causing the pain, but I was starting to think it was this conversation. "Listen, did you need to talk to me about anything else? Because if not—"

"Evangeline or Ivanna is back," she interrupted. "With a vengeance."

"You mean, that spirit's getting aggressive with you?"

The geek eyeballed me and then pretended to be absorbed in his notes.

"In the sense that I can't get her out of my head, yes," Chandra whined. "Ever since that Dr. Geyer got arrested, she's been pulling at that French door like crazy. I see her night and day, awake and in my sleep. I wish she'd just open the damn thing already!"

I thought the timing of the spiritual activity was odd given the new developments in the case. "What do you think is going on?"

"That's what I was going to ask you."

"Me? I'm not the medium here."

"Clearly," she scoffed. "But I've never had a spirit harass me like this. So something must be happening with the case."

If there was a spirit harassing her, it was probably because it knew that the killer was still on the loose. But I couldn't say that to Chandra or anyone else until I could prove it. "You'd have to ask the police."

"They're not going to talk to me."

"I don't know what else to tell you," I said, glancing up as two students entered Dr. Miller's office.

She sighed. "Then I guess I'm going to have to go out to the plantation and find out what the spirit wants."

I had to stop her. If my fears were correct, the murder spree hadn't ended at Oleander Place. "I wouldn't go now if I were you. Even though the case is solved, the police are probably still trying to find evidence to connect Adam Geyer to the scene."

"But I have to do this, Franki. That spirit's trying to tell me something, and it's my duty to figure out what that is."

"What about all those scary ghosts?" I asked.

Angling a wide-eyed glance at me, the geek scooted closer to the student in line in front of him.

"I've been thinking about that," she said. "And you were right. If I'm going to be in this business, I need to overcome my fear of ethereal beings."

This was not the time for personal growth. I had to try another tactic. "But what about Officer Quincy? If he hears you've gone back out there, he'll have you thrown in jail."

"I told Lou all about him," she huffed. "And he said that if that crooked copper lays so much as a finger on me, he'll have his badge."

Damn Lou, I thought. "Wait. Didn't Lou say that you weren't allowed to go to the plantation?"

"That was before the case was solved. Now, why are you so dead set against me going out there?" she asked, her voice thick with suspicion.

If she only knew that *dead* was the operative word. "Look, I can't go into the details, but right now is a bad time to go to Oleander Place."

"Why?"

"I just said that I couldn't get into that!" I exclaimed.

The geek shielded his mouth as he whispered something to a group of students staring at me.

I lowered my voice. "Can't you just trust me on this?"

She hesitated. "I guess."

Thanks for the vote of confidence, I thought. "Good. Then just sit tight, and I'll be in touch soon."

I hung up and breathed a sigh of relief. At least Chandra was out of harm's way. Now I just had to get in to see Dr. Miller so that I could be sure about the others.

* * *

It was ten after five when the geek emerged from the professor's office. To avoid eye contact with me, he held his head so high that he was basically staring at the ceiling.

I stood up and dusted myself off. When I stepped into the doorway, I was met by a bookshelf filled with what looked like rare and expensive books. There was another shelf to my right, forcing me to turn left to enter the tiny room.

An elderly man behind an old wooden desk looked up from a paper he'd been reading. "Are you a student in one of my courses, young lady?"

"No Sir. I mean, Dr. Miller," I stammered. Something about the professor and his antique books made me feel like I was in the principal's office. But since I was pushing thirty, I was thrilled with the *young lady* line.

"Then how can I help you?" he asked, removing his reading glasses.

"I came to talk to you about Troy Wilson," I replied, handing him my business card. "I'm a private investigator."

The already deep lines on his forehead deepened further. "Is Mr. Wilson in some kind of trouble?"

I nodded. "He is."

"Well, I don't understand why you would come to me," he blustered in a burst of impatience. "Shouldn't you go to the police?"

I held up my hand in an attempt to calm him. "I plan to do that, Dr. Miller, but I need some information first. I was hoping you could tell me whether Troy had any history of mental instability."

He rested his elbows on his desk and clasped his hands in front of his mouth. "I think you can appreciate that I'm not at liberty to discuss my students' personal affairs."

I took that as a *yes*. "Certainly."

"It's odd that you would come to see me today," he said, staring into my eyes.

I squirmed like a schoolgirl in my seat. "Why do you say that?"

"I haven't seen Mr. Wilson for several months," he began, leaning back in his chair, "and then he called me out of the blue about an hour ago."

"Oh?" I was anxious to know where this was going, but I was afraid to prod for fear that he would refuse to answer.

"He wanted to say good-bye," he said, looking into my eyes again.

I swallowed hard. "Good-bye?"

"Yes. He said he was going away."

My anxiety level set off on a steady climb. I didn't like the sound of this. "Did he say where?"

"He was deliberately vague." He looked down at his desk. "Of course, I realized that he wanted me to think he was moving somewhere, but I assumed he meant that he was going to some sort of facility."

From the pointed way Dr. Miller was looking at me, I knew *facility* meant mental hospital.

"But now," he continued, "it appears as though he may be going to jail. May I ask what for?"

At this point, my anxiety had reached its peak. I knew I had to leave, and soon. "Like you, I'm not at liberty to say. But thank you, Dr. Miller," I said, rising from my seat. "You've been a huge help."

I exited the maze of books and jogged down the hallway. When I reached the main door, I shoved it open and broke into a run. Then I pulled out my phone and dialed 9-1-1.

Because I knew where Troy was going, and it wasn't to a mental hospital or jail. He was going to Oleander Place.

One last time.

CHAPTER TWENTY-THREE

———

When I pulled onto River Road, it was after seven o'clock. Rush hour traffic had turned the easy forty-five minute drive into an hour-and-a-half ordeal. Although the delay had me frantic with worry, I took some comfort in knowing that the police would arrive at Oleander Place before me.

But as I approached the plantation, I didn't hear any sirens or see flashing lights. To be on the safe side, I pulled over just before the house and shut off the engine. There was an eerie silence in the air that caused the hair to stand up on my arms. Something wasn't right.

I tapped the first number on my call list.

"9-1-1," a woman responded. "What's your emergency?"

"My name is Franki Amato. I'm a PI, and I called in a possible code 30 in progress at Oleander Place on River Road an hour and a half ago."

The woman fell silent as she searched for the record of my call. "The St. James Parish police have already been out there, ma'am. The officers on the scene saw no signs of a homicide."

"Listen, this is urgent. Three people have been killed at the plantation in the past two weeks. And I know another murder is about to happen, if it hasn't already."

"We'll send someone out."

"Thanks." I hung up and shoved the phone into my front pants pocket, praying that the officers would hurry. But I knew from experience that even though I'd called in a possible homicide, the police were hard pressed to find time to deal with possibilities.

As I exited the car, I glanced at the full moon and hoped that the lunar eclipse wasn't happening tonight. Based on what

I'd learned from Chandra's wannabe werewolf clients, people did some pretty crazy things during an eclipse. And the killer I was hunting was already plenty crazy enough.

With my gun in hand, I ran the hundred yards to the hedge and peered through the branches. What I saw took my breath away. The entire house was aglow in a flickering orange candlelight, like a giant jack-o-lantern. And the Southern live oaks that lined the walkway like camouflage-clad soldiers during the day now resembled a platoon of grim reapers forming a pathway to doom.

Doing my damnedest to repress my fear, I made my way along the hedge to the side of the house. Then I ran across the lawn to the first parlor window and ducked down. My breathing was so ragged that I was afraid it would give me away. When I peeked inside, I saw the shrine to Evangeline. It was alive with lighted candles and fresh oleander flowers and draped with pink netting—exactly like the day Scarlett was hanged.

My heart pounded in my chest as I scaled the rest of the house and tiptoed across the back porch to the door. It was unlocked. Pausing to collect myself, I leaned against the wall and glanced at the parking lot. Troy's white car gleamed in the moonlight.

Police backup or no, I had to go in. I pulled back the hammer of my gun and entered the house.

The hallway looked as though it had been prepared for my arrival. It was lined with white candles and oleander petals, creating a glowing, coral-pink carpet to the shrine. Gripping my gun with both hands, I crept toward the parlor. Just before the door, I stopped. Then I turned into the doorway and took aim.

Troy was right where I expected him to be—standing in the courting area and staring at Evangeline's portrait.

"I'm sorry you came here, Franki," he said in a hollow voice, his eyes fixed on the painting. "Now you have to die too."

The second he said the word *too,* I shifted my gun to the left and stepped into the room to greet my target. "Good evening, Delta."

She curled her lips into a cruel smile and pointed an antique double-barreled Derringer right between my eyes with an aim as sharp as the spikes in her hair. "I knew you were too damn stupid to heed my death threats."

"Apparently not stupid enough to believe Adam or Troy were responsible for the murders," I retorted.

She smirked. "I guess I underestimated you. Because you had to be bailed out of your last murder investigation by that old whore—"

"I told you before, she's a stripper," I said through gritted teeth. "And a far better person than you could ever be."

Delta tightened her grip on her gun, and I noticed that she'd pulled back the hammer. That meant it was too risky for me to try to take a shot at her. I knew from my police training that if I fired off a round when her hammer was drawn, she'd have time to shoot back.

"As I was saying," she drawled, "because you weren't smart enough to figure out your last investigation, I thought for sure you'd fall for my Troy trap."

I wanted to look at Troy to see his reaction, but I didn't dare take my eyes off Delta. "Impossible," I spat. "Unlike you, he's too nice a person to harm a fly, much less murder three innocent people."

"I'd say that's a matter for debate," she countered, raising her chin. "After all, he's a mental case with an intense personal interest in poison, which makes him the obvious candidate for the killer."

I grimaced. "He was never anything but a scapegoat to you, was he?"

Delta put a hand to her chest. "In my defense, he handed me the murder plot on a platter. That love-struck loon was obsessed with everything Evangeline—her painting, her personal papers, the records of her death." She laughed. "He was practically begging to be set up."

Out of the corner of my eye, I saw Troy hang his head. I willed him to get angry, to find his strength, because we were going to need it to escape this house of horrors.

"But then one day a real, live Lacour showed up on our doorstep," Delta jeered. "And the little harlot was a carbon copy of Troy's beloved Evangeline."

"Then you did know that Ivanna was a descendent of the Lacour family," I said.

"Of course I did," she snapped. "Her mother mentioned a daughter in her letter, and Ivanna looked just like Evangeline. I'd have to be a buffoon not to put two and two together, especially when Ivanna came back to the plantation on the pretense of taking several tours of the grounds."

"But you figured out that what she was really doing was seducing Troy to get him to help her find the Lacour diamond," I said.

"That imbecile took one look at her and fell hook, line, and sinker," she said, her voice thick with contempt. "He didn't give a damn about what that would mean to me or to my plantation."

I could see Delta's anger rising. If I could get her to look at Troy, I could shoot before she had time to react. I had to keep her talking and her temper flaring. "Then what happened?"

"Troy succumbed to Ivanna's charms, because she was as close as he was ever going to get to living out his fantasy of sleeping with Evangeline." Her brow furrowed. "They started having Friday night trysts—in Evangeline's bed. Ivanna would dress up in Evangeline's pink crinoline dress, and Troy wore pirate clothes, trying to be her Beau."

"So, you caught them in the act," I said, trying to stoke the fire.

Her eyes narrowed to little slits. "If I had, I would have killed them on the spot. Scarlett was the one who saw them when she came up here after hours to do her cleaning." Delta sneered. "I caught her washing the soiled bed linens the next morning. The filthy pigs didn't even bother to clean up after themselves."

Troy's shoulders slumped.

Look at Troy, Delta. Look at him, I thought. My arms were aching from holding the shooting position, and I didn't know how much longer I could keep my gun level.

"At first I thought Scarlett had dirtied the sheets with some white trash boyfriend of hers. But when I confronted her, she told me the whole sordid tale. I assured her that I'd take care of it."

Now I understood why Delta had killed Scarlett. "So when Ivanna was found dead, Scarlett figured out that you'd 'taken care of it' by killing her."

"Yes, and she said she'd go to the police if I didn't pay her off." She frowned. "Can you imagine the nerve of that girl, accusing me of committing a crime and then trying to bilk me out of my money? Why, just for that, even if I hadn't killed Ivanna, I would have wrung her impudent little neck."

I shivered at the callous way she'd referenced Scarlett's hanging. And my mind started to drift to a bad place—thoughts of what she might have in store for Troy and me. But I couldn't go there now. I had to focus on a plan. "What about Miles?" I asked. "Did he try to blackmail you too?"

She snorted. "You bet he did. That good-for-nothing bum demanded fifty thousand dollars to keep his mouth shut."

"What did he have on you? The belladonna you made him grow behind the little mill?"

"He was too stupid to know what that was," she said with a wave of her hand. "The morning Scarlett was killed, when we were pulling artifacts for the photo shoot in the little mill, he looked out the window and saw me entering the house." She shook her head. "That was his problem—sticking his nose where it didn't belong. Just like that Adam Geyer character."

The mention of Adam surprised me so much that I almost jerked my gun. "He came out here?"

"A couple of times. He wanted access to the plantation for himself and his attorney. When I denied his request, he came out after hours, smashed a window, and let himself in."

I was stunned to hear that Adam had broken in to Oleander Place. I guess he'd meant what he said when he vowed to find Ivanna's killer. "How did you know it was him?"

"He set off the alarm. I'd left a few minutes before, so I rushed back in time to see a car speeding away. I had Officer Quincy run a check on his plates. I was about to press charges, but then he left belladonna in his lab and got himself arrested." She gave an incredulous laugh. "Men are such idiots."

So I was right—Delta hadn't framed Adam. Liam had.

"Speaking of idiots," she continued. "How did you manage to figure out it was me?"

I returned her insult with one of my own. "Well, besides your deplorable character, it was your reference to the belladonna. The medical examiner concluded that Ivanna had ingested it. You were the only one who suggested that it might have been put in her eyes."

She smiled. "Thanks to Troy's exceptional thesis, I knew exactly what to do."

I stole a glance at Troy. He was once again staring enrapt at Evangeline's portrait, oblivious to our predicament. Meanwhile, my arms were growing weaker. "But how did you pull it off?"

"It was easy," she said with a shrug. "The day before Ivanna's death, I sent Troy on a wild goose chase to a conference in Nashville. I told him that I'd made an appointment for the following morning for him to meet with one of the attendees, a history professor who'd discovered a letter from an ex-slave detailing Evangeline's death. When Troy heard the news, he was only too happy to go."

So he'd told the truth about attending the graduate student conference on the day Ivanna died, but he'd lied to me about the date of his return.

"Obviously, there was no such professor," she continued. "And poor Troy had no idea that John would be waiting to pull him over on false charges when he tried to come back for his rendezvous with Ivanna."

My jaw dropped to the floor, but luckily my gun didn't. "Officer Quincy is in on this too?"

"I should say so," she said in a haughty tone. "He's my lover. We tell each other everything."

My already shaky arms got even shakier as the skin practically crawled off my body. "What happened when Ivanna arrived?"

"I'd planned to knock her out with chloroform and then douse her eyes with the belladonna. But when she saw me here instead of Troy, she fainted." She giggled. "I couldn't have planned it any better myself."

Bile rose into my throat, but I had to keep my stomach— and my arms—in check. I took a deep breath and said, "So, you put the poison into her eyes and then you positioned her on the bed, just like Evangeline."

Delta pursed her lips. "Not exactly. As I'm sure you know from Troy's thesis, belladonna causes a violent death—confusion, hallucinations, seizures. So, I had to wait that out and try to minimize the damage Ivanna did to the pink room. The torn sheer was no big deal, but I'm still upset about that priceless perfume bottle."

I was sickened by her account of Ivanna's death. I couldn't imagine the terror and the pain Ivanna had experienced, and it was particularly appalling to hear that Delta's only regret was the loss of an antique. "There's one thing I don't understand about all of this."

She lowered her eyelids, as though bored by my curiosity. "Oh?"

"Why would you intentionally drive your family legacy and your business into the ground with these murders?"

"Isn't it obvious?" she asked, surprised by my question. "Haunted plantations are passé. There are lots of us in Louisiana, and we're all struggling to keep the tourists coming. In the meantime, we're competing with haunted houses that spend tens of thousands of dollars every year to create new themes and props, while we're stuck showing the same old things. And those places aren't just for Halloween anymore—they're becoming trendy year around, especially for Valentine's Day."

I looked at her open-mouthed as I tried to comprehend how the murders of Ivanna, Scarlett, and Miles would bring big bucks to Oleander Place.

"There's a haunted house near here that made twelve thousand dollars in one day with their "My Bloody Valentine" attraction. Do you know how much alligator jerky I'd need to sell down at the gift shop to make that kind of money?"

I shook my head.

"Three *years'* worth."

I was starting to think that Delta was more unstable than Troy because none of this was making sense. "But you've lost all your customers thanks to these grisly crimes. How do you expect to attract them now?"

She smiled like a Cheshire cat. "With the big finale."

I didn't want to ask, but I had to. Because I had the distinct feeling that Troy's life—if not mine too—depended on it. "What does that involve?"

Delta face seemed to light up with excitement. "Troy poisoning himself at Evangeline's shrine. Can't you just see it?" she asked. "A handsome young man becomes obsessed with the portrait of Evangeline, a beautiful plantation owner's wife who was poisoned with a cup of oleander tea. He transfers his obsession onto her gorgeous lookalike relative, but then he kills her when he realizes that she can never live up to his beloved. In despair, he drinks a cup of oleander tea to join his unrequited love." Her eyes flashed. "Now that's what I call a Greek tragedy."

More like a horror story, I thought. I glanced at Troy hoping that her gruesome plan had snapped him out of his trance, but he continued his adoration of Evangeline.

"Of course, those fools Scarlett and Miles got in the way, but I did what I could to minimize the damage. I put Scarlett in her red crinoline dress to make for a more striking image, and then John and I threw Miles into the sugar kettle to sweeten the pot." She let out a raucous laugh. "Get it? To sweeten the sugar cane pot?"

I got it, all right, and it nauseated me.

"But once the dust has settled, people will only remember Evangeline, Ivanna, and Troy. Business will boom, and everyone in the country will know about Oleander Place."

I shook my head. "They'll know it as a place where unspeakable things happened. No one will come here."

"What do you know?" she shouted. "Contemporary murders have a mystique about them. They draw huge crowds year around."

She had me there. I could think of lots of places where people gathered to seek pleasure from others' tragedies. It was a vile business—one that a vile person like Delta was perfectly suited for. There was no point in arguing further, and I knew I couldn't hold up my arms much longer. I sighed and said, "We can't keep this up all night. It's time for you to surrender."

"Surrender?" she asked, taken aback. "Why would I want to do that?

"Because I called the police before I came. They'll be here any minute."

"Oh, I know that," she said with a gleeful twinkle in her eye. "John got an automated phone message about your 9-1-1 call."

My heart sank, and my stomach fell. Some police departments had a system that enabled officers to receive phone alerts about 9-1-1 calls regarding specific locations. Apparently, the New Orleans PD was one of them.

"In fact, he's on his way right now to help me stage the poisoning. But I told him to take his time." She smiled. "I said that you and I had a lot of catching up to do."

By this point, I wasn't sure whether my arms were trembling from exhaustion or fear. "Don't do this, Delta. You'll never get away with this many murders."

"You're forgetting that I have police connections," she said. "Besides, you won't have to watch, if that's what you're worried about. Because Troy's going to kill you first."

I stared at her as I processed the news that I was part of the Oleander Place murder plot.

She frowned. "It's a shame you're not blonde, because everyone knows that dead blondes make for a better story. But that can't be helped." She squinted as she sized me up. "The real issue is what to dress you in. Not even a hoop skirt will fit over those hips."

I promised myself that if I survived, I'd make her pay for that last crack. But at the moment, I had bigger problems than my hips to deal with. I'd been following standard police procedure for standoffs—talking the perpetrator down. But that had gotten me nowhere fast. Trying to buy time, I said, "Then I guess you'll have to let me go."

"Sorry, but I warned you." She smirked. "Twice."

As I desperately tried to think of something to say or do, I saw the glow of headlights through the window—but no flashing lights. That could only mean one thing.

Officer Quincy.

Risky or not, I had to take the shot before he entered the house. Otherwise, Troy and I could kiss this world goodbye.

"Too bad I don't respond well to threats," I said. Then I pulled the trigger.

CHAPTER TWENTY-FOUR

————

Instead of gunfire there was silence.

I broke out in a cold sweat as the reality of what had happened dawned on me like a nuclear bomb. My gun had jammed.

I looked from the barrel to Delta.

Her face was as black as her Baron Samedi brooch. "I should blow you away for that stunt," she seethed. "But I'm not going to let the likes of you ruin my plan."

I swallowed hard, trying to choke down the growing fear that I was destined to become part of the plantation's lurid lore.

"Now drop the gun and walk over to Troy," she said, motioning with her pearl-handled pistol.

I let my Ruger fall to the floor and went to his side.

"Go on upstairs." She looked at Troy. "Both of you."

Troy exited the parlor first, and I followed with Delta at my back. As we climbed the stairs, I inched close to him and whispered, "Why didn't you tell me?"

"I couldn't lose Evangeline."

"Silence!" Delta commanded, jabbing the gun between my shoulders.

Troy was worse off than I'd thought. If there was any chance of us making it out alive, it was going to have to come from me. The only thing I could think of was to try to push Delta down the stairs when I reached the second floor.

A door slammed below.

"Delta?" Officer Quincy called.

A fresh wave of fear coursed through my veins. There was no escape now. He'd shoot me if I so much as blinked.

"Up here, John," she replied in a lackadaisical tone. "Franki and I just finished with our girl talk."

I followed Troy onto the landing, fighting the urge to faint. There was no need to ask where we were going. I lowered my head and entered the pink room.

"Franki, sit on the bed," Delta said. "But for heaven's sake, be careful. Antique beds weren't made for people your size."

Too numb to react to her jab, I did as I was told.

Officer Quincy burst into the room. "We need to get this over with quick," he said, handing Delta a pair of latex gloves. "I've been monitoring the St. James Parish PD on my police radio, and our little friend here made a second 9-1-1 call."

Delta sneered. "It's not going to do her any good. I've got the belladonna ready. All I need is for you to hold her arms."

Officer Quincy shoved me backward onto the bed and pinned my torso with his arms and chest.

"Wait!" I shouted, stalling. "Why belladonna?"

She put her hand on her hip. "Because you're Italian like Ivanna. Of course, the *beautiful woman* meaning doesn't apply in your case, but no one will question it when they learn your heritage," she said, slipping on the gloves. "Plus, I want you to die a horrible death."

I was seriously considering bum-rushing her for that first comment, but the *horrible death* one took the wind out of my sails.

"Hurry, Delta," Officer Quincy said. "If they're not dead before the police get here, we'll have a hard time proving Troy acted alone."

"Give me a minute," she snapped, reaching into her Louis Vuitton. She pulled out a small bottle and unscrewed the cap. As she leaned in toward me with the poison, I squeezed my eyes shut and started thrashing.

"Hold her still, John!" Delta yelled.

"I'm trying," he rasped, his voice tense from the struggle. "But she's as strong as a horse."

"The size of one too," she observed.

After hearing their horse comments, I started bucking like a bronco.

"It's no use," he ground out. "I've gotta knock her out."

I kept my eyes closed, waiting for the blow. I heard a thwack, a dull thud, and another thwack. But I felt no pain. In fact, the only thing I felt was Officer Quincy's weight sliding off my body. Then I heard another dull thud.

I opened one eye and saw Chandra high-fiving a balding, beer-bellied man in an island shirt.

"Boston strong!" she cried as they each raised a copper pipe in triumph.

I shot up from the bed and saw Delta and Officer Quincy unconscious on the floor. Woozy from shock, I asked, "What are you doing here, Chandra? I told you not to come!"

"I said I'd trust you, but I didn't say I'd listen to you," she explained as she pulled down her zodiac-themed miniskirt.

I glanced at Troy standing motionless in the corner. "I'm glad you didn't."

"By the way," Chandra began, "this is my husband, Luigi Toccato."

"Call me 'Lou,'" he said, giving my hand—actually, my entire arm—a hearty shake.

"So nice to meet you," I breathed. "You two saved our lives. But how did you do it?"

"Ah, we drove out in my plumber's van," Lou said, kicking Delta's gun out of her reach with his toe shoes. "Then Chandra got one of her visions. She said you were in danger, so we grabbed a couple of pipes from my supplies and came in around back."

I stared at Chandra in awe, remembering how scared she was the last time she came to the plantation. "How did you get up the courage to do this?"

She gazed at her husband. "When Lou's by my side, I can do anything."

"Aw, you," he said, turning as red as a tomato. He leaned over and gave her a smooch.

"Besides," she added, her tone now as hard as the pipe in her hand, "I'm afraid of ghosts, not bitches."

Police sirens screamed up the drive.

Chandra took that as her cue to slip her and Lou's pipes into her super Chanel bag. "Now if you three will excuse me," she began, fluffing her big bouffant bob, "I have a psychic matter to attend to."

* * *

Lou and I watched from the back porch as the police led Delta and Officer Quincy in handcuffs to the parking lot.

"Take your hands off me, you ingrate!" Delta shouted at the twenty-something male officer trying to help her into the back of the squad car. "I'm the widow of the late Chief of Police, Jackson Dupré."

"We know who you are, ma'am," the officer replied in a tired voice.

"Then you will treat me with respect, or you'll answer to my attorney," she snarled. "Do you understand me?"

Lou yawned and scratched his belly. "Why doesn't he just shove her into the car already?"

"My thoughts exactly," I replied.

The back door opened and Chandra stepped onto the porch. "Where's Troy?"

"They took him to the station," I replied. "He'll undergo a psychiatric evaluation and get the treatment he needs."

Chandra frowned at the sight of Delta and crossed her arms.

"What's the matter?" I asked. "Aren't you happy to see the diabolical one get her due?"

"It's not that." She sighed. "That spirit's turning the doorknob again."

"Maybe she wants to come outside to see Delta being taken to jail," I joked. "You know having her around the plantation had to be a living hell for those ghosts."

"That's the problem," Chandra said. "The spirit's standing in front of French doors, but she's not in the house."

My smile faded. "How do you know?"

"Because there's a vase on the floor to the left of her. But when I stood in the corner between the French doors and the pink room a few minutes ago, I realized that there was no vase there."

I rubbed the back of my neck. "I don't think I've ever seen a vase by the French doors. But maybe one used to be there."

Chandra shook her head, jingling her jewelry. "This isn't a vision from the past. The spirit's turning the handle in the present."

"Then maybe she's not at Oleander Place," I suggested.

"Or, maybe she is," Chandra countered, "but she's turning the handle of a different French door."

As soon as she'd spoken the words, I knew where that door was. "The little mill!" I exclaimed. "Miles told me that the windows and French doors were replaced, and the originals are stored there."

"What are we waiting for?" Chandra yelled.

The three of us ran across the grounds. I arrived at the mill first, for obvious reasons.

It didn't take long to find the French doors. They were propped up against a wall in the back corner—beside a large blue vase.

I grasped the knob of the door on the right. It was exactly like the one I'd repaired the day Chandra and I got trapped inside the parlor. "We need to remove the handle."

"I (huff) got (puff) this," Lou said, pulling a pipe wrench from the pocket of his cargo shorts. He bent down in front of the handle.

I fixed my gaze on the back of his head to avoid seeing his... Well, he's a plumber.

Lou stuck out his tongue, gave a couple of tugs with the wrench, and the handle fell into his hand. Battling his belly, he rose to his feet. "Here (huff) you (puff) go."

Like Lou, I was breathless—but with excitement. I shook the base of the handle over my palm, and out tumbled the Lacour diamond.

Chandra gasped and clasped her face. "All this time the spirit was trying to show us where the diamond was!"

"Exactly." I stared with wonder at the coral-pink gem.

She put a hand on my arm. "That means the spirit was probably Evangeline, not Ivanna."

I bit my lip. "I have a feeling it was both of them."

"Well, it sure is a beaut," Lou said, pulling up his sagging shorts. "What're you gonna do with it?"

"Oh, I can't keep it," I said. "It belongs to the plantation."

Chandra's lips formed a tiny pout. "But Delta's going to prison. Surely you don't plan to give it to her?"

"I'm giving it to the police," I announced in a steadfast tone. Although, let's be honest, I really wanted to keep it for myself. "We'd better head out."

When we arrived at the parking lot, I approached the policeman who'd loaded Delta into the back of his patrol car. "Officer, we found something in the little mill that's pertinent to the case. It's the legendary Lacour diamond."

Delta's head turned so sharply I thought it was going to spin all the way around like Linda Blair's in *The Exorcist*. "That diamond is mine!" she shouted at the closed window. "Do you hear me, Franki Amato? Mine!"

The officer shined his flashlight on the stone. "That's some diamond."

"And it's my property!" she yelled. "Give it to me this instant!"

"I can't do that, ma'am," he said, turning to the window. "This diamond is evidence."

Seeing Delta's reaction, a thought occurred to me. "Officer, do you mind if we take a few pictures with the diamond, since we found it, and all?"

"Make it quick," he replied, depositing the gem into my palm.

Delta shot daggers at me with her eyes. "Get your filthy hands off my heirloom!"

Chandra and I snapped several selfies with the diamond as Delta raged.

That'll teach her for making cracks about my size, I thought as I returned the diamond to the officer with a huge grin on my face.

By the time he drove away, Delta's fury had given way to tears, and she was wailing and blubbering about her "precious pink baby."

"What a wuss," Chandra said.

"Yeah," Lou agreed. "Southern steel, my *culo*."

I smiled at his use of the uncouth Italian term for derriere. "Once again, Lou, you took the words right out of my mouth."

* * *

When I entered my office the next morning, there were beignets and a soy latte on my desk. I turned to find Veronica in the doorway. "What's this?"

"A small thank you for your amazing work on the case."

"Are you sure you're not mad that I continued working the investigation?"

"I can't tell you what to do with your day off, but I am upset that you put yourself in danger." She crossed her arms. "Promise me that you'll give me a heads-up the next time you plan to confront a ruthless killer."

"I promise," I said, taking a seat behind my desk. "But honestly, I thought I was covered after calling the police. And besides, you've been so busy lately that I thought you wanted me to handle the case on my own."

"I have been busy," she said as she eased into the armchair. "And the truth is that after I helped you get the investigation underway, I did take a step back."

"I noticed," I said, reaching for a beignet. "I just don't understand why."

She sighed. "Because PIs don't work with partners like the police do. And even though I'd love for us to collaborate on cases, the budget doesn't allow for that yet. So, I needed for you to gain confidence in your ability to work a case on your own." She smiled. "And after bringing down Delta Dupré, you should be able to handle anyone."

I swallowed a big bite of beignet. "I see what you're saying," I began, dusting powdered sugar from my hands, "and I have to admit that in some ways it was pretty great to call the shots. But you're overlooking the fact that I did have a partner on this case."

"Who? David?"

I took a sip of latte. "Chandra."

Veronica rolled her eyes. "Now, I'll admit that she and her husband saved your life, and for that I'll be forever grateful, but—"

"No *buts* about it," I interrupted. "Like you, I have my doubts about her psychic abilities, but no one can deny that her vision of the spirit and the doorknob led to the discovery of the Lacour diamond. And while we're on the subject, I have some sparkly selfies to show you."

Veronica clapped her hands as I handed her my phone. She was swiping through the photos when my Sir Mix-a-Lot ringtone sounded. She looked up. "It's Ivanna's father."

I grabbed the phone and pressed answer. "Hi, Liam."

"I'm calling to congratulate you on your stupendous work on the case," he said. "You should be proud to know that it's a lead story in the Italian news."

"You're in Italy?"

Veronica looked as surprised as I was.

"I had Ivanna buried beside her mother," he said, the pain evident in his tone.

"I'm glad." I wanted to ask him about the belladonna, but I didn't feel right about doing it after he'd mentioned the burial.

"I also wanted you to know that the police called me this morning." He paused. "They've released Adam."

Liam had just presented me with the opening I needed. "Did they ask if you'd planted the belladonna in his lab?"

There was silence on the line. "As far as they're concerned, the case is closed," he said in a cautious tone. "And as for Adam, the arrest gave him the opportunity to sober up and think about his actions, past and future. So, all things considered, there was no harm done."

I was silent as I wrestled with my conscience. Liam had committed a crime, but what good would it do to turn him in? Adam was already free, but Liam might go to jail—that is, if he came back to the United States. And if he was imprisoned, he could never work for Doctors Without Borders again.

There was a muffled voice over a loudspeaker.

Liam cleared his throat. "That's my boarding call."

I wasn't surprised he was at the airport. "Are you going back to Syria?"

"Afghanistan."

The call came over the loudspeaker again.

This was it—my last chance to insist that he turn himself in. "Liam…"

"Yes?"

But then I thought of all the lives he would save. "Have a safe flight."

"Thank you, Franki," he said softly. "So very much."

I tossed my phone on the desk and looked into Veronica's eyes. We both knew there was nothing to say.

The main door slammed.

"David's here," we said in unison—happy for the distraction.

"Franki!" he yelled, entering the room like a tornado. "You're a hero!"

I grinned. "Chandra and Lou are heroes too."

He curled his upper lip. "They didn't look like it on the news."

"Why not?" Veronica asked. "What do heroes look like?"

"I dunno, but not like cosmic plumbers."

I burst out laughing, imagining them decked out in moons, stars, and plumbing supplies. "I'm sure they looked better than Glenda did when she was on TV after our last murder investigation."

David turned pink and said nothing.

"So, how are you going to celebrate your success?" Veronica asked.

"Work, I guess," I replied.

"No, ma'am," she said, wagging her index finger at me. "You're taking that day off."

"Dude!" David exclaimed. "The Jazz and Heritage Festival starts today. You should totally go."

"I don't want to go to a concert alone," I said. Then I saw Veronica's brows lower with concern, so I added, "I think I'll spend the day with my man."

Her brows shot up. "Bradley?"

I stiffened, and then shook my head. "Napoleon."

* * *

I pulled into my Uptown neighborhood, wishing I could avoid the cemetery. The realization that I had no one to celebrate with except for my dog had really gotten me down. The last thing I needed right now was a bunch of graves reminding me that I was going to die alone too.

It didn't help that Veronica had mentioned Bradley. I knew I shouldn't miss him, but I did. I even found myself wondering whether Chandra had been right about Pauline not being the third person in my relationship. Because there was one other candidate I could think of—my nonna. She was nothing if not a third wheel. And not your ordinary car wheel, either.

I was trying to figure out what the biggest wheel in the world was when my phone rang. I looked at the display before responding, "*Bonjour*, Corinne."

"Have you seen ze news?" she whisper-shouted.

Oh no, I thought. *What have Chandra and Lou done now?* I envisioned Chandra going into one of her vibrating spirit trances while Lou performed some sort of plumbing demonstration. "About my case, right?"

"*Oui!*" she whisper-exclaimed. "Ze FBI took her away in ze handcuffs."

"Ze FBI?" I echoed. I'd suspected Chandra of faking a vision or two, but I had no idea the feds were involved.

Oui, ze FBI," she repeated. "And Bradley helped!"

When she said his name, I finally understood. And I had to pull over to recover from the shock. "Bradley was working with the FBI?"

"He was undercover! He prove zat Pauline embezzle from ze bank and ze children," Corinne gushed. "Now I must go before my manager see me. *A bientôt!*"

I hung up my phone and hung my head. Bradley had said that things weren't what they seemed, and I'd laughed. Even worse, he'd asked me to trust him, and I hadn't. I doubted that he would ever forgive me.

The final scene from *Gone with the Wind* popped into my head. Scarlett was crying on the staircase after Rhett had walked out on her for the last time. Then she looked off into the distance and vowed to get him back because, after all, tomorrow was another day.

"Southern belle bimbo," I said as I shifted the car back into gear and headed for home.

A few minutes later, I pulled in front of my house and slammed on the brakes.

Bradley was in the driveway in a sleek Armani suit and dark sunglasses. He looked like a male model—with a bouquet of yellow roses in his hand.

Because I had my convertible top down, I almost leapt over the side of my car to get to him. But I decided that the occasion called for a more ladylike route, i.e., the door.

He took off his sunglasses, and our eyes locked as I walked up the driveway.

"Franki, I—"

"Sh." I put my finger on his lips. "I already know."

Then I replaced my finger with my mouth.

When we came up for air, I narrowed my eyes said, "But I do have one question."

He ran a hand through his hair. "What is it?"

"How in the hell did you end up working with the FBI?"

He grimaced. "Well, the investigation is still pending so I can't go into details. But what I can say is that I contacted the FBI after a major donor to the 'Shoot for the Moon' fundraiser called about a tax receipt for his donation, and I couldn't find any record of it."

"That's terrible." I looked down. I felt really bad for Bradley, and I was still so angry at Pauline for trying to take advantage of him.

"Hey," Bradley said as he gently lifted my chin with his finger and looked into my eyes. With his free hand he reached into his jacket pocket and pulled out an envelope. "This is for you."

Thinking it was a letter or card, I shivered when I realized that it was an airline itinerary for two from New Orleans to… "Houston?"

He cleared his throat. "Yeah, I got a really, uh, interesting and persuasive call from Father Roman and Carmela about making things right with your mamma."

I put my finger back on his lips. "And you still came here today?"

He took my hand in his and kissed my palm. "Actually, I thought it was charming."

I blinked. Poor man, how could he know? The reality of Nonna was just too unreal for anyone to fathom. He would have to learn for himself. Until then, I thought it best to change the subject. I snuggled up to him and asked, "Do you have to go back to work?"

He sighed. "For a few hours. The bank merger was due to go through this week, but now that Pauline is in the news, I have to do damage control."

I rested my forehead on his. "I'm so sorry."

"I'm not," he breathed and then kissed my eyelids. "Not now that I have you back."

I felt my body go limp and was grateful his strong arms were around me.

"How about dinner tonight?" He kissed the tip of my nose and flashed a devilish smile. "We could go to Nonna Mia."

I instantly regained my strength and punched him in the arm. "When hell freezes over."

He laughed and pulled me closer. "Okay, then. Galatoire's?"

"That's really fancy," I said as he kissed my cheeks. "I'm not sure I have anything appropriate to wear."

He moved his lips a fraction away from mine. "What about that knockout skirt?"

RECIPES

Pink Prosecco Lemonade

Franki Amato loves her Limoncello, but she's also rather fond of Pink Prosecco. In the spirit of excess (I mean, where's the spirit in moderation?), she has found a way to combine them in this delicious pink lemony drink.

Pink Prosecco
Limoncello
Pink lemonade
Strawberry for garnish

In a fluted glass, mix two parts Pink Prosecco, one part Limoncello, and one part pink lemonade. Garnish with a strawberry.

Pink Prosecco with Raspberry Sorbet

Veronica's favorite "ladies' night" drink also involves Pink Prosecco—but with a scoop of yummy raspberry sorbet (It goes without saying, of course, that Glenda substitutes Pink Champagne—and skips the sorbet).

Pink Prosecco
Raspberry sorbet

Place one scoop of raspberry sorbet in a fluted glass. Fill with Pink Prosecco and serve immediately.

Grazie for reading Prosecco Pink!

Dear Reader,

I hope you enjoyed *Prosecco Pink*. The characters in the Franki Amato Mysteries are very special to me because they're loosely based on people I've had the pleasure of meeting during my lifetime—except for the killers, of course! I'm also really fond of this series because it has its origins in a car trip I took from Texas to New Orleans with my parents in the early nineties so that my father could stock up on Italian deli meat at Central Grocery (Italians will go to great lengths for their food).

When I wrote *Limoncello Yellow*, the first book in the series, I got a lot of fan email about Franki. But I actually received more about Nonna and Glenda, LOL! As an author, I was thrilled to get reader feedback. And some of the things people said about *Limoncello Yellow* helped me to make improvements to *Prosecco Pink*. So I would love to hear your thoughts, good or bad, about my books. You can write to me at traci@traciandrighetti.com.

If you would rather not write to me directly, then please consider writing a favorable review of *Prosecco Pink*. These days, authors are dependent on readers like you to stay in business. So thank you in advance for taking the time to write a review. Mille grazie!

Traci Andrighetti

P.S. If you're a Franki fan, I'd love to have you on my street team, The *Giallo* Squad. You can find information about how to join and what you will receive on my website: www.traciandrighetti.com

Book Club Questions
for *Prosecco Pink*

In *Prosecco Pink*, Glenda reveals that she loves pirates (well, any man, really). What's your type?

Are there NOLA sites referenced in the novel that you would like to visit?

What does the color pink symbolize to Ivanna? What does it mean to you?

Do you believe in ghosts? Why or why not?

Was Franki right to be skeptical of Chandra's psychic abilities? Have you ever been to a psychic?

Investigating a murder on the grounds of a plantation has Franki quoting lines from *Gone with the Wind*. Do you ever quote from books or movies?

Plantation homes are common in Louisiana. Have you ever visited a plantation?

Nonna Carmela is up to some new tricks in *Prosecco Pink*. How do you think Franki could stop her meddling once and for all?

Do you think Franki should have forgiven Bradley for not telling her that he was working with the FBI?

Lastly (and most importantly), who do you think ultimately ends up with that fabulous coral-pink diamond?

ABOUT THE AUTHOR

Traci Andrighetti is the author of the Franki Amato Mysteries. In her previous life, she was an award-winning literary translator and a Lecturer of Italian at the University of Texas at Austin, where she earned a PhD in Applied Linguistics. But then she got wise and ditched that academic stuff for a life of crime—writing, that is.

If she's not hard at work on her next novel, Traci is probably watching her favorite Italian soap opera, eating Tex Mex, or sampling fruity cocktails, and maybe all at the same time. She lives in Austin with her husband, young son, and three treat-addicted dogs

To learn more about Traci, visit her online at:
www.traciandrighetti.com

Enjoyed this book? Check out these other novels
available in print now from
Gemma Halliday Publishing:

www.GemmaHallidayPublishing.com

39219478R00165

Made in the USA
Lexington, KY
11 February 2015